PAW AND ORDER

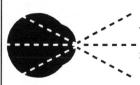

This Large Print Book carries the
Seal of Approval of N.A.V.H.

A CHET AND BERNIE MYSTERY

PAW AND ORDER

SPENCER QUINN

THORNDIKE PRESS

A part of Gale, Cengage Learning

GALE
CENGAGE Learning

Farmington Hills, Mich • San Francisco • New York • Waterville, Maine
Meriden, Conn • Mason, Ohio • Chicago

GALE
CENGAGE Learning

Copyright © 2014 by Spence Quinn.
Thorndike Press, a part of Gale, Cengage Learning.

ALL RIGHTS RESERVED

Thorndike Press® Large Print Mystery.
The text of this Large Print edition is unabridged.
Other aspects of the book may vary from the original edition.
Set in 16 pt. Plantin.

LIBRARY OF CONGRESS CATALOGING-IN-PUBLICATION DATA

Quinn, Spencer.
    Paw and order : a Chet and Bernie mystery / by Spencer Quinn. — Large print edition.
    pages ; cm. — (Thorndike Press large print mystery)
    ISBN 978-1-4104-7263-2 (hardcover) — ISBN 1-4104-7263-9 (hardcover)
    1. Dogs—Fiction. 2. Private investigators—Fiction. 3. Large type books.
I. Title.
PS3617.U584P39 2014b
813'.6—dc23
                          2014026261

Published in 2014 by arrangement with Atria Books, a division of Simon & Schuster, Inc.

Printed in Mexico
1 2 3 4 5 6 7 18 17 16 15 14

To Victoria

ONE

We blasted out of bayou country, Bernie behind the wheel, me in the shotgun seat. Our ride's a real old Porsche, the oldest we've had in our whole career. The last one got blown up; the one before that went off a cliff. And who can remember the one before that? Not me, amigo, except for how loud train whistles turn out to be from up real close. The point is, old Porsches are how we roll at the Little Detective Agency, just one of the things that makes us so successful, leaving out the finances part, where we've run into some hiccups I won't go into now. And don't get me started on hiccups, which is the annoying thing about them, namely that you can't stop. What else do you need to know? Bernie's last name is Little, which is how come we're the Little Detective Agency. I'm Chet, pure and simple.

We came to a crossroads with a roadhouse on one corner. Bernie slowed down and read the sign: "Ti-Pierre's Cajun BBQ." No surprise there: for some time now, barbecue had been in the air, impossible to miss. Bernie tilted up his face — no need to describe his face, the best human face in the world — and took a sniff. "I can almost smell it," he said. Yes, the best human face, not at all like those tiny-nosed human faces you see so often. Bernie had a nose that looked capable of doing big things. So why didn't it? I turned to him, gave that nose a good long look. He gave me a good long look back.

"What's on your mind, big guy?" he said. Then he smiled. "I got it — you're up for one last taste of the local grub before we head for home."

No! That wasn't it at all! Bernie laughed and gave me a nice pat, scratched the spot between my ears where I can't get to. And just like that, one last taste of the local grub was all alone in my mind, whatever had been there before completely gone. I couldn't have been happier, which is how I like to operate.

We pulled into the parking lot at Ti-Pierre's Cajun BBQ. I was just noticing all the bikes in the lot, the big kind that bikers like, when the phone buzzed. Bernie hit speaker.

"Bernie? You called?" Hey! It was Suzie. Hadn't heard her voice in way too long, although it usually sounded warmer than this. Suzie had been Bernie's girlfriend, back when she'd worked for the *Valley Tribune,* the Valley being where we lived — maybe in Arizona, a detail I'd picked up quite recently — but then she'd gone away to take a job with the *Washington Post,* a no-brainer Bernie said.

"I, um, ah," Bernie said. "Sorry."

"You're saying you're sorry?"

"Uh-huh."

"For what?"

"For what didn't happen," Bernie said. For what didn't happen? This was hard to follow. My mind wandered to a morning not long ago when Suzie had arrived suddenly at the houseboat where Bernie and I had stayed while working the Ralph Boutette case and found Vannah on board. Vannah: a story for another time, but I should probably mention that tiny bikini and how the straps kept slipping no matter what she did. My mind wandered on to something else, namely barbecue, and when it came back, Bernie was saying, ". . . crazy to let silly misunderstandings come between us."

"How about serious misunderstandings?" Suzie said, her voice still pretty cold.

9

"Them, too," Bernie said.

There was a pause, and then Suzie laughed. Soon they were both laughing. I like watching humans laugh when they're on the phone, especially when they laugh their heads off and somehow keep the phone in place the whole time. As for what this conversation was about, you tell me. It went on for some time, and then I put my paw on Bernie's knee, just reminding him about what we were here for, namely barbecue.

Bernie glanced at me. "I've got a feeling Chet's hungry," he said.

"That'll be with a capital H," Suzie said, losing me completely. But maybe not Bernie. He laughed again. What fun we were all having! I pressed a little harder with my paw.

"So," Bernie said.

"So," said Suzie. After that came a long pause. Then she went on. "What's next?"

"Headed home," Bernie said.

"Happy trails," said Suzie.

We hopped out of the Porsche — me actually hopping, Bernie using the door — and walked toward Ti-Pierre's Cajun BBQ. They had a deck on one side, so that was where we headed, restaurant decks usually being pretty welcoming to me and my kind. We took the last empty table — all the others occupied by biker guys and gals — and Bernie ordered: beer for him, water for me, ribs and brisket to share. A biker at the next table leaned toward us.

"That your Porsche out there?"

Bernie nodded. I'd been about to lie down in the shade under the table; instead I sat up nice and straight.

The biker leaned a little closer, one of those dudes with a neck thicker than his head, not a look that shows humans at their best, in my opinion. "Piece of crap," he said. He had the most interesting breath I'd smelled in a long time, a rich mix of onions, garlic, pulled pork, whiskey, pot, cocaine, rotten teeth, and strawberry ice cream.

"This is America," Bernie said. "You're welcome to your opinion."

The biker dude turned to the biker gal beside him. Hey! She had the same kind of neck, thicker than her head. Had I ever seen that on a woman before? I was trying to remember when the biker dude spoke in a high little voice. "You're welcome to your opinion." The biker gal thought that was funny. So did a bunch of the other bikers, all of them now looking our way. "My point exactly, pretty boy," the biker said, now back to his normal voice, rough and loud. "This.

Is. America."

Pretty boy? Was he agreeing with me that Bernie had the best face in the world? I went back and forth on that. Meanwhile, the biker dude was saying, "Your piece of crap ride ain't American. Makin' you a traitor, as well as a sexual deviator."

It got very quiet out on the deck at Ti-Pierre's Cajun BBQ, so when Bernie spoke every word was clear. "You're embarrassing yourself," he said.

It got even quieter. I heard the sounds of chairs being pushed back a bit and feet getting gathered underneath dudes, dudes maybe planning to rise in a hurry.

The thick-necked biker's face was real red now and his nostrils had opened up a surprising amount, reminding me of a bull I came across once in a corral I'd regretted entering almost immediately. "Tell you what," he said. "I'll give you a choice. I can either beat the shit outta you here and now —"

"Yeah, do that, Ferdie," called someone from another table.

"— or you can put those airy-fairy wheels of yours up against me and my Harley, say from here to the Pont Greve Bridge and back." He took out a fat wad, counted out some bills, and slapped them on our table.

12

"A thousand bucks says you lose."

Another biker dropped in more money. "Make that two grand."

And one more biker. "Three."

Meaning there was a serious pile of money on the table, how much exactly I'll leave to you, since I don't go past two. I had the feeling that we hadn't walked away with a whole lot of green on the Ralph Boutette case, although the details wouldn't come. Something about emergency car repairs? Maybe. But none of that mattered now. All that mattered was us latching on to that pile of money.

Bernie leaned back in his chair, looking real relaxed, unlike everyone else on the deck. But that was Bernie! "I'm mighty tempted, Ferdie," he said. "But you're too drunk to drive."

There's a kind of silent excitement that can spread quickly through a group of humans. It's got some sweat in it, the sour kind, plus a funky part, male and female. I smelled it now, and the fur on the back of my neck rose up. Ferdie got to his feet, and I smelled one more thing: he had a gun in his pocket, recently fired.

Ferdie — even huger than I'd thought, now that I saw him upright — gazed down at Bernie like he hated him, which made no sense since they'd hardly even met. "Willing to bet I'm too drunk to beat you to a pulp?" he said.

Bernie got a distant look in his eyes, the way he does when he's doing his deepest thinking.

"Yellow, huh?" said Ferdie, which I didn't get at all, Bernie's skin being tanned and a bit reddish if anything.

"It's more the syntax," he said.

"Huh?"

"A little tricky, took me a moment," Bernie said. "But sure, I'm on. Although why don't I just take the money and spare you the pain?"

Ferdie roared. More bull than man, but the sound didn't scare me. I'd seen enough fighting — and done plenty myself — to know that when it came to humans, the silent ones are the most dangerous. Did Ferdie flip the table right onto Bernie and come swarming in, throwing heavy round-houses with his huge arms? Possibly, but I was on my own feet now and facing away from the action, setting up a friendly little boundary, just making it easier for every-body. From behind I heard a *thump thump,* and maybe one more thump, Ferdie still pounding away, and then came a brief pause followed by a snap that reminded me of wishbones on Thanksgiving — my favorite holiday, but no time to go into that now — only much louder, and right after that there was a horrible cry of . . . how to put it? Agony? Not Bernie's of course, but it really did scare me just the same.

I turned. Bernie was on his feet — the money already tucked into the pocket of his Hawaiian shirt — setting the table back up in the proper way. Ferdie lay on the floor kind of . . . how to put it? Writhing? That was as close as I could get. His arm was at an angle you never see. Just the sight of it made a big bearded biker a few tables back puke all over a paper plate stacked with cornbread. I came close to losing my appetite, and in that moment of not concentrating on my job, almost missed Ferdie's biker gal — the one with the thick neck, even thicker than his, I now saw: what a time we were having! — whipping a little pink-handled gun out from under her bra. Luckily for me — and I've had so much luck in my life, starting with flunking out of K-9 school on the very last day, which was how I met Bernie — I can go from just standing around to flying through the air in no time flat, always the best time there is. The next thing I knew I had that little pink popgun in my mouth and the thick-necked biker gal was holding her wrist and calling me names I'm sure she didn't mean.

"Nice work, big guy," Bernie said, taking the gun. A breeze sprang up behind me and after hardly another moment went by, I realized it was my own tail in action. Was I cooking or what?

Bernie held up the gun in a delicate kind of way between his finger and thumb. "Any objection to me confiscating this? Wouldn't want anyone to get hurt."

Judging from the looks on their faces, that didn't go over too well with the bikers. They seemed to be closing in, a dude with one of those teardrop tattoos, like he was always feeling sad, drawing a throwing knife from behind his back.

"I know what you're thinking," Bernie said, his eyes on no one in particular. "I'm making a big fuss about nothing. No way such a pipsqueaky thing could be accurate. You're probably right, but . . ." Bernie's grip on the gun changed a bit: still kind of loose but now his finger was on the trigger. Crack went the gun, but in a very small way. Then came a clang, and the throwing knife got knocked right out of the teardrop dude's hand and fell to the floor. "Gracious me," Bernie said. He stared at the pink-handled gun like he was amazed, then dropped it into his pocket.

Things settled down after that. In fact, it turned out the bikers all had somewhere else to be. By the time the waiter appeared with our order, we had the deck to ourselves.

"Where the hell did everybody go?" the waiter said.

"No one takes time to smell the roses anymore," Bernie told him.

Roses? None around that I knew of, and you can trust me on that kind of thing. But the smell of Ti-Pierre's Cajun BBQ was overpowering. The waiter laid a paper plate of brisket at my feet, and I have no memories from that moment until Bernie and I were back in the car.

He opened the glove box, popped the little pink-handled gun inside, which was where we normally kept the .38 Special, now on the bottom of the sea for reasons I won't go into. Bernie cranked us up, drove out of the lot and into the crossroads, started to turn, and then stopped. He took his hands off the wheel. There was no traffic, but stopping in the middle of the road? Not our usual MO.

Bernie looked my way. "Left is west, Chet. West and home. We're westerners, you and me." I was just finding that out now? It sounded important. "But there's a tide in

the affairs of men." This was getting complicated. I started to pant a bit. Bernie's hands
settled on the wheel. "And east is Suzie."

TWO

"It's a big country, Chet," Bernie said. "Last, best hope."

I looked out from the shotgun seat. Yes, big country was zipping past, this part hilly and so green, compared to back home. As for hopes, I had none at the moment: everything was perfect just how it was. The sun went down and the land darkened from the bottom up until all I could see was a mountaintop off to one side, glowing deep orange.

"Lookout Mountain, big guy," Bernie said. "Battle Above the Clouds, Grant versus Bragg. Littles fought on both sides. Military family, going way back. Kind of shapes your outlook on life, curse and a blessing. Suppose we'd been, I don't know, pharmacists, say, or shoemakers."

I loved when Bernie went on like this! Shoemakers, was that it? I checked Bernie's feet. He was wearing flip-flops. I felt in the picture, but totally. Not long after that, we pulled into a truck stop, had a little snack — kibble for me, tacos for Bernie. Then came a wonderful warm wave of relaxation flowing right through my body, and when that happens, my eyelids get heavy. And after that, what can you do? Clouds came rolling in. I was safe and sound above them. From time to time Bernie's voice drifted in through the clouds, Bernie speaking the way he does when he's thinking out loud. "Should we call ahead?" he said. And then after a while, ". . . but surprises are nice — don't women like surprises?" I shifted around, got even more comfortable, hard to imagine how that was possible. Whatever this was, Bernie would work it out. He was the best out-loud thinker I knew. The worst was a perp name of Joe Don "Einstein" Wargle Jr., whose last out-loud thought that I heard was: "If I jump out this here window, you suckers'll never catch me."

Meanwhile, Bernie had gone quiet. Somehow I got my eyes open long enough to check on him. And what do you know? He was in dreamland.

The next time I opened my eyes, the sky was just starting to lighten in a milky sort of way, too soon for telling whether it was clear or cloudy, and we were on the road. I looked across at Bernie. Sometimes I think you only see humans the way they really are from the side. Actually, I'd never thought that before and wished I hadn't now. I mean, what comes next? All I knew was I really liked Bernie's face from the side; and the front, of course, goes without mentioning. As for what I could see? First, Bernie was real tired, his face pale except for dark patches under his eyes. Second, the eyes themselves were intense, like Bernie was wired about something. I sat right up. When Bernie's wired, I'm wired.

He glanced over at me. "Sleeve of care all knitted back up, big guy?" he said, pretty much losing me from the get-go. I checked the sleeves of his shirt, saw nothing unusual. He was wearing the same Hawaiian shirt he'd had on the day before, the one with the drinking fish pattern — all these fish bellied up to a bar, smoking and drinking, not my favorite when it comes to Bernie's Hawaiian shirts. I looked out instead, saw we were on a freeway with lots of lanes, all those lanes clogged in both directions.

"Our government on the way to work," Bernie said. "Kinda wish they wouldn't bother."

Uh-oh. What could we do about that?

21

There were so many of them. We climbed a long hill, and on the other side a big city appeared, maybe not as big as the Valley, but the river in this city had water in it and ours didn't. "Foggy Bottom," Bernie said. "Where they keep the levers of power. Wouldn't mind seeing one of those levers someday, let alone getting my hands on it."

Kind of a puzzler: what about that time we got stuck in a ditch and Bernie said, "I'll just use this branch to lever us out." He had his hands on a lever that day, no doubt about it, and the fact that the branch had snapped in two and we ended up calling in the wrecker and giving him all our cash and the dude was still grumbling didn't change that. Also, there was no fog I could see now; the sky had turned nice and blue. I made a mental note to drag the very next fallen branch that came along over to Bernie. Then he'd say, "Levers of power, just what I've been looking for. Thanks, big guy!" The day was off to a good start. We crossed a bridge over the river, a white-domed building on the far side. "Jefferson Memorial," Bernie said, and then surprised me by leaning out his window toward the white-domed building and calling, "Come back to life!"

We've had this type of long road trip before, a long road trip where Bernie gets a bit hard to follow after a while. Those road trips always ended well in my memory, just like everything with Bernie. My mind moved on to thoughts of breakfast. But no one ever comes back to life, practically the first thing you learn in a job like mine; although I can think of an exception, which maybe we'll get to later. But all the other times a new smell starts up right away and no matter what the EMTs do — and I've seen them try and try — there's no going back. Turned out I had a hope after all: I hoped Bernie wouldn't be too disappointed when whoever he wanted to come back to life did not.

We drove into one of those neighborhoods that was all about nice houses with space between them and no one around but landscapers. Bernie patted his pockets, reached under the seat, fumbled with some scraps of paper, squinted at a torn envelope. "Two forty-three? Is that what it says? Can't read my own damn . . ." He checked the passing houses, slowed down, pulled over in the shade of a big tree. A taxi came by the other way, the driver pulling over on his side of the street and parking in the shade of his own big tree. The driver — a slicked-back hair dude — took a long look at a blue mini-van parked farther up our side of the street and then glanced over at us. His face, not happy at the moment, looked like it was made of a few hard slabs stuck together. He steered back onto the street and drove off, leaving a faint smell of hair gel behind, a bit like the scent of bubble gum. I'd tried bubble gum once. Not food and not a chewy: I didn't understand bubble gum at all.

We got out of the car, approached the nearest house, a brick house with a tall hedge in front and a gated driveway on one side, the gate hanging part open. A member of the nation within the nation — as Bernie calls me and my kind — had laid his mark on one of the gateposts, forcing me to do the same. Meanwhile, Bernie had gone on ahead. I tried to hurry things along, but that's not so easy to do. Bernie was already knocking at the front door when I caught up to him.

"Kind of a big house," Bernie said. "Maybe we've got the wrong —"

The door opened and a woman — not Suzie — looked out. She was maybe about Suzie's age, had red hair and green eyes — although Bernie says I can't be trusted when it comes to colors, especially red, so don't bother remembering this part — and wore a dark business suit. I knew right away that she was the type of woman who had a certain effect on Bernie.

"Yes?" she said.

"Uh," said Bernie. "We're, um, looking for Suzie Sanchez."

"Is she expecting you?"

"Not really. It's kind of a surprise."

The woman gazed at Bernie. With some humans, you can see into their eyes a bit, get a feel for what's going on behind them. This woman was some other type. "Are you a friend?" she said.

Bernie nodded. "I'm Bernie Little. This is Chet."

My tail got ready to start up, but the woman didn't look at me. "The private detective?" she said. She looked past us. "That must be the famous Porsche."

"Wouldn't know about famous," Bernie said.

The red-haired woman smiled, more to herself that to us, if that makes any sense.

"Suzie mentioned you," she said. "She's our tenant — you'll find her in the carriage house out back." The door closed.

We followed the driveway along the side of the house, past a small green lawn which a squirrel had crossed, and not long ago —

"Chet!"

— and came to another brick house, much

smaller than the first. Bernie gave it a careful look. "Urbane?" he said, stepping up to the door. "Would that be the word?" He was on his own. I waited for the answer. Bernie froze and said, "Oh, my God! Flowers!" "Flowers" was the answer, not "urbane"? That was as far as I could take it. Meanwhile, Bernie was glancing around wildly. He spotted some yellow flowers growing in a window box, sprang over and snatched them out, then returned to the door, the flowers in one hand and a surprising amount of that moist black potting soil on his shirt. Bernie's other hand was in knocking position when the door began to open from the inside. A lovely big smile spread across Bernie's face and then just hung there in the strangest way when a man stepped outside. The man wore a suit, had a neatly trimmed little beard but no mustache, a look that always bothered me, no telling why, and carried a briefcase made of fine, lovely-smelling leather that aroused a funny feeling in my teeth right away, a feeling that only gnawing can satisfy, as you may or may not know. He paused, rocking back slightly on his heels. We've seen that before. Bernie's a pretty big dude, and I'm not exactly a midget myself, a hundred-plus pounder, in fact, as I'd heard Bernie say more than once.

"Ah, um," the man said, and then his gaze settled on the flowers. "A delivery for Ms. Sanchez?"

"Huh?" said Bernie.

I was with him on that: the bearded dude had a strange way of talking. Much easier to understand was his smell, which was all about nervousness, and getting more so. Nothing easier to pick up in the whole wide world of smells than human nervousness — excepting bacon, of course, goes without mentioning, and possibly steak on the barbie, and there's no leaving out burgers, plus those Thai ribs down at Mr. Cho's Tex Mex Chinese Takeout and Delivery aren't too shabby, and . . . where were we again? All I knew for sure was that my position on the front step seemed to have changed a bit, moving me closer to the briefcase. At the same time, the bearded dude was calling over his shoulder. "Suzie? A delivery for you."

"Coming." That was Suzie, no doubt about it, from somewhere back in the house — meaning we'd found her, so everything had to be going smoothly.

The bearded dude raised his voice again. "Bye, love." Then he stepped around us — me getting in a lick of his briefcase, an all-too-quick lick, but the leather was by far the best I'd ever tasted — walked down the street, got into the blue minivan, and drove away. Bernie wasn't smiling now, but his mouth was still open. All of a sudden, he looked like Charlie! Charlie's Bernie's kid back home in the Valley, where we all once lived together as one big happy family — me, Bernie, Charlie, and Leda, Leda being Bernie's wife at the time, but now married to Malcolm, who's real big in software, whatever that may be, and we don't see Charlie much, except for some holidays and weekends. But no time for any of that, and I shouldn't have even gotten started. The point is, I could now see Charlie in every feature of Bernie's face. Okay, not the nose. Bernie's waiting to get that slightly bent part — hardly noticeable, in my opinion — fixed after he's sure that his fistfighting days are over, which I hope is never, on account of how much I'd miss seeing that sweet uppercut.

Right in there somewhere, Suzie appeared. Her eyes — beautiful dark eyes that shone like the countertops in our kitchen after they'd been polished, which had been a while — widened in the way that shows a human is surprised. Cats are just the opposite, but let's leave them out of the story if we can.

"Bernie?" she said. "What are you doing here? I thought you were headed home."

"Uh, home, right," said Bernie. "Surprise type of thing." He thrust the flowers in her direction, then seemed to think better of it, and drew them quickly back, the heads of some of the flowers snapping off and wafting down to the floor, a black-and-white tile floor that I knew would feel nice and cool on my paws once we got inside. Wasn't that the plan? I got a sudden feeling that things weren't going well and started panting just the littlest bit. Bernie noticed all the scattered petals. "Maybe not my brightest idea," he said.

"No, no," said Suzie. "This is wonderful! I just wish you'd called, that's all. I would have been more . . . organized."

Bernie glanced back toward the street. "Is that what we're calling it?" he said.

"Bernie? Whoa. Is something wrong?"

"How would I know? I'm just the delivery boy."

Suzie's face changed and so did her eyes; she started to become a harder kind of Suzie. I preferred the other one. "You're not making much sense," she said.

"No, love?" said Bernie.

"Love?"

"That's what your guest calls you."

29

"My guest?" Suzie's eyes shifted. "You're talking about Eben? He's from London, Bernie."

"So?"

"So he calls everyone 'love,' " Suzie said. "Like Ringo Starr."

Ringo Starr? Had to be some sort of perp. And not even the first Ringo perp we'd run into. Who could forget Ringo Gogarnian, who liked to dress as a mailman and empty out people's mailboxes and was now dressed in an orange jumpsuit? Message to Ringo Starr: heads up, buddy boy. Bernie and Suzie had gotten a bit confusing there for a moment, but now we were humming.

"Meaning you and he aren't . . . ?" Bernie said.

"Aren't what?"

"You know."

"For God's sake — he's a source."

"A source of what?"

"Information," Suzie said. "I'm a journalist, remember? Journalists have sources."

"Oh," Bernie said.

"That's it?" said Suzie, her voice closer to its normal self, which actually reminded me of music. "Just oh?"

Bernie thought for a moment. Then he held out what was left of the flowers.

"How nice," Suzie said. "You're giving me

my own flowers."

Of course it was nice — Bernie always came up big in the end. As for me, I was already in the house, feeling the tiles under my paws, pleasantly cool just as I'd expected. I also seemed to be . . . how to put it? Munching? Close enough. I seemed to be munching on some of those petals that had fallen on the floor. They tasted a bit like grass, drier perhaps, but with a faint hint of lemon that was really quite pleasant. What was the name of this city again? Foggy something? I was liking it just fine.

THREE

First, we were hungry. Lucky for us, Suzie had a little kitchen at the back of her place, and soon we were chowing down: yogurt for Suzie, bacon and eggs for Bernie, bacon and kibble for me, and then a bit of bacon for Suzie, which she and I ended up sharing. So nice to see Suzie again! I'd missed her.

After that, we were sleepy, even though it was morning. No problem for me: whatever regular hours happened to be, we don't keep them in this business. Bernie and Suzie went upstairs to her bedroom and closed the door. I made a quick recon of the whole house — not much to it, bathroom and another small bedroom on the upstairs floor, kitchen, office, and living room down below. Then I lay by the front door and closed my eyes. Warm air, actually almost hot and much damper than the air we've got back home in the Valley, leaked in under the door, and with it came sounds from the street: a car going by, a truck, and a bicycle making just a faint airy *whirr-whirr-whirr,* very pleasant to my ears.

A door opened, not too far away, thumped softly closed. Then came footsteps. A woman, moving away, wearing sneakers: other than that, I had no info. She stopped. Silence. There's a silence when something's ended. This was the other kind, when you're still in the middle.

I heard the soft grunt of a woman bending down or leaning forward. After that, a real faint metallic scratch, just about at the outside range of what I can hear. That scratch was followed by another, slightly louder. After that: a pause, a soft thud, like from a real small door closing, and then the footsteps came my way again. A door opened and closed. Another bicycle went by with another nice *whirr-whirr-whirr.*

Everything got quiet. It was quiet upstairs, too. Quiet was the ideal sound for sleeping, but for some reason I felt restless. I got up and did a complete recon of Suzie's place again, and then another. I was just passing her bedroom door for way more than the second time, when it opened and she tiptoed outside, buttoning up her blouse. Human tiptoeing: always something I love to see, although why they do it is a complete mystery.

"Shh," she said in a little whisper, making the sign Bernie and I had worked out for quiet, namely a finger across the lips. "Let him sleep, Chet — he's so tired." She gently took my front paws, which seem to have risen up and planted themselves on her chest, and encouraged them back down to the floor. We headed downstairs, Suzie still on tiptoes. Funny how noisy human steps could be, even with only the toes touching down. Yes, you had to feel for humans in some ways, but wasn't it amazing how so many of them kept breezing along like they were aces?

Downstairs in her office, Suzie checked her watch, didn't seem to like whatever it was telling her, and began gathering up stuff real quick: phone, laptop, shoulder bag. I hung right beside her, even quicker, and for no particular reason except that it felt good. We bumped into each other a few times, and then Suzie laughed and said, "Want to ride with me, Chet? The big lunk'll be zonked till noon."

What was this? Ride? I was already at the front door. The big lunk part I didn't get at all.

■ ■ ■ ■

Hadn't been in Suzie's little yellow Beetle
in way too long. Last time I'd seen it had
been back in the Valley, that sad day with a
U-Haul hooked on behind and Suzie on her
way to her new gig — a no-brainer, Bernie
said, although how did that match up with
the look on his face as he'd watched her go?
But now we were all back together! So
everything was cool, except that all the other
times I'd been in the Beetle, she'd had treats
in the glove box, and now there were none.
Not a scrap of food anywhere in the car, for
that matter. I didn't even need to bother
digging under the seats. Suzie was the tidy
type of human. The untidy types could be
bothersome at times — take Nestor "Messy"
Ness, for example, now on parole because
no one at Northern Correctional could bear
to share a cell with him — but there was
also something to be said in their favor.

We stopped at a light. "Here's a crazy
thing," Suzie said. "I really did like getting
those flowers!" She laughed. "Does that
mean I need to toughen up?" Suzie turned
and gave me a close look. I gave her a close
look right back. She smiled. "Forgot what
it's like having you around." Then came a

nice pat, so nice I never wanted the light to change. What a weird thought, because then how would we ever . . . something or other. "We'll have to pick up some treats along the way, won't we?" You had to love Suzie. Did she need to toughen up? Not with me around, amigo.

"Along the way": had to be immediately, ASAP, stat, in a hurry, now, or even sooner. What else could it mean? But we didn't seem to be making any stops. We hit some traffic, made a few turns, and soon a big open area appeared on one side, with lots of grass and — and what even looked like a nice swimming pool, the longest I'd ever seen, with a very tall and narrow stone tower at one end! Swim and a snack? But that was life: just when you think it can't possibly get any better, it does. That thought was still in my mind as we drove past the stone tower and turned onto a side street, away from the water. What was going on? I studied Suzie's face for some clue, found none.

Lots of humans are completely unaware that you're staring at them. You can stare at them all day if you want, which I don't, except when it comes to Bernie, of course. Suzie wasn't the unaware type. Her eyes shifted my way.

"I swear sometimes, Chet, I can feel you thinking right along with me."

Good news. Now we'd be clearing up this snack and swim problem. She took a deep breath, let it out slowly, making a tiny sound at the end. That was a sigh; we've got pretty much the same thing in the nation within. It means there's a problem. Slim Jims are a primo treat, but I'm not fussy: a simple biscuit would do. Problem solved!

"The truth is . . ." Suzie stopped, gave her head a little shake, started up again. "Bad to even say it out loud. But what if — at least for the moment — I'm in over my head?"

I raised my eyes, saw nothing over Suzie's head except for the roof of the Beetle. We were in the car in the usual way. No worries.

"Can't do this job without an ego," Suzie went on. "At the same time, you can't let your ego get in the way."

What a lovely voice Suzie had! I realized how much I'd missed it. As for what she's just said, I was no wiser than before, maybe less. And totally cool with it!

"Meaning," she said, "I can't ignore the question of why someone like Lanny Sands would want to meet me. He's one of those insidermost insiders, the kind you can never get to . . ." Suzie pulled over, parked a few spaces away from a restaurant with sidewalk tables, all empty. She took out her notebook, flipped through the pages, her eyes going back and forth real fast. Meanwhile, a taxi was coming up the street on the other side. It stopped, and a man wearing a suit and a baseball cap got out. He went over to the restaurant, sat at one of the tables.

"Should have known he was the ball-cap-and-suit type." Suzie snapped her notebook shut and started to get out. I started to get out with her — no point in making her go around and open my door from the outside: I like to make things easier for everybody.

Suzie held up her hand. "Sorry, Chet. You'll have to stay put."

Stay put? Had I ever heard such a thing? Did I even understand what it meant? All I knew for sure was the doors were closed and the windows, while open enough to let in a steady flow of air, weren't open nearly enough for what I had in mind. I was just about to start charging back and forth across the front seat and maybe doing things to the Beetle that might not be right, when Suzie glanced back at me. "Won't be long — I promise." Suzie has a wonderful voice, like music, if I haven't mentioned that already. Not music like "Death Don't Have

No Mercy." More like "If You Were Mine," one of our favorites, mine and Bernie's, especially when Roy Eldridge comes in with his trumpet at the end. The feeling I get, all the way through my ears to the tip of my tail and back again, and I'm sure the same thing happens with Bernie, except for the tail. Too bad Bernie didn't have a tail. He said so himself on a day I won't forget: Bernie, high up in a tree in our yard, taking down a hanging branch with the chainsaw. He leaned way out and said, "A tail would come in handy right now, big guy." The moment after that, Bernie, the ladder, and the chainsaw were all in separate motion. Bernie ended up landing on the roof of Leda's convertible — this was toward the end of their marriage — not a scratch on him, and the branch came down on its own with the arrival of the monsoons, so everything was cool. But the point was . . .

While I tried, although not my very hardest, to remember the point, I found I now had my nose stuck out the partly open window on the shotgun side. A waiter was bringing coffee to Suzie and the ball-cap-and-suit guy; and not just coffee, but some sort of baked goods — goods: what a perfect name! — that reminded me of crullers. The next thing I knew, I was finding to my amazement that the window was in fact open just wide enough, if I squeezed and squeezed and — ah!

"Oh, my God," said the ball-cap-and-suit guy, leaning way back in his chair, hands up for protection. Protection from what? Not me, I hoped. Then I noticed I'd somehow come to a stop with one paw, or maybe two, on his foot. I got that problem fixed, and pronto.

"Chet!" Suzie said, grabbing my collar and urging me toward her end of the table. "How did you —" She glanced over at the car. "Never mind. Sit. Be good."

I sat. I was good.

"Your dog?" said the ball-cap-and-suit guy.

"Belongs, if that's the word, to a friend," Suzie said.

"Eben St. John, by any chance?"

"No," Suzie said. "But you know Eben, Mr. Sands?"

"Call me Lanny. Haven't had the pleasure of meeting him yet, but I know of him."

"Plus you know I know him," Suzie said.

Lanny Sands — if I was following this right — shrugged his shoulders. He didn't have much going on in the way of shoulders, but he turned out to be one of those big-headed types, an interesting combo. That was life: interesting things flowing by all the time. "Lucky coincidence," he said, taking a bite from one of the cruller-like things.

Croissant? Was that it? With the two twisted-up ends? One of which fell off and practically bounced right up into my mouth? Still totally sitting, as anyone could plainly see, I inched his way.

". . . carriage house of yours?" Lanny went on, talking with his mouth full, a very cool human thing in my opinion. "I had a friend who wanted it, but you got there first."

"That's why you wanted to meet me?" Suzie said.

Lanny laughed, a few croissant crumbs getting spewed my way. They treated you right in this town.

"And exact my revenge," Lanny said. He laughed some more. "The truth is I've been following your work — you're good."

"Yeah?" Suzie said. "You wanted to praise me in person?"

"Any harm in that?"

"Not that I can see," Suzie said.

Lanny looked down, started moving his silverware around. The knife clinked against his water glass with a sound that seemed strangely loud to me. "The story you did on the Neanderthal reenactors is probably my favorite," he said.

"Thanks," Suzie said. "But I'd actually like to get into more serious stuff."

His head rose. "Such as?"

"Politics," Suzie said. "Isn't that what this town is all about?"

"After real estate," Lanny said, polishing off the rest of his croissant in one bite — kind of a big one there, dude — and washing it down with coffee. I'd tried coffee once — actually, a paper filter full of coffee grounds — and that was enough.

"And now that I've got you here," Suzie said, taking out a device and laying it on the table.

Lanny shook his head. "We're off the record."

"Can I quote you anonymously?"

"About what?"

"The election."

"No," Lanny said. "And the election is two years away."

"Meaning imminent in your world," Suzie said.

"My world?"

"The inside baseball world."

"I'm not part of that," Lanny said.

"Come on," said Suzie. "You're the Sandman."

"I hate that nickname."

"Isn't it a compliment? Your arrival on the

42

scene means lights out for the opposition."

"That's the cartoon version of how things work here."

"Then give me the grown-up take," Suzie said. "How about these terrible poll numbers of the president's, for example? As his childhood friend, college roommate, former campaign manager, you must have some opinion."

"Haven't seen the president since last Christmas," Lanny said. "And I no longer follow the polls. I'm retired."

"Aren't you a little young for that? What do you do with all your energy?"

"Travel. Play golf. Meet interesting people, like you. My advice is to stick to the feature stories. What's wrong with giving the people some lighthearted relief?"

"Nothing," Suzie said. "What do you say specifically to these polls showing that if General Galloway is the opposition nominee, he'll win at least thirty-nine states, with two toss-ups?"

Lanny gazed at Suzie in a way that reminded me a bit of one of Bernie's gazes, the kind that goes deep inside. I got a good clear view of his face: a roundish sort of face with very light-colored eyes. It showed nothing in particular, but under the table — and I always check out what's going on under tables — one of his legs suddenly started up, going a mile a minute. Which isn't actually that fast — we'd done two miles a minute out in the desert, and more than once. We know how to live, me and Bernie. But that wasn't the point. The point was that Lanny's top and bottom halves weren't in sync. We watch for that kind of thing at the Little Detective Agency.

"He's not nominated yet," Lanny said. "And our opponents have a long and happy history of shooting themselves in the foot."

Uh-oh. I'd seen perps do that, and more than once. Maybe this town was tougher than it looked.

"Picking someone other than the general would be shooting themselves in the foot?" Suzie said. "Is that what you're saying? And what kind of strategy depends on the other guy screwing up?"

"Strategy's beyond my grade level," Lanny said. He raised his hand. "Check!"

"I'll get this," Suzie said.

"Nonsense," said Lanny, paying the waiter. He rose. "Let's stay in touch."

"Why?" said Suzie.

Lanny laughed again. "You're going places," he said. He sat back down, lowered his voice. "In fact, if General Galloway is the nominee, I may have something for you during the campaign. As long as you don't jump the gun."

"What sort of something?" Suzie said. "And what do you mean by jumping the gun?"

"Asking premature questions, like you're doing right now." Lanny rose again. "How's that landlady of yours, by the way?"

"Lizette Carbonneau? You know her?"

"Seen her at parties," Lanny said. "Are she and Eben close?"

"I don't think they know each other," Suzie said. "Why?"

"No particular reason," said Lanny. "You'll find this is a small town, that's all. Remember student government in high school? It's the same type of people, but exactly."

"Am I meant to understand that in the context of Eben and Lizette?" Suzie said.

Lanny smiled. "It was just an idle remark, and not particularly original," he said, "signifying nothing."

He walked off down the street. Suzie watched him go. I watched both of them, no need to turn my head even as the distance grew. That's how we roll in the nation within. I'm sure your eye setup has its good points, too.

"I actually liked high school," Suzie said.

I pressed up against her. I liked high school, too, especially the one near our place on Mesquite Road, where I'd once snagged a baseball in the middle of a game. And then done it again the very next day!

FOUR

"Suzie Sanchez, girl reporter," said Suzie.

Back in the car, stop-and-go traffic and a cat was eyeing me from the rear window of the car ahead. Ever had a cat eye you? Cats always send the same message, a message about them being on top and you on the bottom. Even the way they move sends that message! Once — true story — I was digging a hole — can't remember exactly where or why and it doesn't matter — and really making progress, all paws chipping in to the max and clods of earth and sod soaring sky high, when I happened to notice a cat on someone's porch, perhaps a porch associated with the very lawn I was digging up, it now occurs to me, although it did not at the time, but that's not the point. The point was the way this cat, so perfectly still, was watching me, so perfectly in motion, if that makes any sense. I froze for a moment, standing, if I'm remembering right, on just two of my paws, one front and one back. That was when the cat yawned, an enormous yawn somehow right in my face despite the distance between us. At that moment, I lost all interest in the hole! True story! And just walked away. A good thing in the end, because by the time the dude with the shotgun came charging onto the porch, I was out of range.

". . . speaking of high school, my very first piece on the high school paper," Suzie was saying, "an exposé of janitorial salaries that made the principal — Chet? What are you doing?"

What was I doing?

"Not digging at the seat, by any chance?"

Digging at the seat? Me? Of course not. My front paw was poised like this because . . . just because. Up ahead, the car with the cat in back swung onto an exit ramp and disappeared from view. My paw came down and rested comfortably on the seat, a seat that felt slightly rougher than before, hardly at all, not worth a second thought.

"Good boy," Suzie said.

That was me! I gave the side of her face a nice big lick. She laughed. "Stop it — we'll have an accident." So I stopped, if not then, at least not too long after. Suzie was the best! When I was with her I didn't even miss . . . uh-oh, but I did. I did miss Bernie, just a bit. Then more and more. I curled up on the seat and thought about him, all nice thoughts. Suzie's voice flowed by me, kind of like a bubbling stream Bernie and I had come across on a missing wilderness camper case, of which all I remembered was an encounter with a mule named Rummy, plus the glimpse of a golden seam in a mine just before it caved in.

". . . the ways of the school committee in my little town being very good prep for DC, as it happens," Suzie was saying. "But maybe not this particular story, whatever it actually is. Eben says he's going to have something spooky for me." She laughed a laugh you hear from time to time, soft and not particularly happy. Human sounds can be confusing. "Literally spooky, maybe? Like with real spooks?"

Spooks? Oh, no. I knew spooks from Halloween, my least favorite of all the holidays, Thanksgiving being the best. Everyone zonked out in front of football on TV and leftovers out the yingyang, just for the taking: hard to beat Thanksgiving! But Halloween, with masked humans on the loose — like everyone's suddenly a perp! — is the worst. And the humans in those white-sheet spook outfits? The worst of the worst. We no longer go out on Halloween, me and Bernie. Bernie even likes me to stay in the kitchen when the trick-or-treaters come knocking, likes it so much that he once tried closing the door on me. A door he'd already taught me to open! No one's funnier than Bernie. But bottom line: if Suzie was dealing with spooks, I felt bad for her.

". . . then there's this outfit of Eben's," Suzie was saying. "Consultants, Chet — the town's crawling with them. They all want something, meaning Eben wants something, but what? Aside from what he's not going to get, of course."

I had no idea. And I didn't try too hard to make one happen. My mind was on other things, namely the news about all these crawling types in this burg. I scanned both sides of the street, saw not one crawler, although an old guy stepping out of a bar on the next corner looked a little wobbly. He blinked in the light as we went by, but he didn't go down. Once I saw a whole roomful of crawling humans. This was at a New Year's Eve party where Bernie and I hadn't actually been invited but showed up anyway, on account of a perp name of Playboy Boyovich possibly being on the scene, which turned out to be the case, and was he surprised to see us or what? So were the other partygoers, for that matter, all of them naked — which never shows humans at their best, in my opinion, no offense — and playing some sort of gigantic board game that covered the whole floor. Which reminds me of the point of all this! Whoa! Chet the Jet catches a break! But I've had a lot of luck in life. Complaints? Not a single one, amigo. Start me up!

Back to where we were before. Which was . . . something about . . . oh, so close, in the slow flickering shadows right at the edge of my mind, just out of reach. Does that ever happen to you?

". . . all so Byzantine," Suzie was saying. "In fact, I've been reading about Byzantium lately. Thinking of pitching a thumbsucker on Byzantium as a sort of handbook to twenty-first-century DC." She glanced over at me. There was a tiny vertical line on her forehead, right between the eyes. That meant she was worried. Why would Suzie worry? We were all back together, me, Bernie, Suzie. I gave her knee a quick head push.

Suzie laughed. "Nothing like the direct approach," she said. "That's you, Chet." What was that about? You tell me. And while you're at it, please clear up the pitching thumbsucking thing. I knew pitching, of course, baseballs being one of my very favorite balls, so interesting when you start getting inside, most likely why the guys at Sportz 'n Sudz, a bar we no longer frequent in Vista City, talk so much inside baseball. Thumbsucking? I knew that, too, on account of Charlie when he was little. The moment that tiny thumb came out of his mouth, I'd be right there on the spot to give it a lick. How do you like that? Actually, it's possible, I realize now, maybe kind of late in the game, that Leda did not like it one bit. Was that around the time she and I started to not get along so well? And maybe Bernie and Leda, too, now that I thought about it? Uh-oh. I stopped that thought at once, stopped it cold and blew it to smithereens forever. But the point was I hadn't followed Suzie at all.

". . . and so," she was saying, "let's do it the way you do it — how does Bernie put it? In the nation within the nation? Let's be the opposite of Byzantine. Thanks, Chet."

Huh? What was this? All I knew was that Suzie was giving me a pat — nice, but way too short — then whipping into a U-turn. The line on her forehead was gone. But the opposite of Byzantine? I was lost. At that moment, we shot forward.

"Chet!"

And practically right away I realized I was resting a paw on Suzie's driving leg, maybe even pressing down somewhat, for reasons unknown. I sat up at once, tall in the shotgun seat, a total pro, even though we weren't actually working any sort of job. I work with Bernie.

We crossed the river and not long after entered a world of office parks. We've got the same kind of world back home in the Valley, except not so green.

"Welcome to Maryland," Suzie said. "Most of what you see around you is about elephants versus donkeys."

Oh, no. Up until then I'd been liking Maryland a lot. But I'd had encounters with both those creatures — it's that kind of career, amigo — and if elephants and donkeys were in the picture, we had problems.

"Fun times, Chet. Election two years away, president's numbers in the toilet, and the opposition jumping up and down with glee."

That did sound like fun, the toilet part especially, and there can never be too much of jumping up and down. Suzie turned into a mostly empty lot and parked in front of a low brassy-colored office building with those brassy-colored windows you can't see through from the outside. I don't like them, hard to say why.

"Feel like actually waiting in the car this time? I'll be quick."

Suzie looked at me; I looked at her.

"Right," Suzie said. "But the leash is non-negotiable." She popped open the glove box and took out the leash she'd kept just for me back when she was still in the Valley. I was kind of surprised to see it still there, also not that happy about it. Suzie smiled and gave me a quick scratch between the ears, not hard enough but blissful just the same. "Come on, Chet. I know you can do it."

We got out of the car. Suzie came forward with the leash. Of course, I could do it! And not only that, I could do it like you've never seen.

"Chet?"

Yes, that was me, pure and simple. At the moment, I appeared to be wriggling around the parking lot on my back, just one of my tricks, and one that happened to scratch all the itches Suzie hadn't taken care of.

"There'll be a little treat if you're good."

Not long after that, we went through the front door of the office building, me upright and leading — and on the leash, I suppose, although all my attention was on an almost whole croissant Suzie had suddenly produced from her pocket. Almost whole or not, it was all gone — down the hatch! — by the time we came to the elevators. "Down the hatch," was what Bernie used to say to Charlie, back in the high-chair days, a high chair I hung around quite a bit. That little spoon of Charlie's! He missed the opening to the hatch just about every time. Honey-coated Cheerios — Charlie and I grew up on them together.

The elevator opened and we got in. Or, more accurately, Suzie got in and I lingered at the entrance, one paw raised. Am I at my best in elevators? Maybe not. Elevators are a lot like crates, as I'm sure you've noticed, and crates are out of the question for me. But just as Suzie was starting to give me some sort of look, I caught a whiff you don't usually catch in elevators, namely a whiff of guinea pig. I sniffed up that whiff, if you get what I mean, all the way to the back of the elevator.

"Good boy, Chet," Suzie said as she pressed a button on the wall panel.

Suzie, just the best! And always nice to hear *Good boy, Chet,* although why now was a puzzler, a puzzler I ignored completely, on account of how occupied I was with the guinea pig smell. No actual guinea pig had been in the elevator — the scent wasn't nearly strong enough — meaning it had been left by some human who spent time with guinea pigs. Why would a human do that? I'd had some experience with guinea pigs. Take Peony, for example, a guinea pig who'd cropped up in a case some time back and of which I remembered nothing but Peony, with whom I hadn't gotten along. Guinea pig teeth are surprisingly sharp; let's leave it at that.

The elevator rose and came to a too-quick stop, the doors sliding open. Hey! I almost puked! We got out, walked down a hall, and stopped before a door. Suzie read the sign: " 'World Wide Solutions,' " she said. "Eben has a lot of good points, but modesty's not one. Not much modesty in this town, now that I think of it. Possible story idea, Suzie girl." Or something like that, way too hard to follow. Suzie opened the door and we went inside.

You get to know offices in this line of work — Cedric Booker, the Valley DA has a basketball hoop in his! Which had got me a bit too excited, and the next thing I'd known Cedric's basketball was all shriveled up, nothing ballish about it. A story for another time.

This particular office had no hoop. Instead, there was just the usual reception part and an inner office at the back. No one sat at the reception desk, which bore a vase of flowers, the plastic kind without a trace of flower smell. Wasn't flower smell the whole point of flowers? There were lots of human things that I didn't understand. I was trying to think of another one beside the plastic flowers as we approached the closed door of the inner office.

Suzie knocked. "Eben?"

No answer, but a man was in there: I could smell him, and also smell that lovely leather briefcase. How nice a few moments with that briefcase, preferably alone, would be! Was that in my future? This was shaping up as a fine day.

Suzie turned the knob, opened the door. The inner office was smaller than our office back home on Mesquite Road but much tidier, no papers scattered around, no piles of this and that, nothing on the desk but a closed laptop — in short, it was all as neat as Eben's little trimmed beard. Eben was sitting behind the desk, kind of slumped in his chair. One of his eyes was open and the other closed, like he was winking. Except he wasn't.

"Eben?"

I went closer, possibly pulling the leash from Suzie's hand, but that's the kind of thing that happens when I smell blood. It was seeping, although hardly at all, from a small round hole just behind one of Eben's ears.

"Oh, my God!"

Eben's open eye shifted very slightly in Suzie's direction.

"Eben! What happened?" Suzie, now right beside me, touched Eben's shoulder, a light touch, but enough to make him tip sideways, right off the chair and onto the floor. Suzie's eyes got huge and frightened, and she covered her mouth with her hand, something you see women do, but men never.

The death smell started up almost at once, which was always how this goes down. So we had the blood smell, the death smell, and also — almost overwhelmed but definitely in the room — the guinea pig smell. I had the craziest thought of my life: the guinea pig did it.

I needed Bernie.

FIVE

"Bernie?" Suzie said into her phone. "Come on, pick up. Please."

We were still in Eben's office but had moved a little farther away from Eben's body. His face was getting whiter and waxier, which somehow made his neatly trimmed beard more and more prominent, almost like the beard was alive on its own or something like that. I wished I hadn't had that thought. It went away.

"Bernie? Bernie? Wake up!"

Right about then I smelled one of those smells Bernie and I had worked on. Who wouldn't like working on smells? For one thing, it involves treats, often a Slim Jim. No other thing actually comes to me, but aren't Slim Jims enough? This particular smell, the one I was picking up at the moment, was metallic and gunpowdery. I followed it to the foot of Eben's desk chair, a roller chair pushed back from the desk a bit. A shell casing lay beside one of the little chair wheels. I sat beside it and barked, just this clipped and not very loud bark I use for smell work.

Suzie looked down at me, saw the shell casing, and put the phone away.

"You're really something, you know that?"

How nice of her! And even nicer was the Slim Jim, coming next. But it didn't! Instead, Suzie turned and went into the outer office. I followed, followed very closely, the leash now forgotten by Suzie and dragging on the floor. Suzie opened the top drawer of the reception desk. The Slim Jims were in there? Made total sense to me. She reached in and . . . took out a notebook? She flipped through it, found no Slim Jims that I could see. Things were taking a bad turn. Suzie placed a finger on one of the notebook pages and picked up the desk phone.

"The building manager, please," she said.

Not long after that, we had a bunch of uniformed cops in the room. There was some back and forth, some huddling over Eben, and then Suzie showed them the shell casing. Meaning one of the cops had the Slim Jim responsibility? But no. They got started with crime scene taping, picture taking, gum chewing, all the usual cop things. The cop with the most gold on his uniform made a little motion to Suzie and led us out to the hallway.

"You who called it in?" he said.

"Yes," said Suzie.

"Name?"

"Suzie Sanchez. And yours?"

The cop didn't seem to like that. His eyes, like little raisins — I'd tried a box of raisins once, found them too sticky for my taste — got even littler. "Lieutenant Soares." He turned those raisin eyes on me. "This your dog?"

"A friend's, actually."

"Looks like a K-9 type."

I was! I was the K-9 type! Was Lieutenant Soares on Slim Jim duty? Maybe he wasn't so bad after all. He turned back to Suzie, seemed to be waiting for her to speak. When she did not, he said, "How about you take me through it?"

"Through what?" Suzie said.

"Your relationship to the deceased, for starters."

"He's — he was an acquaintance."

"And the purpose of your visit?"

"Eben was a consultant. I was consulting him."

"What did he consult about?"

"International politico-economics."

"Is that what you do?" Lieutenant Soares said. "International politico-economics?"

"In a sense," Suzie said. "I'm a reporter for the *Washington Post.*"

"Ah," said Lieutenant Soares. His eyes shifted one way, then the other. That's a sign of thoughts getting batted around in the human mind. Lieutenant Soares opened his mouth and looked on the point of saying something — I'd have bet anything it was about Slim Jims! — but at that moment the elevator opened down the hall and a man stepped out. He came toward us, a quick-walking dude in a dark suit. Lots of dark-suited dudes in this city; I thought about making what Bernie calls a mental note, but nothing came next and I dropped the whole shebang.

Hey! The quick-stepping dude turned out to be the intense-type of human who pushes a sort of energy wave in front of him, a wave I could feel in a hard-to-explain way. Hadn't run into one of those since Pepperpot McGint, a tiny booze-truck hijacker who'd put up the best fight of anyone I'd ever seen one-on-one with Bernie and now was breaking rocks in the hot sun, probably lots of them and real fast.

This new energy-pushing dude — he had

a big bony nose, something I always like to
see in a human — stopped in front of
Lieutenant Soares. "You in charge?" he said,
flashing some kind of ID.

Lieutenant Soares squinted at the ID in
an unfriendly way and then said, "Yeah,"
also in an unfriendly way.

"I'll be taking over now."

"Didn't catch your name."

"But you just saw it." They stared at each
other. "Ferretti," said the new guy. "Double
R's, double T's, Victor D." He pushed past
us and entered Eben's office. Lieutenant
Soares muttered something that didn't
sound nice and followed. We did, too. By
that time, Ferretti was already in the inner
office.

"Whoa," said one of the cops, holding up
his hand in the stop sign.

"It's all right," said Lieutenant Soares.

Ferretti ducked under a strip of crime tape
in one easy motion and stood over Eben.
He gazed down at him for a long time.
Everyone else stopped what they were doing and gazed at Ferretti. He turned slowly
away from Eben and then paused, his eyes
on a potted plant in the far corner of the
room.

"What have we here?" he said, ducking
back under the yellow tape and walking over

to the plant. Something lay half-buried in the blackish earth. Ferretti snapped on plastic gloves, reached into the pot, and pulled out a gun. He blew off the dirt in two puffs and held it up, a real small gun with a pink handle.

"Twenty-two?" said Lieutenant Soares.

Ferretti nodded.

One of the cops raised the shell casing. "Twenty-two," she said.

When we got back to Suzie's place, the red-haired woman — Lizette the landlady, had I gotten that right? — was outside the main house, watering flowers with a hose. Spray me! That was my first and only thought.

"Hi, Suzie," she said.

"Hi, Lizette."

"Is something wrong?" Lizette said. "You look . . . not yourself."

"Terribly wrong," Suzie said. "A friend of mine's dead."

Lizette's eyes opened wide, glittering and green. "I'm so sorry. Who . . . ah . . . ?"

"A consultant named Eben St. John," Suzie said.

"The name's not familiar," said Lizette.

"He was shot," Suzie said. "Murdered."

"Oh, my God," Lizette said, putting one hand to her chest. The other steered the hose nozzle back and forth in a steady rhythm over the flowers. "Shot? Murdered? What happened? Do they know who did it?"

Suzie started in on a long explanation. I watched the flowing water from the hose. Spray me! It didn't have to be for long: a quick spritz would do.

But no. When I tuned in again, Lizette was saying, ". . . distance between him and the flowerpot?"

"Ten feet or so," Suzie said.

"Ruling out suicide."

"That's what the police thought."

"Who was in charge?" Lizette said. "I — I happen to know some people on the force."

"A lieutenant named Soares."

Lizette shook her head.

"I hear you also know Lanny Sands," Suzie said.

"The political guy?" Lizette said. "I know who he is, of course, but we've never met. Where did you hear that?"

"I must have got it mixed up," Suzie said.

Lizette looked about to say something, but at that moment she noticed that I seemed to be in the flowerbed.

"I get the feeling he wants me to spray him," she said.

"A safe bet," Suzie said.

And the next thing I knew — yes! Spray,

spray, and more spray! Nothing wrong with Lizette, in my opinion. They both watched me getting sprayed, the sight maybe relaxing them a little.

"Your imposing friend find you all right?" Lizette said.

"Imposing friend?"

"The rather big gentleman who belongs to this dog," Lizette said, turning the nozzle and cutting off my water supply. "Bernie Little — your boyfriend from back home, if I understood right."

"He did," Suzie said.

What was this? A rather big gentleman who belonged to me? As I shook off the water — sending my own spray right back on Lizette and Suzie, fun on top of fun! — I went over all my belongings. There were my collars, black for dress-up and gator skin for every day, gator skin replacing my old brown one on a case that's way too complicated to go into now, but let's just say I never wanted to see a huge green dude name of Iko ever again in my life. Then I had my water bowl at home, plus my food bowl, and don't forget the portable water bowl for the car. The Porsche itself: a belonging? What else could it be? And shared with Bernie, the way I like to do things. Hey! That meant the house on

Mesquite Road in the Valley was mine, too! Mine and Bernie's, of course, goes without mentioning by now. And I'd be happy to share my collars and bowls with him if he wanted. I'd actually seen him drink from the portable water bowl on several occasions, the latest being toward the end of the Police Athletic League picnic. Other than those, I had no possessions, so I'd gotten nowhere on this problem, whatever it was.

". . . considered journalism myself at one time," Lizette was saying. The light caught her green eyes in a way that seemed to green them even more. Lizette was one of those humans you wanted to stare at, hard to say why.

"Oh?"

Lizette smiled. She had very white teeth, small and even. "In a former life. Now I'm with a Web developer."

Suzie nodded. "Where was this, if you don't mind my asking?"

"Excuse me?"

"This former life."

"Ah," said Lizette, "you've picked up the remains of my accent?"

"But I can't place it."

"I'm from Quebec originally," Lizette said. "I went to winter carnival once in Montreal, back in college." Suzie said. "I loved it."

"Where did you stay?"

"A B-and-B," Suzie said.

"Next time try the Château Frontenac — old Montreal at its best."

"Thanks," Suzie said.

One of those strange silences that seem to settle in from above now came over us. "So awful about — what was his name again?"

"Eben St. John."

"So awful," Lizette went on. She rubbed her forehead with her fingertips, leaving a dark smear of garden soil. "If there's anything I can do . . ."

I stepped out of the flowerbed, careful not to damage hardly anything at all.

"Will you just look at him?" Suzie said, her voice quiet.

For as long as she liked! We were in Suzie's room, just inside the door, watching Bernie sleep. He lay on his side, face toward us, eyes closed, eyelashes crusted over with a surprising amount of eye gunk. That was Bernie, of course, always doing things in a big way, just another reason for the success of the Little Detective Agency, except for the finances part, which may have come up already, but it comes up a lot in real life, too, if that makes any sense, so . . . so something or other. Meanwhile, Bernie's breathing — he's a wonderful breather, hard to explain how exactly — was slow and regular, mouth open just a bit, drool leaking from the downward corner. He looked great. Suzie went over to the bedside table, picked up Bernie's phone, checked the screen, sighed.

She put the phone down, but too close to the edge of the table and it fell to the floor, landing with a not loud but sort of hard *clack-clack*. Then came something very scary I'd seen once or twice and had hoped never to see again. Bernie went from being totally still to totally in motion, springing from the bed with a kind of — yes, growl — and grabbing Suzie by the wrist so fast I didn't really know what had happened until it was over. Suzie cried out. Bernie's eyes, which were all blurry, slowly cleared. He let go of Suzie's wrist, sat down on the edge of the bed with a heavy thump.

"Oh, my God," he said. "I'm sorry." He hung his head. I hated seeing that.

"What . . . what happened, Bernie?" Suzie said, rubbing her wrist. "Was it a bad dream?"

"I don't know." Bernie took her wrist, gave it a kiss. I moved in a little closer. Don't think for a moment that I had a problem with Bernie kissing Suzie's wrist. It was just that . . . that . . .

"I haven't had an . . . episode in a long time," Bernie was saying, "didn't think I'd ever . . ."

"Episode?" Suzie said.

Bernie shrugged his shoulders.

"Like a flashback?" Suzie said.

"I guess that's what they call it."

"To the war?"

Bernie nodded. A long time ago, before we'd gotten together, Bernie'd been to the war and had some bad times. I knew from the wound on his leg, which I may have mentioned before. He limped a bit, but not often, only if we were working real steep country, or he'd had to run for a long time. And Bernie didn't have to run much, running being my department, amigo. He brings other things to the table.

"Want to talk about it?" Suzie said.

Bernie shook his head. He rose, rubbed his face hard with both hands, and then . . . then gave himself a sort of shake. Not my type of shake that goes from nose to tail and back again — impossible what with Bernie having no tail — but a pretty good shake, and in fact a great one for a human. But that was Bernie.

"You're all right?" Suzie said.

"Yeah." And I could see it. Bernie was back to normal Bernie, just the way I love him. He glanced at me — his expression changing slightly — and back to Suzie. "What have I missed?"

Six

"Eben?" Bernie said. "The Brit who was here this morning?"

"Yes, Bernie," Suzie said. "That's what I'm trying to tell you." She gave him a sideways look, maybe enjoying the way his hair was all messed up. And his eyebrows, too! Have I mentioned Bernie's eyebrows? They have a language of their own. "How about more coffee?" Suzie said.

Bernie shook his head. A vein throbbed in one of his hands, something I hadn't seen in a while, the last time being the only missing kid case we'd ever worked where we didn't get the kid back. That vein had throbbed in Bernie's hand; he'd whipped us into a screaming U-turn; we'd roared through the night, pedal to the metal; and gotten there too late. I'll never forget when we opened that broom closet. We'd taken care of justice later that night ourselves, me and Bernie. I won't forget that either. Or the name of the kid: Gail.

Back to Suzie's kitchen. The vein throbbed. Bernie said, "You discovered the body?"

"Chet and I, yes."

"Are you all right?" That had to be meant for Suzie: dead body discovery was part of my job.

"I think so," Suzie said. "I'm kind of stunned, if you want the truth."

"Um," Bernie said. "Uh." Then he reached across the table and patted Suzie's hand. Their fingers kind of wound around each other, almost like living things. Whoa. But, of course, they were living things. I'd meant more like . . . like dancers, say. Finger dancers? Back up, big guy. You're in way over your head.

". . . a Lieutenant Soares from Metro Police," Suzie was saying.

"What was he like?" Bernie said.

"Seemed competent, but he wasn't in charge for long. A plainclothes guy showed up pretty soon and took over."

"A detective captain?"

"I don't know. I sensed the usual uniform slash nonuniform tension. Ferretti was his name, double R, double T, Victor D. He seemed even more competent, now that I think about it."

73

"How so?"

"For one thing, he hadn't been there for more than a minute or two before he found what I'm assuming is the murder weapon."

"Which was?"

"A gun."

"What kind of gun?"

"A pistol or revolver — I can never hold the distinction in my mind for some reason."

"A pistol has an ammo clip, whereas —"

"And please don't explain it again. A twenty-two, by the way, which matched the shell casing Chet found on the floor."

Bernie gave me a nice smile. I moved closer to him in case a treat was in the cards. Something something part of success is just showing up, Bernie always says. Cards themselves I never wanted to see in the cards. We once had a very bad night with cards, me and Bernie, although more Bernie if you want the actual truth, the problem having to do with inside straights, a complete mystery to me, and I guess from how it turned out, a mystery to Bernie, too. He gave me a nice scratch between the ears, hitting that spot I can never quite reach. No one hits that spot like Bernie. I forgot whatever it was I'd been wanting.

". . . point I'm making," Suzie went on, "is that this Ferretti guy was pretty sharp."

"And he's satisfied it's a murder?"

"I think so."

"What was the distance between the gun and the body?"

Suzie's eyes shifted.

"What?" Bernie said. "What was that thought?"

"I spoke to Lizette — the landlady — on the way in. She asked the same question in almost those exact words."

"Maybe she's a PI in disguise," Bernie said. "And the answer?"

"Ten feet, maybe a little more. Ruling out suicide, right?"

"How about robbery?"

"It wasn't mentioned."

"Did they check Eben's wallet?"

"Not before we left," Suzie said.

Bernie gazed down at the table. "What, ah, were you doing there?"

"Interviewing Eben," Suzie said. "I told you he was a source."

"On what story?"

Suzie was silent. Bernie looked up at her. Their eyes met. The way they were staring at each other bothered me in a way I could never explain, so I checked what was happening outside the window. And wouldn't you know it? The very first thing I saw was a bird flying by, a real strange-looking bird, and birds are not my favorite creatures to begin with, not even close. What's with those angry little eyes? Would I be angry if I could soar around the big blue sky twenty-four seven, whatever that is? There's a no-brainer for you, and who doesn't prefer a no-brainer to . . . to . . . a brainer?

Meanwhile, the bird flew past the window and out of sight. And then, whoa, it came back the other way, flying real slow and . . . what was this? Actually stopping outside the window? The bird hovered there for a moment or two. What were those tiny hovering birds we sometimes had near the patio flowerpots back home? Hummingbirds? I listened hard and sure enough picked up a faint hum from this bird outside the window. Humming, yes, but it didn't look much like the hummingbirds I knew, bigger for one thing, plus its wings, instead of a beating blur, weren't moving at all. As for angry bird eyes, this particular bird didn't seem to have any eyes at all! And also — but before I could get to the and alsos, the bird flew away again, wings perfectly still, and this time did not come back.

Back at the kitchen table, Bernie and Suzie were still looking at each other in that way I didn't like. Suzie said, "I wish I could tell you, Bernie."

"Why can't you?" Bernie said.

"He never really told me anything," Suzie said. "It was more like tantalizing."

"Oh?"

"He said when the time was right he was going to have a scoop for me, a spooky kind of scoop as he put it."

Spooky? Didn't I already know that? Whoa! Was I ahead of Bernie? What a thought!

"Spooky?" Bernie said. "What's that mean?"

"I don't really know," Suzie said. "There were no specifics — I got the impression he was feeling me out."

"Feeling you out," Bernie said, in a way Suzie didn't like one little bit, easy to see in her eyes.

This was hard to follow. Even worse, they were angry at each other. The next thing I knew, I was barking, and barking pretty loud. It was all sorts of things, like them being angry at each other, and the strange bird, and . . . and —

"Chet!" Bernie said.

They were both looking at me. The anger faded from their eyes. "What's bothering him?" Suzie said.

"No idea," Bernie said. He got up, went to the window, and glanced out. "Maybe he's thirsty." Bernie filled my portable water bowl at the sink, set it down beside me. I wasn't thirsty at all, but what with Bernie being so nice, I lapped up a little sip, just to be nice back. The next thing I knew I was thirstier than I'd ever been in my life! I slurped my way right down to the bottom of the bowl absolutely nonstop — even getting sprayed a bit! And by my very own self! What a life!

There was a knock at Suzie's front door. And just when we were all getting along so well! Suzie went to answer it. Bernie mopped up the floor. I gave myself a quick, businesslike shake and was practically finished winding it down when Suzie returned, not alone: she had Lieutenant Soares with her. His little raisin eyes went to Bernie, then me, and back to Bernie. I actually smelled raisins.

"Didn't realize you had company," Lieutenant Soares said. "You might want to —"

"I'd prefer Bernie's presence," Suzie said. "Lieutenant Soares, my friend Bernie Little."

"The one who belongs to the dog?" said Lieutenant Soares.

"His name's Chet," Bernie said. They didn't shake hands.

Suzie sat down at the table. Lieutenant

Soares took the chair Bernie had been using. Bernie leaned against the counter. I sat at his feet. A mouse made scratching sounds in the far wall. Nothing else was happening.

"I looked you up," Lieutenant Soares said to Suzie, "read some of your work online. That story you wrote about those Neanderthal reenactors was pretty funny."

"Thanks."

"That was how it is, or you made some of it up?"

"I don't make anything up, Lieutenant."

Soares nodded, a kind of nod with his head tilted to one side. Bernie, the best nodder there was, had one just like it. What did it mean? You tell me.

"Glad to hear that, and no insult intended," Soares said. "Fill me in on Eben St. John."

"What about him?" Suzie said.

"A telling anecdote would be nice," Soares said.

"Telling anecdote?"

"The kind of thing that conveys the essence — the way you did with those Neanderthal guys and the bone marrow episode."

I felt a change in Bernie. He didn't move, or go tense, or anything like that, but something inside him had switched on to the max. It was a change I'd felt in him before, the last time being just before we'd walked into an ambush at the old airplane graveyard out in the desert. All those bullets ricocheting off all those planes! I'd never heard such a racket, and I'm counting on it being a one-time-only event.

"I don't have an anecdote like that," Suzie said. "All I can tell you is that Eben was well educated — he had a BA from Oxford and a PhD in economics from Georgetown — spoke several languages, and was an expert on Russia and Eastern Europe."

"What do you know about World Wide Solutions?"

"That was his consulting company."

"Who was behind it?" Soares said.

"Behind it in what way?" said Suzie.

"Funding," Soares said. "Ownership."

"I was under the impression that Eben owned it himself."

"Uh-huh."

"Are you saying that's false?"

"Just gathering information," Soares said.

"I should be doing that myself," Suzie said. "Are there any suspects?"

"Too soon to say." Soares's glance went to Bernie, then back to Suzie. "How would you characterize your relationship with Mr. St. John?"

"We were acquaintances," Suzie said, "as

I think I mentioned before."

"You did," Soares said. "My apologies. Mind telling me the purpose of your visit? We've got his appointment list and you weren't on it for today."

"I was following up on some earlier conversations."

"About . . . ?"

"About a possible story."

"And the subject matter of the story?"

"Do you really expect an answer?" Suzie said. "That's not how journalism works."

"This is a murder investigation, Ms. Sanchez."

I knew Bernie was going to say something even before he opened his mouth, not because I was actually following all this blather, no offense, but because I felt it coming. We're partners, which should be pretty clear by now. "So?" he said.

Soares turned slowly to Bernie. "Bernie, was it?" he said. "Are you familiar with murder investigations, Bernie?"

"Familiar enough to know you're out of line," Bernie said.

Soares smiled, the first smile I'd seen out of him. He was one of those smilers who could do it without showing teeth. "Which side of murder investigations are you most familiar with?" he said.

Bernie smiled right back. His smile showed teeth: big beautiful white teeth that might even have been half-decent for biting, although I was still waiting for Bernie to bite anybody. What a day that's going to be! "Been on both sides," Bernie said.

"Telling me you're a cop?" Soares said.

"I'm a private investigator."

Soares's lips turned down at the corners. Humans never look their best that way, in my opinion.

"But he was a cop," Suzie said.

Hey! I'd heard about that, wanted to hear more. But no more came. Soares didn't seem interested in Bernie's cop days, maybe hadn't been listening to Suzie at all. His eyes were fixed on Bernie. "Where you based out of?" he said.

"Arizona."

Hey! I'd heard about that, too, and quite recently. I had an amazing thought, not me at all: Was the Valley somehow in Arizona? Or the other way around? The thought went away, and none too soon.

Soares held out his hand. "License?"

Bernie came closer, gave him our license. Soares squinted at it for what seemed like a long time. "You're not authorized to work DC."

"Correct."

"Just noting the fact."

Soares handed it back. For a moment, they were both holding onto it, it being our license. That stuck in my mind, no telling why. Bernie didn't return to his spot by the counter, instead stood behind Suzie, his hands on the back of her chair.

"Ms. Sanchez," Soares said, "I'm going to lay my cards on the table."

I changed position to get a better view and watched closely, but no cards appeared, a good thing considering our luck with cards, a subject I may have already gone into and promise to leave alone from now on. Instead, Soares took a small leather-bound notebook from his pocket — a very nice-smelling leather that reminded me right away of that one quick lick I'd gotten of Eben's briefcase — and paged through it.

"Did you know Mr. St. John kept a diary?" Soares said.

"Of course not," Suzie said. "I told you — we weren't close."

"Yet," Soares said.

"Yet?" said Suzie. "What is that supposed to mean?"

Soares reached across the table and handed her the leather-bound notebook. "Care to read the entry dated the sixteenth of last month, top of the left-hand page?

Maybe aloud as a courtesy to your friend Bernie here."

Suzie gazed at the notebook. Her eyes lost that dark countertop shine. Bernie, still standing behind her, could have looked down easily and read for himself, but he did not, instead kept his own eyes on Soares. Suzie closed the notebook and laid it on the table. "I know nothing about this," she said.

Which made two of us. It suddenly struck me that I knew less and less all the time because there was more and more to . . . but the thought didn't quite come. I'm a lucky dude in just about every way.

Soares picked up the notebook and slipped it back in his pocket. "Happened to memorize it," he said. "Quote — Today I came so close to telling Suzie how I feel. Reticence will be the death of me. Unquote."

Impossible to follow. All I knew was that Bernie's hands no longer rested on Suzie's chair, and he'd backed away a step or two.

"Anything to say to that, Ms. Sanchez?" Soares said, gazing right into her eyes.

She looked away. "It's news to me," she said.

Soares rose and laid a card on the table. Finally! But it was just one and no betting ensued, meaning we lost nothing. "Don't be a stranger," he said.

Seven

There's silence, which I enjoy although it just about never happens, not completely. Then there's human silence, which also can be enjoyable, but sometimes not. During those times of sometimes not, human silence feels like the ceiling's coming slowly down on your head. That was the kind of silence we had in Suzie's kitchen after Lieutenant Soares left.

"Let's go for a walk," Suzie said, her voice quieter than usual.

"Okay," said Bernie, also on the quiet side.

Who was first to the door? You can bet the ranch.

There was a screened porch at the back of the big house and Lizette was sitting in it, a book on her lap. She raised a coffee cup as we went by.

"Lizette's French Canadian," Suzie said when we were on the street.

"I thought I heard an accent," Bernie said. He glanced back. "How'd you find her?"

"Her?"

"Meaning the rental."

"Through a friend," Suzie said. "Do you like it?"

"Sure," said Bernie. "This friend have a name?"

Suzie stopped dead. "Why are you doing this?"

"Eben St. John, right?"

"I'm not going to be interrogated," Suzie said. "What's wrong with you right now?"

Uh-oh. Angry at each other again? How was that possible with Bernie and Suzie? All of a sudden, I thought of Bernie and Leda. Oh, how I wished that hadn't happened. I began to be unsure about this burg, wanted to be back home in the Valley. I thought of my best pal, Iggy, who lives next door. Bowling him over would be fun, or making off with his treats.

"That's what I'm asking you," he said.

"I don't understand."

"Don't you?" Bernie said. "For starters, did he ever work up the nerve to spill his quote inner feelings unquote? And —" And then came something or other I missed on account of that strange bird was back, now humming faintly over the crown of a large tree across the street. It just hung in the air in a bothersome sort of way. I crouched and started barking, didn't know what else to do.

"CHET!"

Normally when Bernie speaks my name like that, I dial it down, at least a little, but at the moment I was too upset — yes, I admit it — upset about this strange bird, and this burg, and whatever was going on with Bernie and Suzie. So I kept barking and finally Bernie followed my gaze up to the top of the tree across the street and . . . and said, "Must be a squirrel up there. Take it easy, Chet."

Squirrel? What squirrel? This wasn't about a squirrel. It was about that strange bird — a bird without eyes, by the way, in case I've left that out — that strange bird that . . . that was no longer visible, in fact had somehow vanished. I went silent.

Bernie turned back to Suzie. "Well?" he said.

"This isn't like you," Suzie said, meeting his gaze and maybe even doing it one better, if that makes any sense. I was almost overcome by the weirdest urge of my whole life, namely a strong and sudden desire to bowl them both over! At the very last second, I went with a yawn instead, a huge one, and felt a bit better.

"What isn't?" Bernie said.

"This cold relentlessness," Suzie said. "Or maybe it is like you, but just being aimed my way for the first time."

"Cold relent— ?"

Suzie raised her voice over Bernie's. "Yes, Eben did work up his nerve, as you so charmingly put it about a dead man. Happy now?"

"And?" Bernie said.

"And what?"

Bernie's voice rose, too. "And what did you tell him? Did you spill some feelings back his way?"

All the color left Suzie's face, except for a small pink patch on each cheek. "Why the hell did you bother coming here?" she said, and then turned and ran back the way we'd come, down the driveway to the carriage house and out of sight.

Bernie watched her go. His face was redder than I'd ever seen it, like . . . like he'd absorbed all of Suzie's color. Why did thoughts like that come to me sometimes? I really wished they wouldn't.

Bernie looked down at me. "I suppose it's all my fault."

I looked up at him. This looking at each other thing went on for some time and then

Bernie made a fist and pounded it into his open hand so loud it sounded like a gunshot. A bird burst out of the tree across the street, not my strange bird but an ordinary bird with eyes and wings that flapped.

"Come on, Chet, let's go for a ride." A ride? But no ride-type excitement in his voice at all? I almost didn't get what he was talking about.

We went for a ride, Bernie kind of slouched behind the wheel, me sitting tall in the shotgun seat, a total pro even if we weren't on any sort of job. But if we weren't, why not? We had a dead body, no doubt about that, and dead bodies were part of our business plan at the Little Detective Agency, unless I was missing something.

We got on a big highway, fought some traffic, then took a ramp and found some two-lane blacktop, which was Bernie's favorite when it came to roads. Soon we were in lovely country, green and rolling, and Bernie was sitting up straighter in his seat. He was quiet for a long time, but finally turned to me and said, "I disgraced myself, big guy." Over my head, and totally. "So why do I still want to know what she felt about him? What does that say about me, beyond the fact that I don't have two brain cells to rub together?" He'd lost me completely. "Not to mention," he went on, "the degree of self-involvement on my part. That's what jealousy is, no two ways about it. Plus the poor bastard's dead, for Christ sake! I'm like some plutocrat on the *Titanic,* pissed off he can't get room service." Had Bernie ever been harder to understand than this? Not that I remembered. He was on the opposite of a roll. Opposite of a roll? Whoa! I was having my own problems. I lay down on my seat, curled up, watched the passing sky, clouds moving one way, us another. I felt a little pukey and closed my eyes. That was better. From time to time Bernie said things like, "And what about this murder, any hope of redemption that way?" And: "If we had the whiteboard I could start making boxes, Eben in the center, Soares over on the right, and Suzie where, exactly?" Plus: "No reason to include her at all, maybe better to erase the whole board." As well as other stuff that helped me get to sleep and stay there.

The sun was going down by the time we turned onto Suzie's street, which I recognized from all sorts of smells I won't bother going into now, plus a hydrant I'd noticed near where we'd parked before, a hydrant I wanted to try out in the very near future.

And what do you know? Bernie parked right near it again! Like my thoughts were . . . were making things happen! I hopped out of the car, laid my mark high up on that hydrant, above all the other marks laid on it by fellow members of the nation within. Always best to be on top, in case that's news to you. When that was done, I thought: Slim Jim. I thought Slim Jim as hard as I could, but no Slim Jim appeared.

We walked toward Suzie's place, me and Bernie. The light of the setting sun made a kind of golden outline around Bernie. Did he look good or what? Plus he was walking just like Bernie at his best, strong and fast, with hardly a limp at all.

"Here's what I'm going to do, big guy. Plead insanity. Never been jealous in my life, so what else could it be? Step one — full apology, no ifs, ands, or buts." Wow! Hadn't heard the no ifs, ands, or buts thing since the very end of the Chins Malone case, Bernie telling Chins he was going down no ifs, ands, or buts about it and Chins pushing on the detonator handle anyway, a wild look in his eyes. After that came wilder things, too wild to remember.

"Step two," Bernie went on, "short and simple. I'm going to tell her I love her and want to marry her and spend the rest of our lives together. Finding the right words will be the problem." He slowed down, came to a stop, gazed into the distance. "What would be the right way to put that? Some guys have got the silver tongue, Chet, would knock it out of the park. Eben, for example." Bernie smacked his forehead. "Oh, my God — did I just say that?"

I had no idea what he was talking about. All I knew was that I'd never seen him smack his head before and never wanted to see it again. Normally, when someone smacks Bernie in the head, they've got to deal with me. That didn't seem the way to go. But why not? And what about those guys with silver tongues? There were scary things in this life. I was trying to forget all about them as we came to Lizette's house and headed down the driveway to the carriage house.

"Think it could be this, Chet? That I've never cared for another person — Charlie excepted, of course, but that's different — the way I —"

Whatever that was about — way too complicated already — I never got to hear the end of it, because at that moment Lieutenant Soares stepped out from behind some bushes, a big cop on either side of him.

"Bernie Little?" Soares said.

"You know it's me," Bernie said.

"Just a formality," said Soares. "Got a minute?"

"For what?"

"The Eben St. John murder case."

"Go on."

The sun dipped down beyond the bottom edge of everything, as I'd seen many times, and it got much darker, as it always did. I could barely make out Lizette, sitting motionless in her screened porch. Most of the remaining light seemed to have gotten caught in the eyes of Soares and the other cops. Not Bernie's, for some reason, which had gone very dark.

"The murder weapon was a .22 automatic," Soares said. "Or did you know that already?"

"I knew it was a .22."

"How?"

"Ms. Sanchez told me."

Soares nodded. "Did she describe the weapon at all?"

"In what sense?"

"Any sense, really," Soares said. "But I was thinking visually."

"You're losing me."

"My apologies. Specifically, the gun we found at the scene, the .22 automatic, which forensics now tells us is the murder weapon beyond any reasonable doubt, has an imitation pearl handle, pink in color." There was a long pause. All the humans on the scene, the cops and Bernie, began to smell different. "Unlikely as it seems," Soares went on, "you being a big macho guy and all, but do you happen to own a gun that fits the description?"

"No," Bernie said. "I'm in possession of a gun that fits the description, but I don't own it."

"You're saying it's unlicensed?"

"I'm saying what I said."

"And how did that come to be," Soares said, "you in possession of a gun not your own?"

"Someone was using it to threaten the public safety," Bernie said. "I relieved that person of the gun."

"Where and when was this?"

"Recently and not in your jurisdiction."

Soares gave Bernie a long look. Now his eyes, and the eyes of the other cops, had darkened like Bernie's. "I'm not sensing a high level of cooperation," he said.

"Why not?" Bernie said. "I don't even have to talk to you."

"Then you're either just a nice guy, or I've aroused your curiosity."

Bernie said nothing.

"Nothing wrong with curiosity, not in this business," Soares said. "I'm curious, too. Take a guess about what?"

Bernie stayed silent.

"Forensics found two sets of prints on that pink handle," Soares said. "One match turned up in the IAFIS database — a petty criminal named Bella Lou LaPierre from Breaux Bridge, Louisiana. Another set, mostly on top of Bella Lou's, we couldn't identify until we contacted the licensing unit of the Department of Public Safety in Arizona. They turned out to be yours."

What was this? Something about Arizona again? Other than that, I had no clue, but whatever was going on was making everyone sweat even more. Maybe not visibly, but the air was getting tangier in a not unpleasant way.

"Care to explain?" Soares said.

"I can't," Bernie told him. "But the gun I have is locked in the glove box of my car."

"Mind if we take a look-see?" said Soares.

We walked to the street, Soares leading, then me and Bernie side by side, followed by the two big cops. I didn't like having them behind me, also didn't like having

Soares in front, and was trying to figure out what to do about that when we got to the car. Soares stood to the side and made the now-it's-your-turn gesture with his hand.

Bernie stepped up, took out the keys, unlocked the passenger side door. Then he leaned in, stuck a key in the glove box, turned it. Nothing happened. He tried again. This time the glove box door popped open. One of the big cops came closer and shone a flashlight inside.

I saw Bernie's shades in there; our own flashlight; the manual, all frayed and worn, and also useless, as Bernie had said many times; a bent cigarette; and — hey! — a partly chewed chewy. But no gun, if that was what this was all about.

"Bernie Little," Soares said. "You're under arrest for the murder of Eben St. John."

EIGHT

"Why are you doing this?" Bernie said.

"Why am I arresting the obvious suspect in a murder?" said Lieutenant Soares. "Is that the question?"

"I had nothing to do with it."

"Explain the gun."

Bernie glanced back toward the street. "Someone stole it while I was inside sleeping," Bernie said. "We should go take a look at the glove box again."

"For what?"

"Signs of a forced opening — what else?"

"I'll make a note of it," Soares said. "We're impounding the vehicle in any case."

The bigger of the big cops took a set of cuffs off his belt.

"That's not necessary," Bernie said.

The cop turned to Soares, the cuffs dangling from one of his huge fingers.

"We're playing this by the book," Soares said.

Bernie laughed in his face. Oh, how I loved that!

The cops moved in closer. I was on my feet, right beside Bernie. Were they planning to cuff Bernie? How could that be anything but wrong? The fur on the back of my neck stood straight up.

"Hands behind your back," Soares said. "Turn around."

Bernie didn't move. A low growling started up.

"This can be hard or easy, your call," Soares said.

Bernie gave him a long look. The growling grew louder. Bernie's gaze shifted in my direction. "All right," he said. "But first I'll get Chet inside the house."

The cops turned my way. I bared my teeth, not sure why. Untrue: I knew, all right. Then came a bark, very loud, very angry. The smaller big cop stepped back, at the same time reaching for his gun. Oh, yeah? I got ready to spring.

"Chet! Sit!"

Sit? What sense would that make? Definitely the wrong play at a time like this. What was getting into Bernie? First had to come me grabbing that gun arm and then we'd have Bernie doing what needed to be done, like maybe taking a swing at —

"CHET!"

I sat. Squad cars — one, two, more — drove up, turned into the driveway, lights flashing, sirens off.

Bernie turned to Soares, raised his hand in the stop sign. "I'm walking Chet to Ms. Sanchez's house, just to keep your trigger-happy pal here from making a career-ending mistake. Then you can do what you want." He touched my back. "Come on, big guy."

We walked right between the big cops, me and Bernie, kept going to Suzie's place. I heard the cops following behind us, but Bernie didn't look back so neither did I. Before we got to Suzie's door, it opened and Suzie hurried out, one foot still struggling to get itself into a sandal.

"Bernie?" What was this? Suzie didn't look happy to see him? She looked beyond us toward the cops and the flashing lights. "What's going on?"

"Take Chet inside," Bernie said, his voice the normal Bernie voice, nice and calm. "Then call Cedric Booker and get him to recommend a DC lawyer."

"For who? I don't understand."

"For me," Bernie said. "I'll explain later."

Suzie backed toward the door.

"Chet," Bernie said. "In."

Everything was so strange. All that really

got through to me was "in." I went into the house. Suzie followed, then paused in the doorway.

"Close the door," Bernie said. "Don't let him out."

"But what's happening?" Suzie said.

"They're arresting me."

"For what?"

Bernie didn't answer. Soares stepped up from behind and put a hand on Bernie's shoulder.

"Murder," he said.

Suzie took a quick sharp breath. "Eben's murder?"

Soares smiled.

"Shut the goddamn door," Bernie said.

Suzie closed the door. There was a moment of silence, and then I heard a familiar sound, the click of cuffs clamping down.

"Chet?" Suzie said, her eyes on me but sort of strangely unseeing. "Want water or something?"

Something? I wanted something, all right: Bernie!

Suzie went into the kitchen. I guess I followed. All I knew was that I'd been in the hall and now I was in the kitchen. My mind was on other things, namely: Bernie! Suzie filled my water bowl with nice cold water. I could smell how nice and cold the water was, but I didn't go near it.

Where was Bernie? I tried to remember what had happened to him and couldn't. I trotted — this was my real fast trot, pretty close to a run — out of the kitchen and into the living room, and then into and out of all the other rooms on the first floor, and after that I ran up the stairs — yes, running now — and tore in and out of all the rooms up there. Lots of Bernie smell around — I must have mentioned Bernie's smell, the best human smell I'd ever come across, apples, bourbon, salt and pepper, plus something funky deep down underneath — but no Bernie.

Next thing I knew I was downstairs in the kitchen again. Suzie was on the phone saying, "I don't know Cedric, but the point is —" Or something like that. By then I was running into and out of all the rooms on the first floor. Again? Or for the first time? I ran faster and faster, and coming down the stairs — again? or for the first time? — I almost bumped into Suzie, on her way up. I went still. She put her hand on my head, real gentle.

"Got to calm down a bit, Chet. Everything's going to be all right."

I liked the feel of Suzie's hand but was

having some trouble hearing her, on account of the voice in my head shouting, *Bernie! Bernie! Bernie!*

Suzie's lips moved. She might have been saying something about a treat, possibly of the biscuit type. Suzie was the best; I'd never ever want to hurt Suzie. Then all at once, there on the stairs with Suzie, her gentle hand on my back, I remembered someone I did want to hurt: Lieutenant Soares. Oh, yes! And don't leave out the big cop with the cuffs, and the slightly smaller cop, the trigger-happy one. At that moment, I remembered everything!

I flung myself down the rest of the stairs in one leap, bounded to the front door. Closed and bolted. It had a round knob, and I was getting much better at those, but we'd only just started working on bolts, me and Bernie, and I couldn't bring back what Bernie had told me — couldn't bring it back now when I needed to the most! All I could remember was the lovely sound of his voice as he took one of my front paws in his hand and — and showed me something or other about bolts. So I ended up clawing at the bolt on Suzie's door for a while and then —

"Chet! It's okay, try to calm down."

— ran through the kitchen to the little laundry room at the back of Suzie's house.

Beyond the laundry room was the back door, not only unbolted but even slightly opened. I stuck my nose in, nudged the door open some more, and found a second door, a door of the screen type. It had one of those really easy press-down levers, but I didn't bother with that, simply burst through the screen and into the night.

"Chet! Chet!"

And once outside, I was on the move, big-time. *Zoom:* right around to the front of the house and up the driveway, where I pounced on Bernie's smell right away, all mixed together with cop smells — which always have lots of sameness about them, a promising subject for some other time — but there was no missing Bernie's smell, which always stood out in the nicest way.

"Chet! Chet!"

Who was that? Suzie, perhaps? And did I also hear her running footsteps? Possibly not. As for human running: good luck with that. Once we had a client name of Shockwave Jones — second best sprinter in the whole country at that time but now breaking rocks in the hot sun — who'd bet Bernie double or nothing on our fee that he could beat me in a race. The fun we'd had with that! The look on Shockwave's face when I turned back and circled right around him and then flashed on by again! I was halfway through my Slim Jim when Shockwave crossed the finish line. Had he sold off some of his 'roid supply to pay the bill, perhaps to a DEA undercover, which led him to his present whereabouts? I had some hazy memory of that, but our race was sharp in my mind as —

"Chet! Chet!"

— I reached the spot where the cop smells and Bernie's smell got mixed up with car exhaust smells, meaning . . . meaning I had a car to follow. What could be easier? Cars leave a scent trail that no one could miss. I pelted off down the street at speeds Shockwave Jones would never know, following a typical car scent with one difference: this one had just a hint of doughnut added, something you found just about every time with cop cruisers.

Down the block, across the first cross street in a single bound, or maybe two, paws hardly touching down on the pavement, still warm from the heat of the day: I was on the move! Do I love being on the move? Yes, but this wasn't quite like that, on account of the voice in my head: *Bernie! Bernie!* So I still loved it, but I was out of my mind at the same time, if that makes any sense, although I'm pretty sure it doesn't. But what can I do?

All I know is what I did then, namely fly down that block —

"Mom! There's a huge dog on the loose!"

— and one or two more, across another street, a street with lots of headlights on the move, and sudden blasts of honking, and then . . . and then I lost the scent. When you lose the scent, you double back real quick, which was what I did —

HONK! HONK!

"Someone call animal control!"

— and found the scent again — I was smelling only for doughnuts now, so much car smell around it was impossible to tell one from another — practically right away, on the far side of this crossroads. Yes, they'd made a turn onto this street, maybe kind of busy. I flew down the sidewalk, or maybe along the side of the road, the sidewalk having come to an end sometime back, my mind on doughnut scent and nothing else. Except for: *Bernie!*

Honking and running; shouting and running; squealing brakes and running. Running and running and running: that was me, a runner, pure and simple. And what was this, not far up this street? A blue light? Yes! Blue lights meant cop stations, of which I'd seen plenty during my career. Next thing I knew I was right under that blue light, barking at the closed door, the air almost pure doughnut.

The door opened and a cop looked out. "What the hell?" he said.

A man spoke behind me. "It's all right, officer. I'll take care of this."

I turned and saw a man in a green uniform getting out of a van. A normal sort of guy, smaller than most, but he was holding a long pole with a big loop on the end. I knew that kind of pole from several scary episodes in my past. Dogsnatcher was the name of the pole, making the little guy in the green uniform a dogcatcher, someone whose whole life was about rounding up those of us in the nation within and putting us where no one would ever want to go. The little guy moved toward me in a casual sort of way with a casual sort of smile on his face — but also with surprising speed — and whipped that loop right over my head and around my neck and —

But no. When it was almost too late, what with me at my slowest, my mind on other things, I bolted sideways and the loop glanced off me. And in that sideways bolt, I picked up the very faintest smell of Bernie. I followed it at top speed down a paved alley that ran beside the cop station and ended at a parking lot around the back. More Bernie smell here, no doubt about it. The trail led to the rear door of the station, closed just like the front one. Bernie was on the other side of that door! I rose up, clawed at the handle, but it was one of those pulls, impossible for me. I clawed and clawed, and barked my head off, and —

And totally forgot about the dogcatcher, a real big mistake on my part. *Whoosh.* That nasty loop slipped over my head and tightened around my neck. I turned and twisted and growled and fought, getting nowhere. At the other end of the pole, the little man in the green uniform didn't seem to be putting any effort into this at all. The total effort was coming from me. That made me mad, and in my madness I struggled harder and harder, and then harder than that, until my breath was gone out of me and the loop was too tight for getting any breath back in. The eyes of the little man showed nothing, except maybe a hint of enjoyment. He flipped me over onto the ground. Flipped me? How was that possible? But it happened.

The loop loosened slightly and I sucked in some air. I was still doing that, still lying on my side — but with rough and bloody plans taking shape in my mind — when a man with a big strong nose climbed out of a car parked all by itself at the very back of the lot. He wore a dark suit and walked in an intense sort of way, pushing an energy wave in front of him. I knew this man: Mr. Ferretti, double R's double T's, Victor D.

He came over to where we were, me and the dogcatcher, and said, "What have we here?"

NINE

What we had here was me lying on the pavement in a parking lot behind the cop station where the cops had taken Bernie, unless I was missing something. But what? Doughnut smells and Bernie smells mixed up together could only mean one thing. Bernie was in that building! I had to get inside and that was that.

The little dogcatching man in the green uniform blinked and said, "Huh?"

Ferretti moved in, leaned down, and gave me a close look.

"Need you to back up," the dogcatcher said. "For your own safety."

Ferretti raised his head slowly, transferred his gaze to the dogcatcher. "Excuse me?" he said.

The dogcatcher didn't seem to like that gaze, had trouble meeting it. "I'm an authorized animal control officer performing my duty. You need to back up."

"Yes," Ferretti said, not backing up an inch, which I took to be a very small distance. "I got that part on the first go-around. Pertinent fact — I know this dog. His name is Chet."

"He belongs to you?"

"I didn't say that. But I'm in position to contact the owner."

"Save him some money, sooner you do," the dogcatcher said. "Tell 'im to contact the facility, arrange a pickup."

"The facility?" Ferretti said.

The dogcatcher moved the pole in a way that twisted me back up to my feet. "Animal control. We're online."

"Seems like a lot of trouble," Ferretti said.

"Huh?" said the dogcatcher. Certain humans — take Presto Figueiroda, for example, who'd stolen a shipment of scratch tickets without one winner in the whole truck — said *huh* a lot. The dogcatcher was turning out to be that type.

"Trouble for everyone concerned, including you," Ferretti said. "I propose that I simply relieve you of the fugitive here and now."

"What fugitive?"

"Chet, here. I was being facetious."

The dogcatcher's mouth opened in a way that made me think he was about to say *huh*

110

again, but he did not. He just stood there, mouth open.

"My intention being," Ferretti went on, "to take Chet off your hands and simply return him to his owner, slicing through all the red tape."

The dogcatcher shook his head. "No can do."

Ferretti's voice, not gentle to begin with, got even less so. "You're losing me."

"It's against regs," the dogcatcher said. "Even if you was the owner, which you ain't. This is an open case on my docket, and it don't close till I make delivery."

Ferretti sighed. "The whole goddamn town is organized like that," he said. "Which is why we are where we are."

"Huh?"

"Never mind." Ferretti took out a badge, held it so the dogcatcher could see. "All you need to know is that I'll be taking over now."

The dogcatcher licked his lips — his tongue was pointy and very small, even for a human — leaned forward to squint at the badge, squinted at it for a good long time, and then looked at Ferretti, looked at him in a whole new way.

"You want the rig, too?" he said.

"Rig?"

"Lasso rig," the dogcatcher said, giving

111

the pole a little shake that made the loop rub against my neck in a way I didn't like.

"I don't think that will be necessary," Ferretti said.

He wiggled his finger in the signal that means "come," and we followed him, the dogcatcher holding the pole out to the side, the loop digging into my neck. I thought about doing this and that, but no good thises or thats occurred to me before we reached Ferretti's car.

"Just so happens," he said, opening the front passenger-side door, "that I picked up a sandwich in case this turned into a long night. A steak sandwich, to be precise." Which I'd known the moment he'd opened the door, actually just before. He produced the sandwich, removed the paper wrapper, picked a nice big piece of steak from between the bread slices — and then another! — and dropped them on the floor. "Let's see if he likes steak."

"Of course he —" the dogcatcher began.

"Meaning take that thing off him."

"I wouldn't advise —"

"And I wouldn't consider your advice, so we're in sync," Ferretti said.

Whatever that was, the dogcatcher didn't like it one little bit; his head snapped back like he'd been slapped. Slap him, Mr. Ferretti, slap him! A crazy thought, maybe, but it was still on my mind when the dogcatcher reached over and slipped the loop off my neck. He stepped quickly away but not out of leaping distance. I got my paws under me, coiled up my strength, and —

"How about that steak, Chet?" Ferretti said.

— jumped right into the front of Ferretti's car. He closed the door, went around to the other side, got in, and turned the key. Those two pieces of steak were history before we started rolling.

We drove in silence through streets I didn't know. They got nicer as we went along, more trees, more hills, more big houses. The shotgun seat of Ferretti's car was bigger than the shotgun seat in the Porsche, and really just as comfortable, but not so homey, if that makes any sense.

Ferretti glanced over at me. "My late wife was allergic." He drummed his fingers, long and bony, on the steering wheel. "Is there a way to end up with you when this one's in the can?"

Me end up with Ferretti? Was that it? Made no sense to me at all. I was with Bernie, now and forever. As for allergic, it's a mystery, although we hear that a lot in the nation within.

"But first things first," Ferretti said after a while. "Can't let the tail wag the dog."

I lost track of things for a while after that. Tail wag the . . . ? Had I heard right? Nothing wrong with my hearing. In fact, it's probably much better than yours, no offense. I was very conscious of my tail at that moment, and almost certain it was fixing to wag me and wag me good. My tail has a mind of its own, maybe something that Ferretti didn't realize. I gave him a careful look. From the side his face reminded me of a cliff I knew out in the desert — a cliff that had turned out to be kind of dangerous for me and Bernie, but no time for that now. The point is that the dangerous cliff had a big nose-shaped rock sticking out of it, so if a cliff face could look like a man face, then Ferretti was the guy, if you get what I mean, and I wouldn't blame you at all if you don't. I actually wouldn't blame you for anything. You've been very patient so far.

When I started paying attention again, we were in some suburb, a real nice one with big houses spread far apart and lots of woods between them, meaning maybe we were out in the country. Ferretti turned down a dark lane that led through some trees and came to an end at a small meadow.

On the far side of the meadow stood one of those big houses. A party was going on in the backyard, which bordered the other side of the meadow. Lots of people all dressed up, candlelight glinting on glasses and silverware, music, laughter, plus there'd be leftovers out the yingyang: it looked like fun.

But we didn't get out of the car. Ferretti cut the lights and the motor and just sat there, watching the party.

"Same old question," he said. "Who's using who?"

That was an old question? Brand new to me. I tried to figure it out, got nowhere. Meanwhile, Ferretti unwrapped what was left of the steak sandwich and took a bite. I made up my mind that Ferretti was a pretty good guy. Hadn't he shared his sandwich with me before? No reason he wouldn't be doing it again, and soon. Except he didn't, even though I waited politely, keeping my mouth almost closed.

"What I'd like to know," Ferretti said, speaking with his mouth full, which I knew was not polite from Leda telling Charlie many many times, "is who planted that pink popgun in the flowerpot."

I kind of remembered the pink popgun in the flowerpot. Other than that, I had zip.

Ferretti took one of those little plastic

dental floss packs out of a cup holder and began to floss his teeth. "Same person who pulled the trigger, or is the setup more complicated?" he said. Or something like that: humans aren't easy to understand when they're flossing their teeth. I've had my own teeth flossed lots of times by Janie the groomer, who has the best business plan there is — she comes to us! — but no time for that now, on account of the flossing suddenly freeing up a surprisingly large piece of steak and launching it with amazing speed in an arc that ended on the dashboard right in front of my face! I've had a lot of luck in life and it didn't seem to be running out anytime soon. I made quick work of what had to be the last of the steak — unless . . . whoa! unless Ferretti had some more hidden away in his mouth. I didn't take my eyes off him until he finished flossing and flicked the used floss out the window.

He glanced my way. "What's so interesting?"

Strange question. What wasn't interesting? Ferretti: a bit of a puzzler. Also I wasn't liking him quite as much as before, not sure why.

The look on his face changed. "You've given me an idea," he said. I had? I tried to remember my last idea, was still working on it when Ferretti went on. "What's needed here is a cat's paw, and who could play that role better than your —"

Some movement at the party caught Ferretti's attention. I was vaguely aware of that, also vaguely aware of a newcomer at the party, a tall, silver-haired dude, one of those dudes who holds his head up high. He came striding across the lawn, attracting a ring of men and woman, got involved in a lot of handshaking and cheek kissing. But all that was vague in my mind, which had pretty much been taken over by one thing and one thing only: cat's paw. I'd had experience with cat's paws, more than once and never good. What makes them so quick? Also the tip of my nose is quite sensitive; just thought I'd throw that in, mainly because the tip of my nose was suddenly remembering how sensitive it was.

Back to the silver-haired dude, now holding a champagne glass. We'd had a whole set of champagne glasses back before the divorce. Was it my fault they'd been in a tray on an end table when my tail had happened to spring into action?

"There's our boy," Ferretti said, lowering his voice and leaning forward. He watched the silver-haired dude doing nothing much

— talking, sipping, laughing. Women seemed to like touching his arm. "We've had twelve generals who went on to become presidents, some of them not half bad," Ferretti said. "So why not Travis Galen Galloway? The president's numbers are in the toilet. Look — he can just about taste it."

That toilet thing again? And now tasting was a possibility? This party looked interesting. But that was as close as I got. Ferretti started the car and backed away. "Nice party," he said, "if you like parties where you need a check for fifty K to get in the door."

We drove back into the city. Ferretti was quiet for a long time. Then he said, "Let's give it a whirl."

I got a little nervous. Once Bernie had tried the giving it a whirl thing and we'd ended up down at the bottom of a well, just the two of us and for way too long.

Ferretti got on his phone. "What I told you before might happen?" he said. "Make it happen."

I heard the faint voice of a woman on the other end. "Will do."

"One more thing," Ferretti said. "Is our little birdie still in sector B?"

"Affirmative."

"Bring her in."

"Yes, sir."

Ferretti clicked off, turned to me. "Wouldn't do to get hoisted by our own petard."

That sounded right to me, although I'd only ridden a hoist once, on a downtown construction site where Bernie and I were working a case involving stolen copper pipe, a snap to solve on account of copper being one of the easiest smells out there.

"But FYI," Ferretti went on, "be prepared for much more of that in future. Getting hoist by your own petard probably tracks one for one with technological progress."

That one zipped right by me. Meanwhile, the neighborhood began to look familiar, and soon we came to Suzie's street. The yellow Beetle was parked in front of Lizette's big house, and the driveway gate stood open. Ferretti slowed down, stopped in a pool of shadow. Then he hit a button and my window slid down.

"It's been real."

Humans said that from time to time, a complete mystery to me.

"Out," he said. "Go."

I knew out. I knew go. I went out, leaping through the open window and trotting up the driveway to the carriage house. The sound of Ferretti's car rumbling off grew fainter and fainter and finally faded to nothing.

Ten

Lights shone in the carriage house, and I heard voices inside. I stood at the door, and after a while found I was out of ideas. I barked, just a single bark, and waited. When nothing happened, I waited some more. Then it occurred to me that nothing was still happening, and I barked again, maybe louder this time. The door opened and Suzie looked out.

"Chet!" She clapped her hands together. "You're back!" She opened her arms and I jumped right into them, so happy to see her.

Suzie's surprisingly strong for a not-very-big human, but it's possible she staggered just a bit. I didn't know. I was too busy licking her face.

"Chet, easy there, easy," she said, and I immediately dropped down, all paws nice and peaceable on the floor, and if not immediately then the next best thing.

Lizette came into the hall, a glass of white

wine in her hand. She glanced at me, then looked out into the night. "He came back by himself?"

"Chet can do all sorts of things," Suzie said, kicking the door closed with her heel, one of my favorite human moves.

"Your friend Bernie seems very attached to him," Lizette said.

"They work together," Suzie said. "You could almost call them partners."

I understood everything except "almost." Things not understood are best forgotten: that's one of my core beliefs, and it's the core beliefs that keep you operating at a tip-top level. Another of my core beliefs is that Bernie is the greatest, now and forever. If I have any other core beliefs, they're not coming to me at the moment.

"I think you told me Bernie's a private eye," Lizette was saying.

"That's right," said Suzie.

"Does he have any police training?"

Suzie nodded. "He was a lieutenant with the Valley PD."

"And decided to go out on his own?"

"Something like that," Suzie said. "This was long before he and I got together."

"At least he's got some contacts in law enforcement," Lizette said.

"What do you mean?"

"Just that they may come in handy," Lizette said. "Going down the road."

Suzie voice sharpened. "There won't be any going down the road, Lizette. I told you — Bernie's innocent. He was asleep in this house when Eben was killed."

"Oh, I believe you, of course," Lizette said. She took a sip of wine. The wine's reflection seemed to turn her green eyes yellow in a way that reminded me of cats. I don't like being reminded of cats. "But can he prove it?"

Suzie gazed at Lizette, didn't answer.

"Sorry if I'm being too nosy," Lizette said. She gazed back at Suzie. "You're in love with him — I can see it — and sometimes that clouds the judgment."

"My judgment is unclouded," Suzie said. "Bernie's innocent, and if we have to prove it, we —"

There was a knock at the door. I knew that knock, the best knock in the world, the knock of a guy who could put his fist right through the door if he wanted to, but hardly ever did. Bernie!

"Who is it?" Suzie called.

Humans! They don't have an easy time.

"Me," Bernie called back.

Suzie threw open the door. And there was Bernie, all by himself and uncuffed, looking just great, except for being so tired and worried and angry. But not angry at us, goes without mentioning. He gave us a quick little smile. Even though he was facing Suzie at the time, the smile was meant for her and me both, actually a bit more for me.

"They let me go," he said, stepping inside. Leaping into his arms even harder than I'd leaped into Suzie's was next on my list, but before I could make a move, Bernie put his hand on my head with the exact pressure I like, and the next thing I knew he was scratching the spot I can't reach, and right away scratching the spot I can't reach became my whole list, A to Z, whatever that might mean.

"On bail?" Suzie said.

He shook his head, at the same time closing the door with his heel just as Suzie had done. Whoa! Was there something alike about them? What a thought!

"All charges dropped," Bernie said. "I'm no longer a suspect."

Suzie stepped forward, gave Bernie a hug. Because of how I was standing, I could see Lizette, standing at the entrance to the hall. She seemed to lose control of her wineglass, almost dropped it, some wine slopping over the rim. The movement caught Bernie's eye, and he looked her way, maybe noticing Lizette for the first time.

"Uh," he said, "didn't realize . . ."

"I've been keeping vigil with Suzie," Lizette said. "So glad this . . . this misunderstanding is all cleared up." She turned to Suzie. "You two need some time."

Lizette moved toward the door. Bernie stepped aside to let her pass. "Thanks for helping," he said.

"I really didn't do anything," Lizette said.

Bernie opened the door for her. She walked out, wineglass in hand, the wine making tiny waves, back and forth.

We hung out in Suzie's kitchen, Suzie at the table, Bernie leaning against the counter, me lying by his feet. He was wearing his favorite sneakers, the ones with the paint smears. I lost myself in their smells.

". . . right through the screen door," Suzie was saying, or something like that. I searched my mind for anything having to do with screen doors, came up empty.

"How long was he gone?" Bernie said.

"Hours and hours."

This sounded like somebody's fun adventure, but I was having trouble keeping my eyes open. You'd think a big strong dude like me could keep his eyelids — real tiny things, when you came down to it — open as long as he liked, but you'd be wrong. No offense.

So lovely to sleep in the world of Bernie's sneaker smells. The first little smell stream that came along was all about the desert back home: mesquite, greasewood, those lovely little flowers with a scent a lot like Suzie's, and javelina, best of all. I followed that desert smell stream until a nice fat javelina appeared on a butte made of cloud. I rose into the sky, a wonderful feeling that happened only in dreams.

Meanwhile, I could hear Bernie, somewhere down on earth, so . . . so I had the best of both worlds! Hey! I finally got what that meant! What a life!

". . . definitive evidence it couldn't have been me," he was saying.

"What definitive evidence?" Suzie said.

"No idea. All Soares told the lawyer Cedric found me was that definitive evidence had turned up, and they were letting me go. He wouldn't answer any questions."

"This is crazy," Suzie said. "Is Soares saying he has definitive evidence that you were asleep in this house when the murder happened?"

"How could he?" Bernie said. "It must be something else."

"Like?"

"I don't know. But it must have been ironclad. The murder weapon was mine, at least in a sense, and it had my prints on it — normally a slam dunk."

"What does 'in a sense' mean?"

Bernie started in on a long and complicated story about some biker bar down in bayou country. It seemed vaguely familiar, but back out in the desert I was soaring through the blue sky, the cloud javelina in my sights. Just as I was coming down on him, he saw me and snarled, showing his tusks. Whoa! Tusks that were way bigger than normal, and . . . what was this? Made of buzz saw blades? I flapped my wings frantically to get higher in the air, out of reach, but of course, I had no wings, so I didn't go higher, instead drifted down and down toward those horrible —

"What's he whimpering about?"

"Sometimes he has bad dreams. Chet? Wake up, big guy."

I opened my eyes. Bernie was leaning over me, giving me a gentle shake. No whimpering was going on, and no whimpering had been going on — you can bet the ranch. Whimpering is not my style. I went over to my water bowl and lapped up water, lapped it up as noisily as possible, for reasons unknown to me.

Bernie went over to Suzie, still sitting in her chair. He raised his hands like he was about to lay them on her shoulders, then seemed to change his mind, and stuck them in his pockets instead. Was something wrong between them? I tried to remember.

"I don't like being set up," Bernie said.

"But how could it be a setup?" Suzie said.

They were talking to each other but not looking at each other. Instead, they were both facing in my direction, eyes on me. I stopped drinking — all the water was gone now, or at least not in the bowl — and eyed them back.

"Why not?" Bernie said.

"No one knew you were going to be here, not even me," Suzie said. "Plus assuming someone took the gun from your glove box, how could they have counted on a gun being there in the first place?"

Bernie was quiet for a long time. Then he shrugged and said, "I don't like being set up." His voice got quieter and harder at the same time in a way that made the fur on the back of my neck stand straight up. "And I'm going to do something about it."

"Like what?" Suzie said.

"Like track down Eben's killer," Bernie said. "What else?"

"How are you going to do that? Can you

even operate in DC?"

"I hope I can operate here, at least," Bernie said.

"Here?"

"In this house."

"I don't understand."

"That's what worries me," Bernie said.

Suzie rose and faced Bernie. "Are you trying to scare me, Bernie?" she said.

He gazed down at her. "Last thing I'd want," he said, his voice kind of husky, like something was in his throat. "But suppose Eben was killed because of the story you two were working on."

"I wasn't working on a story with Eben," Suzie said. "He was a source."

"Same thing."

"It's not the same thing."

Bernie raised his hand. "Okay, okay, have it —"

"And I don't like being talked to like this."

"Huh? Like what?"

"Talked down to," Suzie said. "Patronized. I don't need protection."

"Everybody needs protection at some point in their lives," Bernie said.

"Yeah? What about you?"

Uh-oh. Something was wrong between them, no doubt about it. How could that be, now that we were all back together? I started panting, nothing I could do about it, and turned to my water bowl again. Empty. Right, I'd known that. But there seemed to be lots of water pooled on the floor, so I got going on that.

There's a vein in Bernie's neck that jumps sometimes — hardly ever, actually — and what happens next tends to be very bad if you're a perp. But no perps were around, so therefore? Whoa! We'd come to a so therefore. The way we have things divided at the Little Detective Agency, Bernie handles the so therefores, me bringing other things to the table. I was home free.

Bernie took a deep breath. The neck vein throbbed one last time and went invisible. "Yes," he said, "sometimes I need protection, too."

And who was always on the spot to do the protecting? It's not a secret.

"Give me a for instance," Suzie said.

"Right now," Bernie said. "Right now is a for instance. When a setup falls apart, it's in the interest of whoever's behind it to wipe out the traces. The point is we're in this together, Suzie. Even if that sounds like a stupid cliché."

Suzie gave him a long look. Did her eyes soften? Maybe just a bit. But they both began smelling more like their normal selves. I stopped panting.

"You're not the smoothest talker, Bernie."

"So I've heard."

"It's actually one of your best characteristics."

"I didn't know that."

"And there's another good one."

Uh-oh. Suzie had gone way off course, probably because she hadn't caught Bernie's keynote speech at the Great Western Private Eye convention, sometime back. True, there'd been some snoring in the audience, but not in the front rows, and there'd definitely been applause at the end. Don't forget about my hearing, better than yours. I'm sure you bring other things to the table.

If Bernie was upset that Suzie had dissed him, he didn't show it. That was Bernie, every time! In fact, he had a little smile on his face, was even shuffling his feet a bit, the same way Charlie had when he'd won the fifty-yard dash at field day. The last field day that I'd be attending, according to Bernie, but that's another story.

"All right," Suzie said. "You win."

"I don't want to win," Bernie said.

"No?"

The little smile left Bernie's face. He and Suzie watched each other in an unblinking sort of way that made me want to blink. I could feel their thoughts, sort of mingling in the air between them. Suzie went to the cupboard and took out . . . what was this? A bottle of bourbon? I'd never seen her touch bourbon. Wasn't wine her drink? This town — Foggy Bottom? Had I gotten that right? — was turning out to be a strange place where strange things happened.

Suzie put the bottle and a couple of glasses on the table. "I got this in case you ever came."

"I came," Bernie said.

That was followed by more gazing at each other, and then they sat down. Suzie opened the bottle and poured a little into her glass, quite a bit more in Bernie's.

"I talked to my editor," Suzie said.

"About what?" said Bernie, swirling his drink around. Bourbon smell got stronger right away.

"Confidentiality agreements in our business and what happens after a source dies."

"And what did he say?" Bernie said.

"Sheila's her name," said Suzie.

"Damn."

"Yeah, damn." Suzie took a pretty big sip of her drink. "She said it's a judgment call."

"Sure," said Bernie. "Otherwise reporters could end up taking important secrets to their graves."

"People take important secrets to their graves all the time, Bernie. You must know that." She drained her glass.

Bernie was quiet for a long time. Then he said, "What's your call?"

Suzie was silent.

"If it helps at all," Bernie said, "I'm going to work this case, with you or without."

"See right there?" said Suzie. "That's bullying."

Bernie lowered his head. I hated seeing that.

Suzie breathed in a long, slow breath, let it out even slower. "Eben was still sizing me up, as I told you. But what I didn't tell you is that he had some contact he was gearing me up to meet."

"Who?" Bernie said.

"He didn't say," Suzie said. "Eben had to be very cautious because the contact's life is in danger."

"Why?"

"On account of what he knows."

"Which is?" Bernie said.

"Quote, something that will change the course of history," said Suzie.

"That's Eben talking?" Bernie said.

"Yes."

"Kind of on the melodramatic side."

"I thought so," Suzie said. "At the time."

Eleven

"Step one," Bernie said at breakfast, bright and early the next morning. "World Wide Solutions."

"What about it?" Suzie said.

"The name," Bernie said. "It has *solutions* right in it, and solutions are what we're after."

Bernie's always sharp, but it was clear right from the get-go that today he was at his sharpest. Is that why Suzie balled up her paper napkin and threw it at him, as a kind of prize? I always like a prize myself, and without really knowing how — although a leap right over the kitchen table might have been involved — I'd somehow snatched that balled-up paper napkin out of the air. I stuck a twisting landing, and sat up nice and straight facing Suzie, whose eyes were open wider than normal, and Bernie, who'd reached out to steady an orange juice glass that had gotten a bit tippy for some reason.

Meanwhile, the paper napkin was dissolving in an unpleasant sort of way in my mouth, but I wasn't sure what to do about it. I'd completely forgotten that I actually disliked chewing paper! Can you believe it?

"He's a big ball of id, isn't he?" Suzie said.

"Id?" said Bernie.

Suzie reached for another napkin like she was going to do the same thing all over again — which would have suited me just fine, doing the same thing all over again being one of my go-to moves — but then thought better of it. I was with Bernie on this id thing, totally out of the picture. At the same time, I liked the sound of it. Big ball of id — why not? I couldn't have been in a finer mood when we stepped outside and headed toward the Porsche.

A beautiful day, sunny, not too hot, all very nice except that some of the trees seemed to be turning from green to yellow and brown and red, a new one on me, and somewhat unpleasant in a way I couldn't possibly describe. I let Bernie and Suzie go on ahead and took a moment to do what I had to do, first against a lovely-smelling bush at one end of Lizette's garden, then a quick splattering back and forth over one of those flowering vines that climbs the side of a house, reserving just a splash, as high as I could manage, right into a sort of raised-up bowl. What were those raised-up bowls called? Birdbaths? I wasn't sure, but before I got anywhere on the problem, I noticed Lizette, sitting motionless on her screened porch, eyes on me. I paused, one rear leg raised way up, and gave her one of my very friendliest looks. She turned away and picked up her phone.

I trotted out to the street and . . . and what was this? Suzie settling into the shotgun seat? I love everything about Suzie except her forgetfulness in this one little area. I went over to let her know in the nicest possible way that —

"Chet! You'll wake the dead!"

Uh-oh. I got a grip and pronto. I'd seen it happen once already in my career — a perp name of Wixie Fryar getting lowered into a coffin by these other perps who thought they'd done him in, when all at once . . . I didn't even want to go there and for sure never wanted to see another dead dude wake-up scene again. Those fluttering eyelids and nothing but the whites of the eyes behind them? Uh-uh. I hopped onto the tiny shelf behind the front seats — totally inappropriate for a hundred-plus pounder such as myself — without the slightest objection and sat up straight and tall, a no-

136

nonsense pro and on the job. Bernie stepped on the pedal and we were off.

"What do you think goes on in his mind?" Suzie said. Or something like that. I had no idea who they were talking about, soon lost interest in the conversation. High above I caught a quick silvery flash, saw the strange bird making a turn in our direction. Birds had tried to poop on me more than once, but this one didn't. That didn't make me trust him.

We crossed the river and soon were back in the world of office parks. Maryland? Was that it? And all this around me was about elephants and donkeys? I couldn't pick up a single sniff of either one, meaning the case was going well so far.

In the front seat, Bernie reached over and patted Suzie's hand. "This is fun," he said, "working with you."

What? Working with Suzie? And just like that, things took a real bad turn for the worse.

"Chet?" Bernie said. "A little space, big guy."

Space? With just my head poking through between the seats, I was giving them plenty, much more than enough. Any possibility of squeezing my shoulder through? Took some doing, but —

"CHET!"

And maybe a sharp swerve, plus a scream-like sound from Suzie, and some loud honking, not necessarily in that order. I got myself back on the shelf, twisted around like I was much more interested in the goings-on in the next lane, and spotted a big member of the nation within hanging out the window of a pickup. I let him have it full blast. He let me have it back, the same way. I felt better.

Bernie turned off the highway and parked in front of a brassy-colored office building that looked familiar. Before we got out of the car, I remembered the whole visit from before, the smell and taste of Eben's briefcase most of all. Hey! I was on fire! Who wouldn't want to work with me, first and only?

A man in a yellow uniform and yellow cap stood outside Eben's office, scraping the sign off the door.

"Anything I can help you with?" he said. And what was this? He gave off a strong scent of hair gel, a smell that reminded me of bubble gum? It got me thinking.

"Are you a cop?" Bernie said.

In a yellow uniform? I didn't get that.

Neither did the dude with the scraper, unless I was missing something. "Me? A cop?"

"I thought there'd be a cop on guard," Bernie said. "And crime scene tape."

"They were just leaving when I got here. All done, apparently. Maybe you can reach them at the station." He turned to the door, raised the scraper. Meanwhile, I was still thinking, hoping for an actual thought sometime soon.

"We don't want to reach the cops," Bernie said. "We're friends of Eben St. John's."

The man turned back to us, looked blank. His face was kind of like slabs put together, if that makes any sense, but it was hard to tell on account of the shadow under the bill of his baseball cap. A thought came to me at last: I'd like to see him without that cap on his head. I waited for follow-up, but none came.

"This was his office," Suzie said.

"Ah," said the man. He glanced at what remained of the sign. "World Wide Consulting, was it? I'm doing the renovation."

"World Wide Solutions," Suzie said.

"Right," said the renovation man. "By lunchtime, it will be —" He took out his phone, read from the screen. "— Terrapin Exports."

"You don't waste time," Bernie said.

139

"The early bird catches the worm."

The renovation dude was right about that. I'd seen it so many times, the poor worm struggling to stay in the ground, the bird with its weird skinny bird feet firmly planted, tugging away. Then another bird comes gliding down, way too late. I've often encountered worms — like anyone else whose job requires digging now and then — and eaten my share, but I would never bother to hunt them down. Just between you and me, they're not that tasty.

". . . quick look around," Suzie said.

"Look around?" said the renovation dude. "Afraid I'm not authorized to —"

A woman called from inside the office. "Mr. York? Is someone there?"

The renovation dude opened the door. I glimpsed a tall older woman standing at the desk, putting papers in a box. She had swept-back wings of white-and-black hair — a very nice color combo, in my opinion, and not just on account of it being mine, too, although mostly — but what really jumped out at me were the glasses she wore, glasses of the kind they call cat's-eye. I'm sure the name alone gives you the chills. If this was a case — but how could it be? Was anyone paying? — then we were suddenly in trouble.

"Associates of . . . of the previous tenant," said the renovation dude, Mr. York, if I was getting this right.

The woman gazed out at us. Not us, exactly: her eyes went to Bernie, then to Suzie, and back to Bernie, somehow missing me.

"What can I do for you?" she said. "I assume you've heard the sad news?"

"That's why we're here," Suzie said. "We're trying to find out what happened."

"I didn't know . . . the deceased," the woman said. "I represent the building owners."

"Who must want this to go as smoothly as possible," Bernie said.

There was a long pause, Bernie and the woman eyeing each other. Then the woman spread her hands in that gesture humans make to show you're going to get zilch out of them. "I don't see how I can help," she said. "But please come in."

By that time, I was pretty much inside the office anyway; actually completely inside. Bernie and Suzie followed. Several boxes lay on the floor, packed with papers, folders, framed photos, plus pens and pencils and other desk stuff. I sniffed out that guinea pig smell right away, weaker than before but still hanging around.

"You're packing up Eben's stuff?" Suzie said.

"At the request of his head office," said the woman.

"The police gave you the okay?" Suzie said.

"Would I be doing this otherwise?"

And maybe a bit more chatter along those lines, whatever they happened to be, but meanwhile Bernie was pacing off the distance between the desk and the flowerpot where Ferretti had found our gun. I hadn't seen Bernie's pacing-off thing in way too long! I trotted over and pitched in, pacing in my own way. Did the woman at the desk glance over in alarm? Maybe, but I'm too busy concentrating on my job to be sure.

". . . head office of World Wide Solutions?" Suzie was saying.

The woman nodded. "Somewhere overseas, I believe," she said.

"Did they give you a shipping address?" Suzie said.

There was another pause, this one much shorter, before the woman said, "My instructions were to leave everything with the building superintendent for pickup."

Bernie and Suzie exchanged a look. I got the feeling he was telling her something in a silent sort of way. That was bothersome.

Why not me? I liked Suzie just fine, but didn't she have somewhere to go?

Suzie turned to the woman at the desk. "Maybe we could help you."

"Help me?"

"Sort through things. We knew Eben personally, as I mentioned."

The woman shook her head. "Oh, I couldn't do that," she said. "I'm not authorized. It could cost me my job."

"How about getting authorized?" Bernie said.

"I don't understand."

"By your boss," Bernie said.

"That would never happen," the woman said. "He's a strictly by-the-book type. The whole company's that way."

Bernie and Suzie exchanged another look. Meanwhile, Mr. York, the renovation dude, was kind of lingering in the doorway, scraper in hand.

Suzie turned to the woman again. "What's the name of the company?"

The woman handed Suzie a card.

Suzie examined it. "Preakness Development?" she said.

The woman nodded.

"We're having a real Maryland-themed day," Bernie said, losing me completely.

"I'm sorry?" said the woman, showing she

and I had something in common, kind of a surprise.

"Terrapin Exports," Bernie said. "Preakness Development."

Some quick blinking went on behind those cat's-eye glasses. Mr. York was inside the room now.

"Not important," Bernie said. "We won't take any more of your time."

"Nice, ah, meeting you," the woman said. "Sorry I couldn't . . ."

"Good luck with the assignment," Bernie said.

Mr. York stepped aside to let us pass, raising his cap in a polite sort of way, and when he did that, I saw that his hair was of the slicked-back kind. At the very moment I ran smack into the thought I'd been waiting and waiting for: namely that I'd seen Mr. York once before, in fact, the day Bernie and I had first driven up to Suzie's house. Mr. York had also driven up — at the wheel of a taxi, if that mattered — and he'd taken a long look at a blue minivan parked nearby. Then there'd been that little scene of Eben coming out of Suzie's house and meeting Bernie, a meeting that maybe hadn't gone well, and . . . But I couldn't take it any further, most likely had already taken it too far. I started barking my head off.

Mr. York jumped back. "What's with him?"

"Do you have a cat?" Bernie said.

"No way," said Mr. York. "I'd have a dog if my building allowed it."

"Come on, big guy," Bernie said to me. "Ease up."

Ease up? I did the exact opposite!

"What the heck?" said Mr. York. "Dogs usually like me."

Bernie! Do a so therefore!

But Bernie didn't. He took me by the collar in that gentle Bernie-like way — and eased me out the door. I knocked off with the barking way before we got to the elevator, or possibly on the ride down, or maybe when we got out on the ground floor.

We drove toward the city, same seating arrangement as before. Maybe we'd soon be dropping Suzie off, getting back to normal. You could always hope, and I always do. It was quiet in the car, no talking, no music. I was in the mood for music! "The Road Goes on Forever," for example, or "Delta Momma Blues." "Don't kid yourself, Chet," Bernie always says, "that one's about codeine and nothing but." Whatever kidding yourself means, exactly, it's not me. I'm not a kid, and also helped take down Twitchy

Tim, a pharmacist gone bad who ran a side business in codeine popsicles, as I'm sure Bernie remembered.

"That was weird," Suzie said after a while.

"Oh, yes," said Bernie.

"Meaning?"

"I don't even know where to begin."

"Try."

The guinea pig smell! Begin with the guinea pig smell! But Bernie did not. Instead, he said, "She never asked for our names."

"So?"

"So maybe she didn't have to."

"You're saying . . . she knew who we were?"

Bernie nodded, just one simple brief movement. I knew that nod very well. It only happened when Bernie was certain he was right.

"Come on, Bernie," Suzie said. "There are much likelier explanations than that. We said we were friends of Eben's. Why wasn't that enough?"

"How about we ask her?" Bernie said.

"Ask her why she didn't want our names?"

"Yeah," Bernie said. "Call Preakness Development and see if they can put you through."

"And then just say, 'Hi, us again — we're

hurt that you didn't card us?' "

Bernie laughed. "Why not?" he said. "If it goes that far."

"If it goes that far?" Suzie said.

Bernie didn't answer. Suzie started up on her phone, tapping at the screen with the look on her face that humans get when they're deep into their gadgets, a look like maybe they're starting to turn into a gadget themselves. Doesn't show them at their best, in my opinion. No offense.

"Bernie?" Suzie said. "There doesn't seem to be a listing for Preakness Development."

"No?" Bernie said, not sounding surprised.

"Not only that — there are no hits at all for them, not a single hit of any kind!"

"Uh-huh."

More tapping. "What's more," Suzie said, "that building is owned by an outfit called Treetop Properties." She looked up, turned to him. "What the hell? Next you'll be telling me that —" She bent over the phone. "But there is a Terrapin Exports."

"Try them."

Suzie made a call. "Hello, Terrapin Exports? I had a question about the new office you're opening at 1643 Ellington Parkway." She listened for moment. "Any plans to?" She listened again, then clicked off. "They know nothing about it, Bernie."

"What bothers me the most," Bernie said, swinging onto an off-ramp, circling around, and heading back on the highway in the direction we'd come from, "is how she came up zip on the Maryland references. That's kind of worrisome."

"More worrisome than the rest of it? How?"

"Not sure," Bernie said. "Did you notice her accent?"

"Accent?"

"Very faint," Bernie said. "I couldn't place it." He pulled off the road, parked again in front of the brassy-colored office building. We were back? Hadn't we just left? A puzzler. But if it was okay with Bernie, it was okay with me.

TWELVE

In the elevator again! Way too much elevator work on this case already. I'm no fan of elevators, couldn't tell you how often they'd made me puke. But not this time: the doors opened just as I was getting the first hints of pukiness. I stepped into the hall, a pukey air bubble rising up through my throat and into the air. Right away I went from feeling not quite tip-top to my tip-toppest. We walked down the hall to the World Wide Solutions office, all systems go, and go is how I roll, if that makes any sense.

No sign of Mr. York, the renovation dude, or taxi driver dude, or whatever he was, but he'd left scrapings on the carpet and there were still some letters on the door.

"He got to 'World Wi' and took a break?" Suzie said.

"Damn it," said Bernie.

He charged forward, turned the knob, turned it so hard it twisted right off. Had I seen that before? Never. But that was Bernie: just when you think he's done amazing you, he amazes you again. The door — what was it left of it — swung open.

No sign of the cat's-eye woman. No sign of much of anything. All the boxes, all the papers: gone.

"Chet was on to something," Bernie said.

"I'd wondered about that," said Suzie.

While I waited to find out what I'd been on to — what an interesting subject! — Bernie said, "And I'm an idiot." That had to be his sense of humor popping up, which could happen just about any time. He went through the office, yanking at the desk and file cabinet drawers. Empty, empty, empty. But that didn't make Bernie an idiot. Nothing could.

"This means they didn't have permission from the cops?" Suzie said.

Bernie slammed a drawer shut and shook his head.

"So therefore," Suzie went on, but I stopped right there. I mean, whoa! Bernie handles the so therefores at the Little Detective Agency, and I bring other things to the table. Didn't Suzie have somewhere to go? And meanwhile, Bernie was listening to whatever she had to say with total interest, like he couldn't look at anyone else if he tried. *Try, Bernie, try.*

But he didn't. The next thing I knew we were back in the hall. Bernie hurried from door-to-door, flinging open the ones that would open, glancing in. I caught glimpses of different sorts of humans surprised at work. Then at the end of the hall, we came to a door that wasn't like the others, just a plain gray door with no writing on it. Bernie rattled the knob. From the other side of the door came sound, faint and low. Call it a moan.

Bernie lowered his shoulder to the door. In a flash, I was pretty much beside myself: I loved breaking down doors more than anything! And what's more natural when you love something than to pitch in and help get it done? We're a team, me and Bernie, in case that's not clear yet. We broke down that door together, side by side, broke it practically to smithereens, smithereens turning up in this job from time to time, just another one of the great things about it. I was so excited about breaking down doors and smithereens and Bernie that I didn't quite see what we'd found on the other side of the door, which turned out to be a sort of storage closet, full of brooms and mops and buckets and other stuff you'd expect. But how about something you

151

wouldn't expect, namely a uniformed cop all tied up in a tight little bundle, his head completely hidden in crime scene tape, wrapped around and around? That's what we found in the storage closet, me and Bernie. Suzie was there, too, wouldn't be right to leave that out. And another thing about her: a lot of people not in our business tend to look shocked when they see a sight like we were seeing, covering their mouths, saying "Oh, my God," that kind of thing. There's something scary about it after all, a face that's crime scene tape and nothing else. But there was none of that with Suzie. Her eyes were as hard as Bernie's eyes at that moment, which means like stone. The crime-scene face man moaned again. I backed up just the tiniest bit, for no particular reason. Don't think for a second that I myself was scared. Not possible. I'm a pro. Please keep that in mind.

"That's it, Nevins?" said Lieutenant Soares. "That's all you've got?"

We were back in the emptied-out World Wide Solutions office, all of us — me, Bernie, Suzie, Soares — on our feet, except for the man from the storage closet, now untied and unwrapped, sitting on the couch for office visitors. He was turning out to be just a normal cop who'd screwed up, name of Nevins, unless I was off the track. That can happen, especially if it's the kind of track that doesn't involve my nose. If my nose is in the picture, you can bet the ranch.

Some people, when they screw up, get what's called a hangdog look, maybe the strangest human expression there is. But that wasn't where I was going with this. Where was I going? I was going . . . cops! Yes, cops, screw-up cops specifically. Screw-up cops don't get that look, the name of which we can do without. Instead, they get the high school screw-up kid look, kind of up from under and mulish. Don't get me started on mules — no way I'll ever forget that mule called Rummy — because there's just no time. The point is that Nevins, the cop from the storage closet, had that look on his face. And did he even smell a bit like Rummy? I thought so. In fact, I was sure of it! What a life!

"Yeah," Nevins said. "That's all."

"You were standing outside the door, as per your orders," Soares said. "You thought you heard a sound coming from one end of the hall —"

"I heard it."

"— turned and took a step or two that way, and got clocked from behind by an unseen attacker."

Nevins stuck his chin out and made a quick nod, kind of chopping and aggressive. It made me want to aggress him right back, but this wasn't my play. I'd seen way too much cop back-and-forth in my time to make a mistake like that.

"And after that you remember nothing until these nice folks came to the rescue?" Soares said.

Nevins's glance went to Bernie and Suzie, skipping over me. If folks come to your rescue, you tend to be fond of them, maybe want to give them a nice big lick. Nevins didn't have anything like that in mind, not even close.

"Yeah," he said.

Soares gazed down at Nevins. "Anything to add?"

Nevins shook his head.

"Go to the ER," Soares told him. "Get yourself checked out. Then take the day."

Nevins pushed himself off the couch and walked out with no backward look. Soares watched him go, kept looking in that direction even after Nevins was out of sight. I heard the elevator's ping.

"You're wondering how to handle the union," Bernie said.

154

Soares turned to him. "Not worth it," he said.

"But potential evidence in a murder case has disappeared before it could be evaluated."

"You can drive a truck through potential," Soares said, losing me completely. Even Bernie looked a bit confused — you could tell from his eyebrows, so beautiful and thick, with a language all their own. "The takeaway will be officer harmed in the performance of his duty."

Bernie nodded.

"I suppose I owe you," Soares said.

"Nope."

"Mind telling my why you came here this morning?" Soares said. "I'm asking real nicely."

"Someone tried to hang a murder on me," Bernie said.

"And you're not the type to let that slide."

"How about you?"

"What about me?" Soares said.

"They used you as their tool."

Soares's eyes turned colder. "You don't even want to get along, do you?"

Bernie didn't answer.

Soares turned to Suzie. "Plan on writing about this case?"

"Of course," Suzie said. "Where are you

in the investigation?"

"Off the record, nowhere."

"And on the record?"

"It's an active investigation. We're pursuing a number of leads."

"Such as?"

"Wish I could share that information."

"For example," Bernie said, "you must have searched Eben's house, apartment, wherever he lived."

"He had a studio off Dupont Circle," Soares said.

"And?" said Bernie.

Soares looked down, like he'd suddenly gotten interested in his shoes. I didn't see it, myself. They were just your everyday cop shoes, scuffed black lace-ups in need of polishing and pronto, shoe polish being one of those smells that adds a little zest to life.

"It was empty."

"Empty?"

"Like he'd moved," Soares said. "Which was what we assumed at first."

"But now you know someone cleaned it out?" Bernie said. When Soares didn't answer, Bernie turned to Suzie. "We're out of here."

Soares looked up. "And headed where?"

"Wish I could share that information," Bernie said.

Soares raised his voice. "Think you're the first hard-ass I've dealt with?"

"I'm done thinking about you in any context," Bernie said.

Then came a silence I knew well, a silence that swells up until there's a sort of explosion and dudes start throwing punches. But that didn't happen this time. Soares held up both hands in the stop sign and said, "No way to fix the past. As for the future, I understand Ms. Sanchez is based here, but is there any reason for you and this champion dog of yours to stick around?"

"Where I'm going is none of your business," Bernie said, real unfriendly. As for me, this particular champ was starting to see Soares in a whole new light.

"Suit yourself," Soares said. Then, as we started to go, he added, "One more thing." He took an envelope from his jacket pocket, handed it to Bernie.

"What's this?" Bernie said.

"A District of Columbia private investigator's license," said Soares. "Good for one year, with certain provisions you'll see in paragraph four, and signed by a duly authorized officer of the department."

"Is that Soares's signature?" Suzie said, reading over Bernie's shoulder. We were standing by the Porsche outside the brassy-colored building. "He's the duly authorized officer of the department?"

Bernie nodded, folded the sheet of paper and put it in his pocket.

"Why would he do this?" Suzie said.

"You tell me," said Bernie.

Instead, Suzie tilted up her head and gave Bernie's earlobe a quick little kiss. That caught my attention big time and I missed some back-and-forth. When I tuned back in, Bernie was saying, ". . . all we need now to make it totally normal is a client."

We started getting into the car. There was a moment or two of confusion and then Bernie said, "Chet?"

In the back? Again? I stepped up to the plate, came up big, took one for the team. In short, I squeezed myself onto that horrible little shelf.

"Do you think Chet resents me?" Suzie said.

"No way," Bernie said. "He loves you."

"Maybe he loves me and resents me at the same time."

"Nah," Bernie said. He glanced my way. "You love Suzie plain and simple, right, big guy?"

What was going on? All so complicated. Sometimes I simply turn my face to the sky and howl. This turned out to be one of those times.

"God almighty," Bernie said.

"He hates me," Suzie said.

Hate Suzie? Impossible. Why would she say that? All I could think to do was: *amp it up!* So I did. Bernie burned rubber out of the parking lot. Were we making noise or what? Heads turned, count on it. But we're used to that at the Little Detective Agency.

Things had quieted down by the time we got back to the city, that strange stone tower straight ahead.

"First in the hearts of his countrymen," Suzie said.

"Not me," said Bernie. "Lincoln's the one."

"That's the sentimental choice."

"Me? Sentimental? That's a first. Should I take it as a —"

Suzie's phone rang, a good thing since it interrupted all that incomprehensible chatter. Suzie said, "This is Suzie," and then listened for what seemed like a long time, sitting completely still. When she finally clicked off, she turned to Bernie and said, "That was Eben's dad," she said. "He's flying back to London with the body."

"Where is he?"

"Dulles."

Bernie pulled a tight U-ee and stepped on it.

We drove up to an airline terminal and pulled over to the curb. The terminal doors slid open, and a small old man came out. He looked around, blinking in the sun. Suzie got out of the car and went over to him. They talked for a little while and then she brought him to the car.

"Bernie," she said, "this is Maurice St. John, Eben's father. Maurice, meet Bernie Little, the private investigator I was telling you about."

Bernie got out of the car, shook hands with Maurice, who looked even smaller next to Bernie. But I liked the way he stood, very straight, bony little shoulders back, head up.

"My flight's in less than an hour, so I don't have much time," Maurice said. "Will you take pounds?"

Whoa. Something about pounds? I knew pounds, never wanted to see the inside of one again. Biting an old man? Not the Chet that I know, but I was prepared to do almost anything to be free.

Thirteen

No biting necessary? Good news, all in all, although just between you and me there's something about sinking your teeth into human flesh that . . . better leave this for now, or possibly forever. The point is that the next thing I knew, Maurice was counting out what looked like money, only way more colorful. It made a nice little wad, nice little wads being just what we always need if we're talking cash money. And we must have been talking cash money, because Bernie took it and tucked it in his wallet, which was where cash money always went. Checks were another matter, getting stuffed way too often in the chest pocket of Hawaiian shirts, a place that's real easy for checks to fall out of, as we'd proved many times at the Little Detective Agency.

"I trust that's enough to get started," Maurice said. He had grayish skin and reddish eyes and gave off a smell that reminded me a bit of Mrs. Parsons, our neighbor back home on Mesquite Road, now pretty much living in the hospital. Whatever she had, Maurice had it, too.

"More than enough, if I'm not messing up on the exchange rate," Bernie said. "This'll take care of the retainer and at least a week's work. If I get results before that, there'll be a refund."

"Results are what I want," Maurice said. His voice rose slightly. "My son, Eben . . ." All at once his throat clogged up, which happens sometimes to humans, and then they can't speak. He teared up, too, often the case during a throat-clogging episode. When humans are sailing along nicely, they've got all their bodily moistures under control, and when they start to go off the rails, the moistures rise up. Just a thought, but it's the kind of thing you watch for in this business.

A tear slid down Maurice's face and dropped to the pavement. I licked it up: a strangely unsalty tear. I felt bad for Maurice.

He took a deep breath. "Thank God, my wife is dead," he said. "This would have broken her heart."

Now a tear or two appeared in Suzie's eyes. As for Bernie, I couldn't tell because he'd sort of bowed his head in a way that made him look even nicer than usual. Maurice dabbed at his eyes. "I beg your pardon," he said. "I don't mean to make a spectacle." He checked his watch. "Is there anything else you need from me?"

Bernie, his head back up, said, "Did your son have any enemies?"

"Personally or professionally?" said Maurice.

"Either," Bernie said.

"I can't imagine him having any personal enemies. Not that Eben was popular in a conventional sense. He didn't push himself forward in the way you so often see nowadays. But no one ever disliked him."

"Was he married?" Bernie said.

Suzie gave Bernie a sharp look, not particularly friendly. What was that about? I had no idea. A big plane flew low overhead, hurting my ears, and then another. Was this conversation going anywhere? Didn't we already have the green, even if it didn't look green? Why not split?

"Eben never married." Maurice turned to Suzie and gave her what you'd have to call a stare. "He had very high standards, was waiting for the right woman to come along."

Bernie caught that stare, gave Suzie a quick stare of his own. Then his gaze went to Maurice and he said, "What about professional enemies?"

"On that I have no information."

"What did Eben do, exactly?" Bernie said.

"He was an international relations consultant."

"Working for an outfit called World Wide Solutions?"

"Correct."

"What can you tell us about them?"

"Nothing."

There was a pause. "You never discussed Eben's work with him?" Bernie said.

"No more than to say, how is work."

"And what would he say in reply?"

"Unobjectionable — work was always unobjectionable," Maurice said.

"But what were the details of this unobjectionable work?" Bernie said. "What was his routine?"

"That was not discussed," Maurice said, his voice maybe sharpening a bit. Was he starting not to like Bernie?

"I don't get all this reticence," Bernie said. "It's like *Monty Python* without the jokes."

Maurice didn't like that. His eyes dried up completely. "Perhaps he was more forthcoming with Ms. Sanchez."

"Why would that have been?" Bernie said.

Maurice's eyes went to Suzie, back to Bernie. He said nothing. Another plane went roaring overhead. Was this an interview? I've sat through many interviews in my career, all of them more comfortable. The worst part was this new python involvement, totally unexpected. I knew pythons only from Animal Planet, but they were a kind of snake, and I'd had experience with snakes out in the desert, none good. If snakes were part of this case, we were in trouble. I took a few careful sniffs, caught not a single whiff of snake, meaning we were safe for now.

Suzie spoke up. "Eben was not more forthcoming. But I didn't know him well, and you did. I was never clear on whether he had any associates —"

"Or if there's a headquarters in London," Bernie said.

"— or who his clients were."

Maurice was silent for what seemed like a long time. Then he licked his lips — thin, colorless lips, just like Mrs. Parsons's — and said, "My son was a good man trying to do good things in a disgusting world."

"Are you suggesting he was some kind of whistle-blower?" Bernie said.

There was a look you saw occasionally when some human or other began to realize what I'd known from the get-go, namely that Bernie was always the smartest human in the room. I saw that look now on Maurice's face.

"You might say that," he said.

Whoa! Did this mean whistle-blowing was a possibility? Nothing hurts my ears like whistle-blowing. Snakes and whistle-blowing on the same case? We were in new territory. I was ready to go home. Hey! I missed Iggy, wouldn't even have minded that annoying *yip-yip-yip* of his. In fact, I would have loved hearing his yips. How did he even make that sound?

"Chet?"

Uh-oh. All eyes were on me.

"Never heard him make a sound like that," Bernie said.

"Is he sick?" said Suzie.

Sick? How ridiculous! I sat up tall and strong, mouth shut, just about. Chet the Jet, unsick to the max. Their gazes moved on, chitchat starting up again.

". . . whistle-blowers work for someone," Bernie was saying. "That's who they blow the whistle on. So if Eben was a whistle-blower, he must have been working for someone."

"My son took a broader view," Maurice said.

"What does that mean?" Bernie said.

Maurice checked his watch again. "I really must be going." He turned and walked toward the terminal. After a moment or two, Bernie went after him — and what was this? Took that fat wad of strange-colored cash money out of his wallet and started to . . . to give it back? I had two thoughts: Hawaiian pants and tin futures, big speed bumps in our financial past.

"What are you doing?" Maurice said, still walking away, the money sort of flapping in his face.

"Take it back," Bernie said. "I can't work for you."

Then came a surprise. Maurice's voice rose, kind of a shout except there was no strength behind it, just mostly air. "Why not? Don't tell me you've got a conscience."

"What does that mean?"

"You got the girl, didn't you?" Maurice looked past Bernie, right at Suzie. "His girl."

Suzie's voice rose back at him. "I'm nobody's girl."

The anger went out of Maurice, just like that. He actually looked kind of sheepish, as humans say, although sheep can be troublesome in my experience.

"I apologize." Maurice turned to Bernie. He gave him a long look, then lowered his voice way down and said, "Aubrey Ross."

"Huh?" said Bernie. "Aubrey Ross?"

"A sort of mentor," Maurice said. "He

brought Eben to America."

"How do I find —" Bernie began, but Maurice was already on his way through the terminal doors. A bunch of bigger people wheeling lots of baggage moved in behind him, and he vanished from sight. Bernie jammed all that cash money back in his wallet and stuck it in his pocket, meaning the interview had gone well, in my opinion.

There was no talking for a long time after that, silence all the way to Suzie's place. Little things about the way humans sit can tell you a lot about how they're getting along, like the tilt of their heads, for example. Bernie's and Suzie's heads were tilted away from each other, just enough for me to notice. *Tilt the other way! Tilt the other way!* But no.

Back in Suzie's kitchen, Suzie sat down at her laptop, Bernie gazed out the window, and I drank my water bowl dry, real thirsty for some reason. I licked the bottom of the bowl for a while, kind of crazy since that's giving back the water I just took from it! Why would anyone do that? The truth is, I was having worries, but forget I mentioned it. My job is to be strong, end of story.

Part of being strong is about looking out

for the team. My team was me and Bernie, although right now we were spending a lot of time with Suzie. Could that possibly mean Suzie had joined the team, maybe at some moment when I was napping? Napping was one of my best things, and I'd hate to give it up. I sat down by the empty water bowl and waited for . . . what? Good news, of course! Why bother waiting for anything else?

Bernie turned from the window, his eyes on Suzie. Her own eyes were going back and forth, back and forth in that machine-like way that means reading is going on.

"What are you doing?" Bernie said.

Suzie looked up, kind of surprised. Was it because of the hardness in his voice? I was surprised myself.

"Researching Aubrey Ross," Suzie said. "Isn't that the next step?"

"Not in my mind," Bernie said.

"What do you mean?"

"First, I'd like to find out why Maurice thought you were Eben's girl."

Suzie's face went very still. "Bernie?"

"If there was nothing to it, why would Eben have gone to the trouble of telling his father? It just doesn't make —"

Suzie rose, smacking her laptop shut. "This is making me sick. It is sick."

They glared at each other. I rose and walked around in a little circle.

Bernie turned to me. "Chet! In the car!"

In the car? Now? It didn't seem right somehow, although how could a car ride ever be wrong? And I got the feeling, hard to explain why, that I'd be back in the shotgun seat. I beat Bernie to Suzie's door. You can overthink sometimes in this business: I'd heard Bernie say that more than once. On my way out, I resolved to cut down on my overthinking.

We walked toward the street, me and Bernie side by side, not going fast. He seemed to be dragging his feet, *scrape scrape* on the path. That made my tail want to droop! How weird was that? I got it up nice and high. As we went by Lizette's house, I spotted her sitting in the screened porch, mostly lost in shadows. I also caught the faintest whiff of some creature, a creature I knew, but maybe on account of Bernie's dragging feet or Suzie's tears, I couldn't concentrate enough to place it. I slowed down a bit, sniffing the air, and as I did a man entered the screened porch from somewhere in the house. Hey! Was it Mr. York? Sure looked like him, that slicked-back hair giving his head a squarish shape in the shadowy light. Lizette rose real fast, like she was surprised

— and maybe not too happy — by the sight of Mr. York. He strode over to her and said something. She slapped his face, good and hard. He slapped her right back, more of a punch, actually, and she fell onto the chair. Mr. York turned and disappeared through a door and into the house.

Whoa! I didn't like any of that. Once some perp smacked his wife, also a perp, right in front of me and Bernie. Bernie decked him with one blow. And then came something crazy, namely the wife whapping Bernie over the head with a wooden spoon. But forget all that, the point being that at the Little Detective Agency we're against dudes taking swings at women. I barked to let Bernie know what was going on.

What was this? He was already out on the street, getting into the car?

"Come on, Chet. Haven't got all day."

Why not? I kept barking.

"Chet! Do you want to ride or not?"

What a question! Of course, I wanted to ride, wanted it more than anything on earth. I amped the noise down to nothing and forgot all about why I'd been making it in the first place. Maybe it would come to me later. Things often did. And when they didn't, how would you know? Wow! Was that overthinking or what, and just when I'd told myself not to. I hopped onto the shotgun seat.

FOURTEEN

Bourbon is Bernie's drink, in case that hasn't come up already. When he's his normal Bernie-type self, he has it with ice. When things aren't going well, the ice gets skipped. We were iceless at the moment, by ourselves on a tiny patio behind some bar that wasn't doing much business, maybe on account of this part of town being kind of sketchy. In fact, there was a good chance we were lost. We'd driven around for a bit, the sun moving from one side of the car to the other, and after a while, Bernie had opened his mouth for the first time on the whole drive and said, "Where the hell are we?" He'd taken the next off-ramp, adding, "I mean that in every sense." Which was a total puzzler, and now here we were on this patio: two tables, one torn umbrella flapping above us in the breeze, a waiter with a cigarette hanging from the side of his mouth.

"I'll have another," Bernie said. "And more water for Chet."

"Never seen a dog so thirsty," the waiter said.

"Uh-huh," said Bernie. "And a pack of cigarettes."

"We don't sell 'em."

"I'll buy a pack from you personally."

The waiter pulled a pack of cigarettes from his pocket, gave it a squeeze so he could peek inside. "Got eight left."

"I'll buy 'em."

"Hell, you can have 'em."

"I said I'll pay," Bernie said. He took a bill from his wallet, handed it to the waiter.

"What's this?" the waiter said.

Bernie gave it a narrow-eyed look, almost a squint. Uh-oh. Didn't see that very often, only during iceless bourbon episodes, and not even all of those.

"Looks like a ten-pound note," Bernie said. "That's the queen. She's actually German by heritage."

"Huh?"

"Never mind," Bernie said, snatching back the ten-pound note — I myself am a hundred-plus pounder, seems the right place to drop in that fact again — and laid a more normal bill on the table, meaning it was green.

"You're offering me twenty bucks for eight smokes?" the waiter said.

"Take it or leave it," said Bernie.

The waiter took it. Bernie stuck a cigarette in his mouth. The waiter lit it off his own cigarette. Bernie sucked in some smoke. The waiter sucked in some smoke. Their smoke clouds rose up under the umbrella and mixed together, then hung there with nowhere to go. And Bernie had been trying so hard to quit! I hadn't seen him smoke a cigarette in longer than I could remember, except for once or twice or a few more times than twice. I don't go past two, a perfect number in my opinion, something worth mentioning even if it's come up before. Run the numbers: didn't humans say that all the time? But the numbers can't outrun me, if you see where I'm headed with this. Fine if you don't. Neither do I.

"Uncle of mine developed a powerful thirst like this pooch of yours," the waiter said. "Turned out to be diabetes."

Bernie gazed at him without speaking. I'd never want that gaze on me.

"I'll get that order," the waiter said, backing away.

Bernie sipped his bourbon and smoked a cigarette, then did it all over again. My thirst finally went away. I lay down at Bernie's feet, angling myself so I could keep an eye on him. Were we on our way someplace or just moving in here to this bar on a permanent basis? I was cool with either.

Bernie gazed up at the underside of the umbrella. A spider web hung between the pole and the umbrella material, a motionless fly tangled in the strands on one side and a fat round spider on the other, kind of flexing some of his legs, in no particular hurry.

"Suppose," Bernie said, "we'd headed west instead of east. No one ever says, 'Go east, young man.' Remember when I pointed that out?"

I did not.

"Why didn't I listen to myself?" Bernie took a big sip, shook his head. "Because I can't be called a young man anymore?" Bernie thought about that, whatever it was. "All these people clinging so desperately to being young — what if that ages them in itself?" He laughed a small laugh, at what I had no idea. "Who wants to be like them? So it's either somehow be forever young, which ain't gonna happen this side of Ponce de Leon, or . . ." He took a deep drag, let smoke out slowly through his nostrils, a great human trick I never tired of seeing.

Ponce de Leon was a new one on me, but would I ever forget Normy de Leon, whose scam had involved stealing garbage trucks and ended with me and Bernie digging him out of a landfill? And he didn't even thank us while we were hosing him down and snapping on the cuffs! Ponce: possibly Normy's brother, and also up to no good? If so, heads up, amigo.

Bernie emptied his glass, looked around for the waiter. No waiter in sight. The sky was starting to darken. Up in the spider web, the fly was gone and the spider had moved over to where the fly had been, its round middle maybe fatter than before and pulsating a bit.

Bernie turned to me. "C'mere, big guy."

I rose immediately, stood by Bernie. He gave me a very nice pat, then a scratch between the ears. "What do think, Chet? What's the next move?"

The next move? I had no idea. Wasn't that Bernie's department? But I knew that Bernie was going through a tough time about something or other, so it was on me to step up. The next move . . . the next move would be to . . . chow down! That was it! We hadn't had even one measly crumb in I didn't know how long.

"Chet! Knock it off!"

Knock what off?

The waiter came hurrying out the back door of the bar. "What's wrong?" he said.

"Huh?" said Bernie.

"That's the loudest goddamn barking I ever heard in my life," the waiter said. "What's he want?"

"Nothing," Bernie said. "We're good. Just bring me another bour—"

"Maybe he wants more water."

"His bowl's half full."

"Yeah, but with the diabetes —"

Bernie lowered his voice. "Don't say that word again."

The waiter raised his hands. "Whatever." He glanced at me. Was I still or had I recently been barking? Tough questions. "Maybe he's hungry," the waiter said. "Got a burger out front the customer hardly touched."

"Uh," Bernie said. "Thanks."

The waiter went inside. It got very quiet on this patio, a rather nice one, all in all. If there'd been some recent noise it had passed on through, but completely. Pretty soon, Bernie and I were munching on burgers, although in truth most of the munching was done by me, Bernie not seeming hungry. He took one bite — mustard spurting onto his Hawaiian shirt, but it was the sunset pattern shirt, the mustard fitting in perfectly — and tossed me the rest, caught in midair and made quick work of. After that, I licked the juices off the patio floor, doing a careful job. Anything worth doing is worth doing well, as Leda would tell Bernie every time she got him to rearrange the furniture, which happened a lot toward the end of their marriage.

". . . I didn't listen to myself then," Bernie was saying, "but what's to stop me from listening now?" We were supposed to listen? I listened my hardest, heard all sorts of things: a toilet flushing, another toilet running — a problem we often had on Mesquite Road — and, yes, a toilet seat banging down on yet one more toilet. It was all toilets in this burg. Not too shabby! Then I heard a fly buzz nearby. I looked up just in time to see it run smack into that spider web and come to a sticky sort of stop. The spider started up on that leisurely leg-flexing thing.

"I'm hearing one thing and one thing only," Bernie said. "And it couldn't be simpler. We're working a case, big guy. We've got a client. We've taken money. What else is there to say?"

I waited to hear. Bernie was silent. After a while, he took out his phone. "What was

the name of that guy? Aubrey Roth? Roe?"
He played with the phone. Time passed.
"Ross!" he said, kind of loud. I woke with a
start, not that I'd been sleeping, more like
dozing. There's sleeping, napping, and dozing, all very nice and different from one
another in ways we don't have time for now.

Bernie gazed at his phone, his face in the
screen glow reminding me of Donald in his
aquarium, Donald being a fish Charlie had
for a while and then not. I'd never meant
what happened to happen, let's leave it at
that.

The waiter appeared. "Another round?"

Bernie, eyes fixed on the screen, didn't
seem to hear.

"Hey, buddy."

Bernie glanced up. "Check," he said, his
eyes looking screeny themselves, if that
makes any sense. Probably not, but of all
creatures, humans are the most like machines, something that takes getting used
to, and I'm not there yet.

Back in the Porsche, me riding shotgun, our
recent seating problems just about forgotten, Bernie brought up machines first thing.
"Amazing what you can find out with one
of these," he said, waving his phone around.
"I'll be able to do this job when I'm in a

wheelchair."

Whoa right there! Had I heard a worse thing in my whole life? True, Bernie limped sometimes on account of his war wound — hardly ever and only when he was very tired or we were working fast on steep ground — but it had never occurred to me that . . . that nothing. I wasn't even going to let myself think it — no big strain, what with thought blocking being one of my strengths. Instead —

"Hey, Chet," Bernie said, laughing and shrugging me away at the same time, "knock it off."

Knock what off? Licking the side of his face? Just one more.

"CHET!"

Then came some braking and honking, maybe shouting from an easily frightened driver in the opposite lane, but all over quickly, no harm done. As for me and Bernie, we don't frighten easily. If you saw me, you'd notice I'm wearing a collar made of gator skin. That sends a message.

A lovely evening, soft and warm, the sky dark on one side, fiery on the other, and wine-colored in between. We drove through a real nice neighborhood, the big brick and stone houses spaced far apart, parked in front of one of the biggest and stoniest and walked up to the door. Bernie pressed a button. I heard chimes inside. How lovely! I hoped no one would come so Bernie would press the button again and I'd hear more chimes. Which was what happened. And then again.

"Maybe nobody's home." Bernie stepped back. At that moment, I heard voices from behind the house. "Let's hit the road," Bernie said.

Those ears of Bernie's: far from small, so you might expect them to do better, but in the end, they were just decoration. I started around the house.

"Chet?"

Bernie followed.

The house had long wings on both sides, fronted by flowerbeds and bushes, almost every single bush and flower marked by the same member of the nation within. I did my best to lay my own mark on top, but there were so many of his that eventually I ran out of ammo. What a disaster! And a first in my career, except for once, stuck deep in the desert and all by myself on a case of which I remembered nothing else. But just think: you lift your leg and squeeze and . . . and nothing comes out, not the teeniest drop! Where do you go from there?

"C'mon, Chet — give it a rest."

I followed Bernie around the house. Just before we turned the corner, I heard a wooden knocking sort of sound that reminded me of good times with Charlie, playing with his blocks back when he was very little. The way those blocks ended up all over the place! In the pipes under every sink in the house! The fun we had! Except for Leda, can't leave that out. "Are you going to let this dog raise your son?" she'd said more than once, maybe her very best idea.

We stepped into the backyard, a huge backyard surrounded by a thick tall hedge, the grass just like a putting green. Two men, both dressed all in white, were playing some sort of game, not golf, in what was left of the late evening light. This game, new to me, was about biggish balls — wooden, judging from the sound they made bouncing off one another; strange clubs that reminded me of the mallet in the tool box back home, used once by Bernie to undent a fender bend, although it ended up adding more; and bent U-shaped pieces of wire stuck in the grass. The men — one short and round, with heavy glasses on his round face and his feet pointing out, duck-style, the other tall and fit-looking — whacked away at the wooden balls with the mallets. Other than that, I understood nothing, but those balls looked pretty interesting, even from a distance.

"Sit."

Me? I looked at Bernie.

"Who else?"

I sat. Bernie stood beside me. We watched. The men played in silence. It's usually easy to tell when women don't like each other, their voices giving them away. Men can be harder, but I picked up a faint scent of something unfriendly between these two, a bit like fear except with a vinegar add-on.

The tall dude stepped up to a ball, whacked it into another ball that went flying. The round dude spoke. "Double tap, I'm afraid. Clearly audible." Something about the way he spoke reminded me of Eben and Maurice. The tall dude gazed down at him. The round dude went to get the knocked-away ball, brought it back, kicked the other ball aside, then tapped his ball through one of the bent U-shaped things. "No beating luck," he said, and held out his hand, like handshaking was in the offing. Instead, the tall dude gave him some money, then walked away, coming toward us. He noticed us and said, "He cheats," as he went by, disappearing around the house.

I heard a car start up and drive off.

Meanwhile, the round dude was rounding up all the equipment and loading it onto a cart, the shadows now falling fast. We just watched, one of our best techniques at the Little Detective Agency. The round dude started rolling the cart our way, saw us, and stopped, one hand reaching into the pocket of his white pants.

"Aubrey Ross?" Bernie said.

The round dude adjusted his glasses. "Do I know you?"

"We're friends of Maurice St. John."

"Is that meant to be a recommendation?"

"You tell me, Aubrey."

Another pause. "Mr. Ross, if you don't mind."

"I'm Bernie Little," Bernie said. "Bernie, if you don't mind."

We moved toward Mr. Ross. His hand stayed in his pocket. He had a gun in there, gun oil being one of those smells you don't miss in our business. It didn't matter now, what with the gap closing between him and us. Just go for it, Mr. Ross. But he did not. They hardly ever do when you want them to. And those other times, when you don't want them to? That's the problem.

"And this is Chet," Bernie said.

Mr. Ross glanced at me. "I had a dog

quite like him," he said. "He was run over by a postal lorry."

FIFTEEN

"Sorry to hear that," Bernie said, and so was I, although postal lorry was a puzzler.

"The experience reminded me of valuable lessons learned along the way," said Mr. Ross. The purple was just about all gone from the sky now, but plenty of it seemed to remain on the surface of his glasses, blocking his eyes from view. A very round dude, Mr. Ross, and also real short: if I stood up on my back legs, I was pretty sure I'd be taller, could rest my paws on top of his bald round head. I gave the idea some thought.

"What kind of lessons?" Bernie said.

Mr. Ross gazed up at Bernie, now mostly just a big, lovely-smelling shadow. "Regarding the unforeseen, mutability, chaos." He paused, then softly clapped his hands. Lights went on all along the back of the house, revealing a long sort of deck or patio, with couches, chairs, barbecue pit, swim-

187

ming pool. "In short," Mr. Ross continued, taking a long look at Bernie in the light, "the limits of management."

Zipping right by me without a trace, whatever that was all about, but I was on to something much more interesting, namely the eyes of Mr. Ross, now visible. They turned out to be very large and round and purple, just like the late evening sky, or pretty close. The only purple-eyed human I'd ever seen! Or maybe it was the purple color of the skin below his eyes, or the eyelids, or . . . never mind. We'll stick to him having purple eyes.

"You left out entropy on your little list," Bernie said.

And once again, this time on Mr. Ross's face, I saw that look, the look of someone realizing Bernie was the smartest human in the room. "For whatever reason, entropy was never a force in my career," he said.

"I want to talk about your career," Bernie said.

"And what, as you Americans are always so quick to ask, is in it for me?" Mr. Ross said.

Americans? That comes up from time to time. In fact, I was pretty sure we were Americans, me and Bernie, but that was as far as I could take it.

"What's your usual?" Bernie said.

"My usual?"

"Inducement. What does it normally take to get your cooperation?"

"Are you offering me a bribe — Bernie, was it?"

"What's your going rate?" Bernie said.

"You think me bribable?" said Mr. Ross.

"Can you fog a mirror?"

I knew fog, I knew mirrors, but that was it. This was Bernie at his most brilliant. And Bernie at his most brilliant is often when we start moving the dial. A very small smile appeared on Mr. Ross's face, just a quick upturn at the corners of his mouth, there and gone.

"Very well," he said. "Consider a donation to a favorite charity, negotiable later or not at all."

"Nothing easier," Bernie said.

Mr. Ross stepped onto the deck, sat on a couch. We followed, Bernie sitting on the end of a chaise longue, me beside him. For company we had some night bugs, drawn by the light, in the way of night bugs. Most of them made a last-minute turn toward one of those cool bug zappers and got zapped, *zap zap zap,* a satisfying sound to my ears.

"This is about Maurice's son, Eben," Bernie said. "He was murdered, which I'm guessing you know. Maurice hired us to find the killer."

"You're a private investigator?"

Bernie nodded.

"But not from around here — Texas, perhaps. I have an ear for accents."

"We're licensed in this district, which is the relevant point."

Mr. Ross glanced my way. Accents had come up already in this case, Bernie saying that Lizette — and maybe somebody else we'd run across — had one. But Bernie didn't sound at all like Lizette. Mr. Ross was way off base, a baseball thing where next came putting your head down, disappearing back into the dugout, and sitting by your lonesome.

"I heard the news, quite naturally," Mr. Ross said, "but through the usual media outlets. I have no pertinent inside knowledge."

"You were Maurice's only suggestion," Bernie said. "According to him, Eben came to the US because of you."

"Some men are resentful by nature," said Mr. Ross.

"You're talking about Maurice?"

"What sort of life would that have been?"

"You're losing me," Bernie said. Which was just one of his rope-a-dope tricks. There was no losing us, me and Bernie, not in the end, which usually involved me grabbing the perp by the pant leg. Those white pant legs of Mr. Ross's had cuffs. I like sinking my teeth into cuffed pant legs above all others, no telling why.

"I refer to the St. John family business, to which seconding Eben was the extent of Maurice's ambition for him," Mr. Ross said. "Imagine a man of Eben's caliber withering away in some provincial office."

"Beats getting shot in the head," Bernie said. "What's the family business?"

Mr. Ross peered at Bernie with those round, purple eyes. "You're one of those only-in-America types," he said.

"Yeah," said Bernie.

Mr. Ross nodded to himself. "The St. Johns own a factory, possibly two or three."

"What's the product?"

"There you have me. Tunnel-boring equipment, perhaps?"

"And what did you have going that was better?"

"Something more intellectual," said Mr. Ross, "giving rein to Eben's analytical gifts."

"Are you talking about World Wide Solutions?" Bernie said.

"That came after."

"After what?"

"After Eben did his bolt."

"What does that mean?"

"Not an American expression?" Mr. Ross said. "I never stop learning. It means to take off unexpectedly. Eben decided to go out on his own."

"But before that, he worked for you?"

"Before my retirement, yes."

"What did you do?"

"I was an employee of the British government."

"I looked you up," Bernie said. "Your last position was third assistant secretary in the embassy's international trade office."

"Correct."

"Sounds no more interesting than tunnel-boring equipment, maybe less."

"For some, no doubt," said Mr. Ross.

"Unless you were doing some tunneling of your own."

Mr. Ross sat up a bit. Bernie had his attention. He had mine, too. Bernie always does, of course, but I meant especially now. Wasn't tunneling a kind of digging? Digging is one of my specialties. When I get front legs and back legs going full speed ahead all at once, I can make dirt fly like you would not believe. That bride up in her childhood tree house, getting her picture taken in her white wedding dress? And me down below, on a quest for some loot Bernie was convinced lay buried in that very yard? You don't forget scenes like that, amigo.

But the point is good diggers have a certain look to them, and it's never short and round — like Mr. Ross, to take a handy example. I was having a real hard time picturing him in the digging business. With those little hands, so soft and pudgy? Not in my lifetime, amigo, a lovely lifetime going on and on in the nicest way. The road goes on forever, and the party never ends.

Back to Mr. Ross, still sitting up straight, gaze on Bernie. "Are you making a suggestion of some sort?"

"Yeah," said Bernie. "I'm suggesting you were a spy, probably still are."

"Spy," Mr. Ross said. "Such a freighted word, so many inaccurate if romantic connotations. I hesitate to even use it."

"I bet you do," Bernie said.

That little smile made another appearance on Mr. Ross's face, real brief.

"You did say you worked for the Brits?" Bernie said.

"I'm British to the core."

"Why would the Brits spy on us?" Bernie said. "I thought we were friends."

"There's nothing simple about friendship," Mr. Ross said.

"Have you ever had one?" Bernie said.

Mr. Ross didn't like that. His face got heavy and . . . and kind of bulldoggish? Whoa! What a connection! No way this dude could remind me of any members of the nation within. But he did! I wished it wasn't happening, but that did no good. Mr. Ross was a bulldog in my mind, now and forever.

". . . putting it this way," Mr. Ross was saying. "If you're sleeping with an elephant, you'd better learn all you can about him — what makes him inclined to roll over, for example. No animus involved — it's mere prudence."

Prudence? That was the name of the elephant? Sounded right. I'd spent time with an elephant name of Peanut, the two of us all alone down in the Mexican desert, and Mr. Ross was on the button. That very thing, an elephant rollover, had happened to me! I'd scrambled out from under Peanut at the very last moment and given her a piece of my mind — a barking piece, better believe it. Then had come a demonstration of what she could do with her trunk, which up till that moment I'd thought was all about rustling around for grub and poring enormous amounts of water into her mouth. If an elephant was now in this case, we were headed off the rails. I checked the air: not a whiff of elephant, and that's a smell that can't be missed, except maybe by someone like you. No offense.

"And how did Eben do in the prudence department?" Bernie said.

Uh-oh. Prudence was the perp? Was that where Bernie was taking this? I'd smelled guinea pig in Eben's office, no doubt about that, but as for elephant, there'd been zilch. I felt a little lost. Sometimes, especially working a tough case like this one, it's good to take a break. I wandered over to Mr. Ross's equipment cart, still out there on the beautiful putting-green lawn. The sounds of Bernie and Mr. Ross talking drifted over to me, but like a kind of breeze, no longer bothersome.

"Excellent question," Mr. Ross said. "Is it possible to be prudent and passionate at the same time?"

There was a short silence, and then Bernie said, "Eben was passionate?" He sounded a little strange, his voice kind of thickened.

"Oh, surely," said Mr. Ross. "He was an idealist."

"An idealist," Bernie said, his voice back to normal, maybe somewhat sharper than normal.

"But with outstanding analytical gifts."

"You mentioned that. Give me some examples."

"I regret I'm unable to."

"Because they don't exist?"

"Because of constraints."

"How about an example of his passion?" Bernie said. "Any constraints there?"

"On that I can speak more freely. World Wide Solutions was his passion."

"Sounds grandiose to me," Bernie said.

"I prefer 'ambitious,' " said Mr. Ross. "Eben sacrificed a lot for World Wide Solutions — possibly everything."

"What was it?" Bernie said.

There was a long pause. "At its core?" Mr. Ross said. "A plea for transparency."

"What does that mean?" Bernie said, and I couldn't have agreed more. What did any of this mean? I returned to what I'd been doing, felt better.

"I can tell you what Eben meant by it," said Mr. Ross. " 'Intelligence for the masses.' "

"Who are the masses?"

"All those global citizens out there — the ones not like you and me."

"I'm not in your league," Bernie said.

Mr. Ross laughed. He had a very pleasant, round little dude sort of laugh. "Eben's point was that intelligence — in the sense of understanding what is really going on in the inner hearts and minds of the powerful — has always been restricted to the few. What a world it would be if the truths were universally known!"

"Maybe worse," Bernie said.

Mr. Ross laughed again. "I happen to agree with you. In fact, I tried to dissuade Eben on those very grounds."

"At the same time persuading him to keep nosing around on your behalf?"

"I wouldn't put it like that."

"MI5? Is that it? MI6? I'm not familiar with the British setup."

"I wish I could help you with that," Mr. Ross said.

"What can you help me with?" Bernie said. "Where should I be looking?"

"Ask questions," said Mr. Ross. "I'll do my best to answer."

"So you want this crime solved?"

"Very much."

"No matter where it leads?"

"I can only hope so."

"But there's no guarantee?"

"Men like you and me don't speak of guarantees," said Mr. Ross. "Haven't we outgrown childish things?"

"Like I said — I'm not in your league."

There was a silence, broken only by a faint but comforting sound, sort of woody and toothy. Then Bernie said, "Have you been in touch with the police?"

"No."

"The chief investigator is a DC lieutenant named Soares. Do you know him?"

"No."

"But a guy from some other department may be calling the shots."

"Oh?" said Mr. Ross. "What other department?"

"No idea," Bernie said. "Did Eben have any enemies?"

"Almost certainly, if you mean institutional enemies."

"What about the personal kind?"

"Not to my knowledge."

"Does the name Terrapin Exports mean anything to you?"

"No."

"Preakness Development?"

"Ditto."

"There may be a man involved in the case — late thirties, six feet, fit-looking, slicked-back hair. Goes by the name of York."

"I know no one matching that description."

"How about a tall woman, mid-fifties, well turned out?"

"Could be thousands of women in this city."

"She wears those funny little glasses. What are they called? Cat's-eye?"

There was a silence. Then Mr. Ross said, "Yes, cat's-eye."

"You know the woman?" Bernie said.

"I know the type of glasses."

"And the woman?"

"I'm afraid not."

"Was World Wide Solutions a one-man show? Or should we be speaking of it in the present tense?"

"Oh, the past tense, certainly."

"Where did the money come from?"

"Money?"

"Takes money to run a setup like that. Was it yours?"

"Mine?" Mr. Ross said. "I'm just a retired civil servant." I heard him rub his soft pudgy hands together. "Anything else? I have an engagement this evening."

"Did he ever mention a reporter named Suzie Sanchez?" Bernie said.

"Not in my hearing."

"What about reporters in general? How did they fit into this transparency scheme of his?"

"An excellent question," Mr. Ross said. "He must have had a role in mind for the media, but he never discussed it with me."

"A role for the media meaning some way of using them?"

"Of course."

"Supposing," Bernie said, "Eben had a contact who knew something that could change the course of history."

"That sounds somewhat overripe."

"His exact words, apparently," Bernie said. "Any idea what that information might be?"

"None whatsoever."

"How about who that contact might be?"

"Similarly."

"Any chance it's you?"

Mr. Ross laughed. "You're dogged, if nothing else." Knees creaked, meaning humans were rising to their feet. "A pleasure to meet you. Here's my advice — graph the point where the follow-the-money and the cui bono curves meet."

"I'd have to go back to school," Bernie said.

Or something like that. I'd been snagged just a bit earlier, namely on dogged. A sharp dude, Mr. Ross, quicker than most to see that Bernie and I were alike in some ways.

We got into the car, a cool night breeze starting up, very pleasant. Bernie turned the key, glanced over at me in the shotgun seat.

"Chet? What've you got there?"

Me? Oh, right. What I seemed to have might have been one of those mallets from Mr. Ross's backyard game, somewhat smaller now, possibly due to recent gnawing. Bernie eyed me for a moment or two and then gave me a pat.

"Good boy," he said.

I sat up my tallest. More patting might have been on the way, but at that moment Bernie's phone buzzed.

"Yeah?" he said.

Mr. Ross's voice came through the speakers. "Mr. Little? I neglec—"

"How did you get this number?"

"Would I ever insult you with such a question? I neglected to ask about this new person involved in the investigation."

"Can't tell you much about him. Name's Ferretti."

Silence on the other end.

"Two R's, two T's," Bernie said. "Do you know him?"

"I'm retired, as I mentioned," said Mr. Ross. "I no longer know anyone."

Sixteen

We pulled away from Mr. Ross's house, drove slowly through his fancy neighborhood. Bernie was thinking. I could feel his thoughts, brilliant thoughts that drifted through the night air and mixed in the most relaxing way with the wind in the trees. So many lovely nights already in my life! And so many more to come!

"Where do we start, big guy?" Bernie said after a while.

Anywhere. Anywhere at all was fine with me. But hadn't we already started? And if so, on what? That was as far as I could take it, and I kind of wished I hadn't begun.

"Do we trust Aubrey Ross?" Bernie went on. "Not as far as we can throw him."

Really? Was that true? Although round in shape, Mr. Ross was on the small side, surely not very heavy. I could picture me and Bernie actually throwing him pretty far, across a room, for example, or even farther.

So was that our next move, circling back to Mr. Ross's place and tossing him around for a bit? Sounded like a plan!

"What's his motivation? Where's he coming from? What does he want? We don't have a clue. But one thing's for sure — he was a spy. What do we know about international espionage? Zip. But here's my guess — there's no real retirement from the spy game, not until they take you out in a box."

Bernie turned down a side street, then another and — and we were circling the block, one of our best techniques! That Bernie! Where did his ideas come from? No telling, but right now were we setting up to throw Mr. Ross around and put him in a box, or just one or the other? Both would have been my preference, but it was Bernie's call. I waited to find out.

We pulled over in a shadowy spot on Mr. Ross's street, his house just in view up ahead. Bernie cut the motor, cut the lights, lit up one of the cigarettes he'd scored off that waiter. The moment I thought of that waiter, I realized how hungry I was, which turned out to be very, very hungry, pretty much starving. Funny how the mind works. You had to control your mind, that was basic in this business, and one of the secrets of our success at the Little Detective

Agency. I told my mind in no uncertain terms, whatever those were, exactly, to shut down all waiter thoughts. And what did my mind do? It jumped to thoughts of Max's Memphis Ribs, our favorite restaurant back home in the Valley. The meat on those bones? Something else! And when you were done with the meat, you still had the bone to work on! Was that a business plan or what? Cleon Maxwell, owner of Max's Memphis Ribs and a good buddy of ours, had to be rolling in green. Although, funny thing, hadn't Bernie lent him a grand or two some time back? What was up with that?

I looked over at Bernie. He took a deep drag, the end of the cigarette glowing bright. Was he worried? I thought so. I was, too. How were we going to shake our money loose from Cleon Maxwell? And then it hit me, maybe the most amazing thought of my life. Cleon could pay us back in ribs! Free ribs forever!

"Chet! What the hell?"

Uh-oh. I seemed to be over on Bernie's seat, kind of sharing it, and perhaps pawing at him at the same time. I backed up, pronto, got a grip.

He gave me a look. "What gets into you?"

What gets into me? How about free ribs forever, buckaroo? Bernie's going to turn that down? I gave him a look right back.

He sighed. "Everything's okay, big guy." He smiled at me, a very nice moment in my day. "I'm guessing you'd like to be back home, huh?"

Back home? I hadn't thought about it. But now I did. And all of a sudden, I was missing everything — starting with the big tree in our front yard. I hadn't marked it in ages! That was bad. I tried not to think of all the members of the nation within taking advantage of me not being there and found I could think of nothing else.

"I knew it," Bernie said. "We'll wrap this up fast, I promise. Although exactly how is —"

Headlights flashed on in Mr. Ross's driveway and a gleaming black car came rolling out, Mr. Ross's round head barely at steering-wheel level.

"Poke a hornet's nest, see what flies out, right, Chet?" Bernie said.

Actually, that sounded totally wrong to me, and I'd had experiences, all bad, with hornets. This must have been one of Bernie's jokes. We fired up, pulled onto the street, lights off. Next would come . . . hey! I had no idea what was coming next, not the slightest notion. Some of our best work got done that way at the Little Detective

Agency. I felt tip-top.

Bernie's the best wheelman in the Valley. He can follow from close behind, far behind, across many lanes, even from in front. And once while going backward the other way, although that once was more than plenty, and I didn't even want to think about it. We followed Mr. Ross onto some busier roads and then a big highway, Bernie switching on the lights and easing back into traffic.

"Never checks the rearview mirror," Bernie said. "Good spycraft or bad? Wouldn't jumpy guys be looking over their shoulders, spies or not? So maybe I've got this all wrong and he's on a pizza run."

Pizza was coming next? That would have been my last guess, if I'd been able to come up with even one. Pizza was a very interesting subject, some pizzas — with broccoli and Swiss chard, for example — being pretty easy to take or leave, while others — with sausage or bacon or pepperoni, for other examples — were unleavable. Closer, Bernie, follow closer. Don't lose him!

But Bernie didn't follow closer, hung back even more. "Is Ross even the pizza type?" he said. "I'm having trouble picturing him scarfing up a slice. DeGaulle would be another. Hard to —"

Mr. Ross cut across a couple of lanes and

swung onto an exit ramp at the last moment. A snap for us to stay with him; Bernie had been following from the inside lane, one of his coolest techniques. I glanced over at him: yes, steering with just one finger on the wheel, and that one finger barely touching. You had to love Bernie.

"Is he headed for the airport, Chet? Is this going to be one of those cases where we go through everything twice?" Whoa! I'd had a nightmare just like that. I was trying my hardest not to let the details come back to me when Bernie said, "The first time as tragedy, the second time as farce," and lost me completely. My mind stayed blank right until Ross pulled up at the same terminal where we'd met Maurice St. John. He parked in front of one of the sliding doors. We got stuck behind a bus, and by the time we'd found a space, Ross had gotten out with a small suitcase and was on his way inside. We jumped out and —

"Hey!" A cop came hurrying over. "Can't park here."

"We're not parking," Bernie said. "We're just —"

"Can't park, can't stop, can't idle, can't do nothin' but load and unload." He whipped out his ticket book.

Bernie glanced into the terminal. Way at

the back, someone waved Mr. Ross past a line. He vanished through a doorway. Bernie pointed at Mr. Ross's car.

"What about him?"

The cop peered at the gleaming black car. "Diplomatic plates," he said.

"So?"

"They never pay."

Bernie shook his head in this way he has, kind of like shooing flies away.

"Tell me about it," the cop said. "Realpolitik sucks. Meanwhile, you got Arizona plates. You pay."

"Yeah," said Bernie. "Maybe first I'll just —"

A black car a lot like Mr. Ross's glided up alongside and a man hopped out on the passenger side. He glanced at us with no interest, got into Mr. Ross's car. Both cars drove off.

"Realpolitik," Bernie said.

"Specialty of the house," said the cop.

Specialty of the house? I knew about that. Take Dry Gulch Steakhouse and Saloon, where it happened to be steak tips. I checked the air, smelled no food of any kind. Not gonna happen, big guy.

Two gleaming black cars in a tidy row are even easier to follow than one. They led us back to the city, onto a broad street that cut through parkland, with big buildings on either side. The black cars slowed down. A gate opened in a long brick wall. I glimpsed a big, lit-up building with columns, lots of gardens and statues. The black cars drove in. The gate closed.

"British Embassy, big guy," Bernie said. "Aubrey Ross has done a bolt. Way out of our reach and gone."

Way out of our reach? I didn't get that at all. Was it one of Bernie's jokes? I checked his face. Not happy. I moved a little closer to him.

Bernie gave me a pat. "He taught us the expression and then gave a demonstration, just in case we weren't getting it. A thoughtful guy."

We drove on. I wondered about the identity of the thoughtful guy and decided it had to be Bernie. Who else?

"But," Bernie said, somewhat later, the two of us parked outside — whoa! the same police station where they'd locked Bernie up? — "we threw a scare into him, didn't we?"

Who, exactly? And now we were going to throw a scare into the cops? Throwing scares into dudes — was that our new MO? I opened my mouth real wide. Teeth out the yingyang? Oh, yeah, and don't leave out big and sharp. Also nice and clean, according to Janie, my groomer, who brushes them in a way that makes me feel good all over, all the way to the tip of my tail, as far as you can possibly get from my teeth, which is kind of a puzzler.

We sat. After a while, I got the feeling we were sitting on the police station. Sitting on a place is in our repertoire, no doubt about it, but had we ever sat on a police station before? Not that I remembered. My take-away? We were better than ever!

The front door of the police station opened, and cops started filing out.

"Shift change, Chet. Not a long shot, more a medium sort of —" Bernie sat up straight. "Is that him? The one at the back, with the high school swagger?"

Hard to follow. I looked at those cops. They all seemed to have some high school swagger! I started to wonder whether all cops in the whole wide world — but never got there, probably a good thing, because Bernie nudged me and said, "It's Nevins, all right. Kind of looks better with crime scene tape wrapped around his head."

And it all came back to me, or at least some, some usually being more than enough, in my experience. For example, I was now pretty sure about our plan: We were going to throw a scare into Nevins. I could practically taste it.

Nevins got into — not an old clunker, exactly, maybe a sort of new clunker, with a dented trunk, like he'd been rear-ended — and drove off. Rear end him one more time, Bernie, rear end the swaggering dude! Hey! All at once, I was on fire. This case would be closing pronto. I leaned forward, front paws on the dash. We followed Nevins, not close enough for rear-ending him, but I held onto the idea. Giving up doesn't come easily to me. In fact, I got confused for a moment and couldn't remember what giving up was. Maybe it would come to me. Some things sometimes did. No time for examples at the moment.

Nevins led us into a neighborhood like lots of neighborhoods I knew, not fancy but also not sketchy, and parked in front of a darkened row house. We pulled over, nicely tucked in between two vans. Nevins got out of his car, walked to the front door of the row house without a backward glance, rattled some keys, and disappeared inside. Not long after, a light went on in a top-floor window. Bernie reached for his door handle, but at that moment a car came slowly down the street, headlights off, like the kind of thing we do ourselves, me and Bernie. Bernie paused and watched the car go by, a familiar sort of car, and I was trying to figure out why when a streetlamp lit the face of the driver, a strong face with a big and powerful nose: my buddy, Mr. Ferretti. Did he have a steak sandwich in there? I sat up real straight, on high alert. I was pretty much starving, if I haven't mentioned that already. Ferretti slowed down even more, head turning away from us and angling up, his gaze on that glowing window at the top of the town house. He almost came to a stop and then drove on.

I barked once, one of my low, rumbly barks, but Bernie was already looking at me.

"What's up, Chet?"

What was up? Ferretti, for one thing, steak sandwiches for two. I couldn't live on air.

"Sometimes I wish you could talk, big guy."

Huh? But I already do, and in so many ways! Bernie had to be tired.

He opened his door. "Let's get to know Officer Nevins."

I hopped out. Nevins was a cop. Cops liked to eat. You take it from there.

SEVENTEEN

We stood by the front door of the row house. There were some buzzers on the side, not many, although more than two.

"Blank, Tina with a smiley face, Mr. and Mrs. Scott, R. Nevins." Bernie pressed a buzzer.

A voice came through the speaker. "Yeah?"

"Pizza," said Bernie.

Sometimes — maybe not often — I'm ahead of the game. Like now: hadn't I just been thinking how cops like to eat? Wow. And pizza was clearly in this case, big-time. What had Bernie said, not that long ago? Something about a pizza-loving perp name of DeGaulle? Hope you look good in orange, amigo. There was only one problem I could see: we actually had no pizza. Other than that, we were in complete control.

The voice again: "Pizza? I didn't order pizza."

"Says Nevins on the box," Bernie said. I

looked everywhere for a box, spotted none.

"I'm Nevins, but I didn't order pizza."

"Maybe someone ordered it for you."

"Huh?"

"Like as a present," Bernie said. "Happens all the time."

A pause.

"It's paid for."

"Be right down."

Bernie turned, put his finger across his lips, our little signal for quiet time. I didn't make a sound, except for the beating of my heart, of course, which never stops going *boom boom, boom boom,* the very nice background music to my whole life. But not the point. The point was that with all this silence going on, it couldn't have been easier to hear footsteps coming downstairs, even though they were the quietest of human footsteps, namely the barefoot kind.

The door opened. Nevins — sweatpants, wife beater, bare feet, and what was this? Pot smell? — looked out, his gaze going to Bernie, me, back to Bernie.

"Hi," Bernie said.

"Where's the pizza?"

"We can still get some."

"Huh? Wait a sec — I know you."

Bernie held up his hand. "No need to thank us," he said. "Silent gratitude speaks volumes."

"Thank you?" said Nevins. "What for?"

"Rescuing you from that storage closet," Bernie said. "You've forgotten the whole episode? Don't tell me you were stoned then, too."

Nevins licked his lips. I always watch for that in a human; it often tells you more than the talk coming out of them. "Too?" he said.

"Weed's one of those real easy smells to pick up," Bernie said.

Whoa! Bernie had just picked up a smell? I gave him a close look. Did his nose seem slightly bigger than usual? I thought so! At that moment, Bernie was more beautiful than ever — and his nose hadn't been small to begin with, not for a human.

Nevins squinted, making a face you wouldn't have called particularly pleasant in the first place even less so. "I get it," he said, kind of inching back in the doorway. "The pizza's total bullshit." Somehow — without the slightest thought on my part — I'd managed to inch the same way even more, and was now pretty much behind Nevins. I'd heard of many pizza toppings in my time, but never . . . I left it right there.

"A pretext, yes," Bernie said. "Shrewd observation. Kind of surprising that Soares doesn't have you higher on the depth chart."

"What are you talking about?" Nevins said.

"The pecking order, who's in line for promotion, who'll be walking a beat for thirty years — all the usual craziness," Bernie said.

Nevins backed up a step, or tried to, but bumped into me, bounced right off, shooting me a wild sort of look. He turned to Bernie. "Who the hell are you?"

"You really don't remember?" Bernie said.

"Try that rescuer shit once more and I'll pop you in the goddamn mouth."

Oh, no. Don't tell me I was ahead of things again, and so soon after the last time! But maybe not a surprise: I know Bernie.

"And we'd be happy to save your ass again, if needed," he said, just as I'd expected.

Part of what came next happened very slowly. Nevins's hands, big and bony, curled into fists. He dropped one of them way down, turned his body, crouching a bit, and launched what's called a haymaker in this business. And while that was going on my only thought was *faster, Nevins, faster!* Not because I wanted to see Bernie hurt — nothing worse than that — but even if Nevins was capable of hurting Bernie, here I was right on the scene to put a dead stop to any of that. No, what I hoped for was just a little action before it was all over. Don't you get in those moods?

Next came the fast part. Nevins's fist was still on the way when Bernie's shot right past it, kind of a blur. Loved that jab of Bernie's. Hook off the jab, Bernie, hook off the jab! And then step inside with the uppercut! Sweetest uppercut in the whole wide world, but it didn't happen. Neither did the hook, the jab being enough, which I knew from how Nevins was lying on the hall floor, out cold. Did he have a glass jaw? I hadn't heard anything shatter — and my hearing is pretty good, probably better than yours — but how could I rule it out? Poor Nevins. Bernie often said that glass-jaw dudes shouldn't get into fistfights, but there'd been no time for a warning.

"How about we invite ourselves up for a quick drink?" Bernie said, stepping into the entrance hall and closing the door behind him. Sounded good to me, although I was more hungry than thirsty, as I may have mentioned, pretty much starving if you want the truth. Hadn't we brought some pizza? For a moment, I got a bit confused.

Bernie picked up Nevins, who'd gone all limp and floppy, threw him over his shoulder and started up the stairs. He grunted once or twice as we made our way past a landing and up to the top floor, but that was only on account of his war wound. I felt bad for Bernie, but what could I do? And then it hit me.

"Chet! What are you doing?"

Getting a good grip on Nevins's wrist, in preparation for dragging him the rest of the way up the stairs, what else?

"Knock it off."

Knock it off? I don't need to be told twice. If knocking it off is what Bernie wants, then knocking it off is —

"CHET!"

I knocked it off. There was one door at the top of the stairs, hanging open. We went on in.

Nevins turned out to be the messy type, often the case with guys who live alone. No one would call our place on Mesquite Road actually messy, but, of course, Bernie didn't live alone. He lives with me, and Charlie on some weekends and every second holiday, meaning yes on Thanksgiving and no on Christmas, or the other way around, or either, or . . .

Back to Nevins. We were in a small living room, things all over the place — clothes, empty bottles, empty food cartons. Bernie sort of unfolded Nevins on the couch while

I made sure the food cartons were indeed completely empty, just doing my job. And they were, all except for the end of what might once have been a spring roll. I made quick work of it, felt hungrier than before. What was that all about? If you kept eating, would you get hungrier and hungrier? No. So what was going on? I left it at that, followed Bernie into a tiny kitchen, too messy to describe, so I won't. But I shouldn't leave out the joint, smoldering away on a counter. Bernie dropped it in the sink, filled a glass with water, and returned to the living room.

We stood over Nevins, watched him breathe. "There are nine billion humans on the planet, Chet. Ever ask yourself — what's the point?"

I never did.

"What would be wrong with scaling back to eight billion? Six? Three? If we could frack pure water out of rock, then maybe none of this would . . ." Had I ever been more lost in my life? But at that moment, Bernie poured the glass of water on Nevins's face, which must have been the fracking part, and everything returned to normal. We were on the job, me and Bernie.

Nevins came to life, all sputtering and annoyed, the way they do at times like this. He sat up, groaned a bit, wiped his face on the back of his hand, gave us nasty looks, and said nasty things I'm sure he didn't mean.

"How about we clean the slate, start all over?" Bernie said. His voice sounded nice and relaxed, and he was standing nice and relaxed, too. I felt nice and relaxed myself. We're a lot alike in some ways, don't forget.

"What the hell do you want?" Nevins said. "I'm a cop. I can arrest you at any moment."

"I'm tempted to see how that would play out," Bernie said. "But it wouldn't be in your best interest."

"Huh?"

"You'd be compounding your mistake."

Nevins blinked, then kind of winced, like the force of just blinking made his head hurt. Maybe I went on a bit too much about Bernie's hook and that sweet uppercut. His jab is not too shabby. I gazed at his hand, now relaxed. Bernie has beautiful hands. You might not think they can do what they can do, but Nevins wouldn't be backing you up on that.

Bernie took a piece of paper from his pocket, held it up so Nevins could see.

"What's this?" Nevins said.

"Private investigator's license for DC and

the surrounding suburbs. Notice the signature."

Nevins gazed at the sheet of paper, rubbed his eyes, tried again. We do some eye rubbing of our own in the nation within, but only in itchy situations. Were Nevins's eyes itchy? He was having a bad day.

"Soares gave you this?" Nevins said.

"Back up to speed," Bernie said. "Good job. The point is Lieutenant Soares has hired us to assist in the Eben St. John murder investigation."

Nevins opened his mouth, closed it, opened it again. "Soares doesn't do things like that — he's a control freak."

"This is a special case."

"Special how?"

"That's what brings us to you."

Nevins went through the mouth routine again. A thought hit me: his mouth was doing it on its own! My tail played the same sort of tricks, but this was the first time I'd seen something similar in a human. Nevins — bleeding a bit from the nose, eyes glassy, reeking of pot, plus those sweatpants hadn't been laundered in some time — was growing on me.

"Who's this 'us' you keep talking about?" he said.

"Chet and I," Bernie said.

"Chet?"

Bernie pointed my way.

"You're what, like partners with a dog?"

And just like that, Nevins stopped growing on me and started shrinking.

"Your point?" Bernie said.

Nevins tried to wriggle farther away from Bernie, but the couch stood against the wall, and he had nowhere to go.

"We'll be filing a report with Soares when all this shakes out," Bernie said, "but at this moment, and not for too many moments more, you've still got a say in your destiny."

"My destiny?" Nevins said.

"Not in a spiritual sense," Bernie said. He glanced at me. "Although do we ever know when the spiritual is in the picture? Maybe the whole point. But forget all that —" Whew! Good news! — "I'm referring to your career in law enforcement."

"You threatening me?" Nevins said.

"Exactly," said Bernie. "My apologies for being obscure. I'm threatening you with exposure unless you play ball."

Whoa! Just like that, out of the blue, we were going to play ball with Nevins? Wasn't this an interview? Was playing ball ever part of interviews? Not that I remembered, but I'm the type who's good to go at any time when it comes to playing ball. Bernie throws

— he pitched for Army before his arm blew out, can still wing the ball a country mile, although we play in cities, too — and I fetch. I crowded in a bit closer. Would Nevins be doing some of the fetching? I didn't know how I felt about that. And then I did. It was a bad idea.

"What the hell?" Nevins said, shrinking back on the couch. "Is he gonna bite me?"

"What a suggestion!" Bernie said, which was my take, too, but exactly. "Why would you even think something like that?"

"On account of how he's practically on top of me with his mouth open wide," said Nevins. "Plus his teeth are huge and he's growling."

Bernie turned to me. "Everything all right, big guy?"

Most decidedly not. I did the fetching, end of story. Once, back in the days when my best pal Iggy still got outside a lot, Bernie had just thrown me a ball when Iggy came pelting over from his place and snatched it right out of the air, a total surprise that led to some back-and-forth over at old man Heydrich's place, old man Heydrich getting a new lawn out of the deal, the grass kind that Bernie hates. We ourselves have the desert kind, not so easily torn up. "That green cost me a lot of green," Bernie said after, maybe on his second or third bourbon, dirt still under his fingernails from laying the sod. Perhaps a joke of some sort. Who wouldn't love Bernie? Besides old man Heydrich, of course, who didn't love anyone I knew of.

". . . Chet?" Bernie was saying. "A little more space, if you can manage it?"

Nothing easier. Just a little was required? Done! I backed off the littlest possible.

"Good boy," Bernie said.

"He didn't do shit," said Nevins.

"You're welcome to your opinion," Bernie said. "The point is Chet likes to see some cooperation, and you've given us zip."

"He's a goddamn dog!"

"Language."

"He's a dog."

"Correct. And very friendly. The last thing he'd want to see would be your career in ruins."

"I don't know what you're talking about," Nevins said.

"Think back," Bernie said. "Back to when you were guarding the crime scene at Eben St. John's office."

Nevins's eyes shifted away, toward the window. I shifted my whole body in that direction. I'd seen perps jump out windows before, higher ones than this. Not on my watch, Nevins old buddy.

"What about it?" Nevins said.

"You told Soares you were standing in the hall, thought you heard a sound coming from the elevator end, turned that way, and got hit on the head from behind."

"So?"

"We're not buying it."

"Why not? Doc said I was lucky, coulda been a skull fracture."

"I know you got hit," Bernie said. "It's a question of where."

"Where? You mean like occipital, cerebellum, like that?"

"I mean in the hall or someplace else," Bernie said.

Nevins's gaze went toward the window again, got interrupted by me. "Fuckin' hell," he said.

Bernie nodded in a sympathetic way.

"Soares put you on to this?" Nevins said.

"No."

"But you're working for him."

"With him," Bernie said. "On the Eben St. John murder, not on personnel matters in his precinct."

Nevins gave Bernie a long look.

"Throwing you a lifeline here, Nevins," Bernie said. Nevins raised his hands, let them flap down to his sides. "Christ," he said. "I couldn't have been gone for more than one minute, ninety seconds tops."

"Tell us about it," Bernie said.

EIGHTEEN

"I'm a human being," Nevins said. "Sometimes you gotta take a piss, orders or no orders."

Whoa! Taking a piss made you a human being? It just so happens I'm an expert in this area, having taken pisses Nevins could only dream of. He needed to do some rethinking, and pronto.

"You know the point where you just can't hang on?" Nevins said. "When you're gonna piss your pants the next second?"

Say one thing for Nevins: some rethinking on his part required, yes, but he had a way of holding my interest. His line of talk made you want to hear more, or at least that was how it worked on me. Pants are not a factor in my case, of course. I wear a black collar for dress-up, and used to have a brown one for every day, now replaced by one made of gator hide, which still gives off the faintest whiff of gator, reminding me always of the scariest night of my life, maybe something we can go into another time.

"Bottom line," Bernie said. "You abandoned your post."

"Kind of judgmental, how you put that," said Nevins.

"Judgmental would be having you shot at dawn," Bernie said.

Nevins got an angry look on his face, like he was about to do something crazy. He dabbed at his bloody nose instead.

Bernie's voice softened a bit. "So you went to the nearest men's room."

Nevins nodded.

"Which, as I remember, is past the elevators on the left."

Nevins nodded again.

"And then?"

"I went back. Couldn't a been more than ninety seconds. Twenty seconds there, twenty seconds back, plus fifty for pissing, max. The longest I've ever done was forty-seven."

"You time your pisses?" Bernie said.

My ears were up as high as they could go. I'd never heard anything as fascinating, and never even expected to.

"Not now," Nevins said. "This was back in the academy. We had a competition. One guy did a minute nineteen."

"He should have his prostate checked," Bernie said.

"Huh?" said Nevins.

"Never mind," Bernie said. "You're back at your post."

"Yeah," said Nevins. "Everything how I left it, tape still up, door closed, and then I hear a sound from inside."

"Not from behind you, as you told Soares," Bernie said.

"Ain't that obvious by now?" said Nevins.

"Nailing it down's a big part of what we do," Bernie said. "Next?"

"Next? What would you adone?"

"Called for backup."

Nevins snorted. Pigs are the best snorters, in my experience, but it's always nice when a human takes a shot at it, and I was enjoying the moment when Nevins almost knocked me off my feet, not so easy to do, my balancing skills being off the charts, according to Bernie. "Pussy," Nevins said.

"You calling me a pussy?" Bernie said.

The room went quiet. Nevins gave Bernie a long look, then turned away. "Naw," he said.

The right answer. Nothing catlike about Bernie. There's only one creature out there that he reminds me of. I think you know.

"So instead of following procedure, you

opened the door."

"Uh-huh."

"And?"

"Stepped inside. And then it's like I said before — I felt this rush of air behind my head, and next thing, I was out like a light."

"All of that now happening inside the office, not in the hall."

"Makes no difference, 'cepting for the procedural part," Nevins said. "Why get Soares all riled up for nothing?"

"Ever considered other careers?" Bernie said.

"You bet," said Nevins. "I got this idea for an invention."

"Yeah?"

"Swear you'll keep it to yourself?"

"I swear."

"A no-hands razor," Nevins said. "Shaves you while you're doing other things, guided by GPS."

"Hmm," said Bernie.

"Looking for investors," Nevins said.

"I'll think about it," said Bernie. Uh-oh: that was my only thought. "Right now," Bernie went on, "I'd like to go back to the moment you took that step into Eben St. John's office."

Nevins shrugged. "Sure."

"Close your eyes."

"What for?"

"To encourage visual recall."

Nevins closed his eyes. He was one of those humans with not much in the way of eyelashes. I like eyelashes. Suzie's are just about the longest I've ever seen, and Bernie's are thicker than you'd believe. Suppose that one day the two of them, Bernie and Suzie, had a . . . I came close to having a not-my-kind-of thought.

"You step into Eben St. John's office," Bernie said, his voice low and quiet. "What do you see?"

There was a long silence. For a moment, I wondered whether Nevins had fallen asleep, but sleeping people have a different smell, and I wasn't picking it up.

Nevins took a deep breath, let it out with a little hum that sounded musical to me. Was Nevins a perp? I was starting to hope he wasn't. "I see," he said, "an office."

"Go on," said Bernie.

"I've got my hand on my gun."

"Smart."

"Thinking of taking it out of the holster."

"On the ball, no doubt about it."

"But you know what?"

"I give up."

"The back office."

"What about it?"

231

"The office inside the office, if you see what I mean."

"Well put. You saw something in the back office?"

"Not for long."

"Why was that?"

"Because next thing I got clubbed on the melon." Nevins's eyes snapped open. "Are you following this at all, for Christ sake?"

"You spotted something just before the melon part."

"What I'm trying to tell you. Someone was in that back office."

"Who?"

"No one I knew."

"Can you describe him?"

"It was a her."

"An older woman? Well dressed, classy looking?"

"Nah. Classy maybe. Wouldn't call her old. Thirty-five, maybe."

"And?"

"No and. Then came boom, on the back of my head. How come you can't —"

Bernie waved aside whatever was in the wings after that. His voice changed a bit, no louder but sort of throbbier, and harder to ignore, not that I'd ever ignore Bernie. "You must have seen something that gave you her age."

"Like what?"

"Her face, for example. That's usually a good way of establishing age."

"Didn't really get a look at her face," Nevins said. "She was kind of turned away from me. Had a nice butt, now that I think of it."

"She had a thirty-five-year-old butt?" Bernie said.

"Got a problem with that?" said Nevins. "Just so happens I have an eye for observation."

"Then you can explain where the classy part comes from."

"Easy," Nevins said. "She had one of those French bobs."

"Lost me," Bernie said.

Which made two of us. Two's the best number, in case that hasn't come up yet, and it's especially the best when you're lost.

"At French bob?" Nevins said.

"Right there," said Bernie.

"My ma owned a salon in Baltimore."

"A haircutting salon?"

"Yeah. A salon."

"French bob is a kind of haircut?"

Nevins raised his hands, made a little motion around his head. "Most expensive one on her list."

"The woman in the inner office had a French bob?"

"How many times I gotta tell you?"

"What color was her hair?"

Nevins stared up at the ceiling. What was this? A pink blob of bubble gum stuck up there? Totally new in my experience. I got the feeling the case was taking a strange turn.

Nevins lowered his gaze. "Auburn, maybe?"

"That's a color?"

"Sure. Reddish brown, or sometimes brownish red. Hers was more like that, brownish red."

"What's the difference?"

"Between reddish brown and brownish red? Mostly the way it takes the light, my ma said. Brownish red ending up brighter."

Bernie went to the window, gazed out. "Your mom still in the business?"

"Retired to Florida," Nevins said. "Husband number four."

Bernie gazed out the window a little longer, then turned to Nevins. "Anything else you remember?"

Nevins shook his head.

Bernie came over, handed him our card, the one with the flower we weren't too happy about, designed by Suzie. "If you think of anything else, let me know."

"What about Soares?" Nevins said.

Bernie looked down at him. "We don't work for Soares. Let's go, Chet."

"Thanks, man," Nevins said.

We headed for the door. Bernie opened it, paused, turned back. "How come the woman had her back turned?"

"Hell if I know," Nevins said.

"If she was standing behind the desk, there wouldn't have been much room between her and the wall."

Nevins nodded, went on nodding for what seemed like too long, the nodding slowing down at the end. "Come to think of it, she might have been hanging a painting on the wall."

"Isn't there already a painting on that wall?" Bernie said. "A clipper ship at sea?"

"Couldn't tell you," Nevins said.

Not long after that, we were back at the brassy-colored office building. It felt kind of late at night, but I wasn't tired, not a bit.

"Want to stay in the car?" Bernie said. "Looks like you're having trouble keeping your eyes open."

What a suggestion! Weren't we on the job? I hopped right out, gave myself a real good shake, the kind that gets the inside of my head all unfuzzed. Late, but there were a few cars in the lot, and lights shone in some of the building windows. We went up to the doors — the revolving kind that you'll never get me into, and a normal one on either side. Bernie tried them, all locked. He took out his credit card, one of his best moves, not the paying part, where once or twice bartenders had taken out scissors and . . . I refused to remember. No, this was all about using credit cards to unlock doors, and Bernie was one of the best, the very best being Fingertips Gertler, the dude who'd taught Bernie and was now breaking rocks in the hot sun. No pockets in the orange jumpsuits at Northern State Correctional, so maybe Fingertips didn't even have a credit card anymore. I felt bad for him, although I could never forget the feeling of his surprisingly plump calf between my teeth, a memory that brought me back to tip-top right away, so there you go. It's nice to feel tip-top after you've been feeling bad, and the quicker the better, in my opinion.

Bernie moved toward the door, credit card extended, but at that moment, a UPS dude appeared in the lobby, coming our way. I know UPS dudes from their brown uniforms, uniforms that sometimes have a baggy side pants pocket full of biscuits. As in this particular case, which I knew before the UPS dude had even opened the door, biscuit smell easily penetrating glass, a fact you may not know. The door opened — Bernie's credit card no longer in sight — and the UPS dude walked out. I sidled over in front of him, just to make sure he hadn't missed seeing me.

"Nice-looking pooch," he said.

"Thanks," said Bernie, catching the door before it closed.

"Can he have a treat?"

I sat, and pronto.

"Hey," the UPS dude said, "it's like he understands."

"A lot like that," Bernie said. "He'd buy stock in your company if he could."

And soon after we were in the lobby, me making all-too-quick work of a biscuit that was on the smallish side, and Bernie smiling to himself. Uh-oh. Was he thinking about some sort of stock buy? We'd had problems with that in the past. A company that made a hat that turned into a pillow? Just one example.

We rode the elevator up to Eben's floor, walked to his office. No one around, no crime scene tape, no light shining under the door. Bernie took out his credit card and presto we were in. There's no one like Bernie.

He closed the door, switched on the lights.

Nice and tidy inside, reminding me for some reason of a model home we'd been in once, something about shady developers. Bernie went right to the back office. The painting of the ship at sea — we'd gone through a pirate movie stage shortly after the divorce, so I was totally up to speed on ships at sea — hung on the wall behind the desk. A pretty big painting: Bernie grunted as he lifted it off the hook and leaned it against the desk.

"Chet?"

Oops. Was I getting a bit excited? But only because I knew where this was headed. What did you sometimes find behind pictures? Safes! We had the same setup back in our office on Mesquite Road. We were going to blow a safe! A first for us, although I'd seen it done. I was loving the thought of a new adventure and at the same time trying to keep all paws still and on the floor — which they did not want to do — when I noticed that there was no safe. What we had instead was a sort of cupboard door, only bigger. Bernie grasped the knob and pulled the door open, revealing a dark, empty space. Round about now would be when he'd take out the .38 Special, but we no longer had the .38 Special; we didn't even have that measly pink popgun. This was going to be a tough case. But not our toughest, which was the only missing persons case we hadn't solved, although we sort of had, only too late. A strange thought popped up into my head: we'd had the .38 Special that night, but it hadn't helped, not until later, when we'd taken care of justice on our own, me and Bernie. So therefore, maybe guns didn't always . . . Whoa! I'd come very close to a so therefore, Bernie's department. I bring other things to the table.

Bernie leaned into the opening, peered down, and then up.

"Chet!" he said, his voice low but kind of — urgent, maybe? — at the same time. "A little space, big guy."

I did my best, but what I saw in that opening was just too interesting, namely a ladder leading up into blackness.

"Well, well, well," said Bernie. Bernie's well well wells were a real good sign: they meant the case was just about cracked. And after, we always had a nice celebration. The nicest celebrations included steak tips.

"Remember how we climb ladders?" Bernie said.

What a question! We'd worked so hard at it, Bernie'd had to clean out the complete Slim Jim supply from the convenience store at the far end of Mesquite Road. Now I

could climb ladders like you wouldn't
believe — except maybe if you'd met me —
and come down even faster, especially by
jumping the whole way.

Bernie swung one leg into the opening,
then paused, reached back and put his hand
on my head, strong and gentle at the same
time. "Me first, Chet," he said.

Him first? Meaning . . . whoa! Not me?
How could that possibly make sense? Going
first was part of my job.

"Chet?"

Panting started up, big-time. Meanwhile,
Bernie grabbed the ladder and began climbing. The next thing I knew, I was right
behind him, every bit as fast, or maybe even
faster. It's a lot like scrambling up the steep-
est kind of hill: you get a good grip with
your back paws and then comes a kind of
surging push. Love that feeling! I surged on
up the ladder, getting my nose brushed once
or twice by the sole of Bernie's sneaker. I
had the craziest thought: why not nip him
on the ankle? Just the lightest possible nip,
as a way of continuing our conversation
about who goes first, if you see what I mean.
But at the last moment, I changed my mind,
not my usual MO at all, and left his ankle
unnipped. I'm pretty sure of that, although
betting the ranch might not be a good idea

on your part.

We came to the top of the ladder, just about side by side, for some reason. A narrow shaft of light appeared, shining not far above our heads. Bernie reached out, gave a little push above that shaft of light. A door opened. On the other side was a small bathroom, not much of a surprise to me, since I'd been smelling bathroom smells all the way up the ladder. The tile floor was at eye level. We climbed onto it and Bernie shut the door. On the inside, the door had no handle of any sort and bore a full-length mirror so you couldn't even tell it was a door. Bernie gave it a poke and it sprung back open. He nodded to himself, don't ask me why, and looked around. A single towel hung on a rail. Bernie — sniffed at it? Yes! Had to love Bernie! I wondered what he smelled. A woman's scent rose from the towel, very faint, but I was pretty sure I knew it.

Bernie took a quick scan inside the medicine cabinet: empty shelves. Then he turned to a normal sort of door, the kind with a handle, and opened it. On the other side was an office. A woman, sitting at a desk, looked up, her face going through lots of emotions, like shock and fear and surprise. I was a bit surprised myself, since this was

241

not the woman who'd left her scent on the bathroom towel. Instead, it was Suzie.

NINETEEN

Suzie rose in a shaky kind of way, leaning on the desk for support. Only one light shone in the room, a desk lamp that lit the lower part or her face but kept the rest of it in shadow. That made Suzie look scary, something I'd never thought I'd see, but of course there are many things I'd never thought I'd see — maybe even more than the other way, meaning things I'd never thought I wouldn't see, or possibly . . . How about we forget this part?

"Bernie?" Suzie said. "What are you doing here?" She glanced beyond us, toward the bathroom. Her voice rose, got screechier than I'd ever imagine hearing from Suzie, like she was afraid of us, which made no sense. "How did you get in? Have you been here the whole time?"

"I'll show you," Bernie said, "if you really don't know."

Suzie's face twisted up in a way that made

her look almost ugly, although I'm the type of dude who can always find some little thing to like in just about every human face.

"Are you stalking me?" she said. Her voice stopped being screechy, went cold instead. "This is turning into a cliché."

"That could never happen," Bernie said.

"Which part?"

"The stalking. That other bit was actually over my head."

Suzie's face untwisted, now looked normal, although in an unfriendly way. "Talk," she said. "Explain what you're doing in a way that makes you look not like a complete jerk."

"How about I just explain the way it is?" Bernie said. "I'm doing the same thing you are."

"What would that be?"

"Have I ever told you about the two miners?"

"Miners with an *e*?" Suzie said.

Bernie smiled. "That's what I like about you — a journalist to the end."

"That's what you like about me?"

"Uh," he said, looking down at his feet, as though . . . as though he could maybe get some help from them? Wow! I understood Bernie like never before. "That's not, um, all, not even the most . . ."

"Go on with the miners," Suzie said. And what was this? She was drumming her fingers on the desk? Always a bad sign, not just with Suzie, but humans in general.

"It was this book I had as a kid," Bernie said. "Two miners who don't know each other start digging into a mountain from opposite sides and they meet in the middle."

Oh. Those two miners. I'd heard this one many times. But here's the thing with me and Bernie: every time is like the first time!

"A metaphor for you and me?" Suzie said.

Metaphor? That came up in my life with Bernie, kind of like one of those soap bubbles that go pop and then you're back in business.

"Just the part about you and me happening to be here right now."

"I know what brought me," Suzie said. She reached into her pocket, took out an envelope, tossed it in Bernie's direction.

"Chet! What the hell?"

Oops. This is — I wouldn't call it a problem, exactly — a sort of thing I have involving objects that get tossed or thrown or flung or winged or hurled — all great methods, never ask me to pick a favorite! — and how I just have to snatch them out of the air, simple as that. I dropped the envelope — hardly damp at all, tooth marks barely noticeable — at Bernie's feet, the way we'd practiced with tennis balls out the yingyang. Next comes *Good boy, Chet,* and a treat.

But . . . but no? No *Good boy, Chet,* no treat, instead Bernie picking up the envelope, smoothing it out, reaching inside, in short, carrying on like we hadn't hit a bump in the road? There are disappointments in life, and my way of dealing with them is to . . . to . . . I promise to get back to that later. At the moment, I'd gotten totally interested in what Bernie was taking out of the envelope, which turned out to be two keys with a little paper tag attached.

"The key to this office?" Bernie said.

"And the main entrance," said Suzie. "It was shoved under my door."

"At home or at work?"

"I don't have a door at work, Bernie. It's a newsroom."

Bernie, the keys held loose in his hand, gave Suzie a look. "Am I too dumb for you?" he said. "Is that the issue?"

"No."

"But you're not saying there are no issues."

"Can we go into that some other time?" Suzie said. "You still haven't answered my question."

"About how Chet and I got in here?" Bernie made a little come-with-me motion, and Suzie followed us into the bathroom, me actually entering first, which is our MO at the Little Detective Agency. He poked the mirror door. It sprang open. Suzie gazed down the dark shaft.

"It goes to Eben's office?" she said.

"Through a door hidden behind the clipper ship painting," Bernie said. "When Mr. York and the middle-aged woman — plus a younger woman who seems to have been on the scene as well — cleaned out Eben's desk, they got there from here."

Suzie leaned a little farther into the shaft. Bernie reached out to put a hand on her shoulder, but paused at the last second, almost but not quite touching her. I wondered about grabbing her by the pant leg — she was wearing jeans — not because Suzie was a perp, no way that could ever happen — but just to keep her safe. Then I thought of grabbing Bernie by the pant leg for the same reason, or maybe no reason at all! This was a very confusing moment in my career.

"So," Suzie said, her voice strange and echoey in the shaft, "anyone in this office had constant access to Eben's?"

"Yup."

"Was it some sort of setup from the beginning? Or more of an ad hoc thing?"

"You ask all the right questions," Bernie said.

Suzie straightened, turned. "And someone wanted me to find out? Is that another right question?"

"Can't think how they'd expect you to find the back passage," Bernie said. "This office itself? Yes."

Suzie glanced around. "But there's nothing here," she said. "It's totally empty."

"Looks that way," Bernie said. "But let's take it apart."

We were going to take this office apart? Of all the things we do at the Little Detective Agency, taking places apart is just about the best, maybe second only to collaring perps.

"Chet! Down!"

We took the office apart. That meant yanking out all the drawers, tearing up the carpets, punching holes in the walls, and a whole bunch of other fun things that I never wanted to end. And even if we found nothing, so what? This was living. I was hit by one of the biggest thoughts of my whole life: why not take apart the whole building? We'd be rich! Hard to explain that last part, maybe, but some things you just know are true.

After that, it got quiet except for our breathing, kind of on the heavy side — mine, Bernie's, Suzie's. Sometimes during a heavy-breathing episode, you pick up a faint scent you might have otherwise missed. And that was just what happened now, the faint scent being that of guinea pig food pellets, tasteless and unsatisfying, as I'd proved to myself more than once. I followed the scent back into the bathroom.

A small bathroom, as I may have pointed out already, with sink, medicine cabinet, toilet. The guinea pig food pellet smell — now with the faint addition of actual guinea pig scent — was coming from behind the toilet. I squeezed my way around the toilet and sure enough, in the little space between the base of the toilet and the wall: some food pellets. There was also a partly rolled-up magazine or something like that. I was licking up a pellet or two just to remind myself of how much I didn't like them, when I heard Bernie in the doorway.

"Chet? What's back there?"

Bernie reached in beside me and picked up the magazine-like thing.

"What is it?" Suzie said.

Bernie held it up.

"A calendar?" she said.

"This year's." Bernie flipped through it.

249

"Nice photos, all snowy winter scenes."

Suzie came closer, looked over Bernie's shoulder. "The writing's Cyrillic?"

"Couldn't think of the word."

"Meaning it's a Russian calendar."

"Must have fallen off the wall, gone unnoticed," Bernie said. "Good boy, Chet."

I'd been waiting for that, and there it was! As for the accompanying treat, a few pellets were still left. I licked them up and felt my very best. Everything comes out right eventually. It's always nicer if eventually turns out to be real soon, of course, goes without mentioning.

"Should we make a list?" Suzie said. We were back at her place, in the living room, Suzie sitting up tall on a bar stool, Bernie slumped on the couch, me curled up at his feet, which always smelled good at the end of a long day and didn't disappoint me now.

"Might help," Bernie said.

"Don't you always work things out on that whiteboard in your office?" Suzie said.

"Yeah," said Bernie. "But I'm flexible."

"Are you?"

They exchanged a look. Friendly? No. Unfriendly? Not that either. Too complicated for me, whatever it was. It made me uneasy, let's leave it at that. I considered a quick chew of the end of my tail, something I hardly ever do, but that was one of Bernie's no-nos, so I put a lid on it.

They looked away from each other, Bernie's gaze happening to fall on me. "Chet — knock that off."

What was this? Somehow the end of my tail had gotten into my mouth, completely without my knowledge or cooperation? And was I chewing on it? Put yourself in my place, assuming your own tail had gotten itself into your mouth, wouldn't you . . . Too confusing? Probably. How about we leave it right there, or perhaps even earlier? Whatever I may or may not have been doing, I knocked it off, and pronto.

Meanwhile, Suzie was taking out her notebook and a pen.

"Before we start," Bernie said, "I've got a question about Eben."

Suzie looked up, turned her dark eyes on Bernie, their shininess totally gone. "Shoot."

"Did you know he was a spy?"

"Spy?" said Suzie.

"Working out of the British embassy for a guy named Aubrey Ross. Now retired, supposedly. I was too clumsy with him and now he's done a bolt."

"I don't get it."

Bernie went into a long explanation about

Mr. Ross, and Brits doing bolts, and lots of other stuff, too hard to follow. When it all finally wound down, Suzie said, "I knew none of that."

"What I thought," said Bernie.

"Eben quit working for the Brits and went rogue?"

"Call it independent. We're going to see more of that — self-declared spies for the global community."

Suzie nodded. "You should be a reporter."

"Can you contract out the writing part?"

Some shininess returned to her eyes. She lowered the pen over her notebook. "Number one. Who slipped the keys under my door?"

Bernie nodded.

"Someone who wanted me to search that upstairs office."

He nodded again.

"And find what?" Suzie said. "It was stripped bare."

"Except for the Russian calendar," said Bernie.

"You're suggesting it was planted?"

"By someone who had to be very careful."

"But there's nothing written on it, no notes or anything like that."

"Meaning the fact that it's Russian is what's important."

They were talking about the calendar I'd found? That was nice. I waited for some mention of the guinea pig food pellets, also found by me, but that didn't happen.

"Number two," Suzie said. "There was a third person involved in the cleaning out?"

"A woman with a thirty-five-year-old butt," Bernie said. "Um, according to Nevins. She also wore her hair in something called a French bob. Ever heard of it?"

"That's how I wear my hair, Bernie."

"Oh."

Suzie smiled a small smile. "Why do I find you charming?"

"You say that like it's a problem."

She gave Bernie a quick look.

"What's that look mean?" Bernie said. I was totally with him on that.

"Can we stick to business for now?" Suzie's gaze went to the notebook.

"Your butt's twenty-five, tops," Bernie said.

Suzie's gaze didn't budge from the notebook. There was a long pause and then she said, "Number three."

Just like that, I was out of the picture, topping out at two, as you must know by now.

". . . did Eben know something that got him killed?" Suzie was saying. "And if so, that leads to number four — who was his source for that knowledge?"

"Yeah," said Bernie. "And number five is who's using us to make this list."

"That would be whoever slipped the keys under my door, no?" Suzie rose, left the kitchen, went to the front door, me and Bernie trailing, although me actually more like leading. She opened the door and looked out. A cool breeze was blowing, carrying the scent of a member of the nation within, and then another. I had a strong urge for some playtime with one of my kind.

"Chet?" Bernie said. "Where are you going?"

Me? No place. Perhaps I'd taken a step or two onto the grass in order to catch a bit more of that evening breeze, and perhaps not. I sidled back into Suzie's doorway, or pretty close.

Suzie herself was eyeing Lizette's place, where lights shone upstairs and down. "I wonder if Lizette saw anything," she said.

"How can it hurt to ask?" said Bernie.

TWENTY

Lizette's door opened and a waiter-type dude — black pants, white shirt, a tray of drinks over one shoulder — looked out.

"Welcome," he said.

In the background: lots of nicely dressed people, drinking, talking, laughing, and eating bits of delicious-smelling food, the small-portion size known as appetizers. In short, this was a fancy party. I have absolutely nothing against the small-portion size. You just have to eat more of them. What could be simpler? Bernie always says that the shortest distance between two points is something or other, and that's become one of my core beliefs.

"Uh," said Bernie, "didn't realize a party . . ."

Suzie stepped right on in, me following; I like when people step right on in. "Don't mind if I do," she said, sweeping up a glass of what they call bubbly from the waiter's drink tray. Once I stood over a glass of bubbly and nosed up the tiny air pops. There's all kinds of fun to be had in life.

Was Suzie suddenly in a fun mood? I got that feeling. She glanced back at Bernie, still wavering in the doorway. "Coming?"

"Well," said Bernie, "I'm not sure we . . ."

Suzie's face was just starting in on a frown, very unusual for her, when Lizette appeared in the hall. She had a sparkling bow in her glossy red hair, cut on the shortish side, and wore a green dress that made her eyes seem even greener. Hey! Lizette was turning out to be one of those humans it was hard to take your eyes off.

"Suzie!" she said. "What a nice surprise. And . . . Bernie, is it? Plus this absolute knockout of a dog."

"Didn't realize you were having a party," Suzie said. "We can come back another time."

"Don't be silly," Lizette said. "The general loves dogs. He'll be delighted."

"General?" said Suzie.

"General Galloway," Lizette said. She motioned behind her. "This is a very modest fundraiser in his honor."

"I didn't realize you were active in politics," Suzie said.

"Tonight's more social than anything

else," Lizette said. "Come join the party!"

Which was exactly what I wanted to hear! Lizette was growing on me, no question about it.

"Uh," Bernie said, quite some distance behind me. I seemed to be well inside Lizette's house, on my way to that screened-in porch and following — more like getting swept along on — a powerful scent trail, and one I'd encountered not nearly often enough in my career, namely the scent trail that flows from a plate or two of shrimp wrapped in bacon.

"Thanks," Suzie was saying, also from somewhere behind me. What was this holdup about? I looked back. "We won't stay long," Suzie said, "but of course I'd love to meet the general. First, I wanted to ask you whether you were home today."

"In and out," Lizette said, raising her glass toward her lips. "Why?"

"Did you see anything unusual?"

"Unusual?"

"Someone lurking around, for example."

Lizette lowered her glass. "No," she said. "Don't tell me you've had a break-in?"

"Nothing like that," Suzie said. "Someone slipped a package under my door and I'd like to find out who."

Lizette's mouth opened, closed, opened

again. "I hope it wasn't — there wasn't anything unsettling in it."

"No," said Suzie.

Lizette watched her, maybe expecting Suzie to say more. When she did not, Lizette said, "I'd be happy to accept any packages for you in future."

"I'm sure that won't be necessary."

"Offer's on the table," Lizette said. "I like to help." She took Suzie's hand. "Let's go introduce you to the general."

They headed in my direction, toward the porch, Bernie trailing. Another waiter went by with a drink tray, and Bernie raised his hand, maybe trying to get the waiter's attention, which didn't happen. For a moment he was just standing there, hand curled like he was holding a drink, even though he wasn't. I waited for him to catch up and fell in beside him. Not that he looked a little lost — we're dealing with Bernie, after all — but I got the idea he could use some company, namely mine.

We moved onto the porch, a pretty big space with lots of wicker furniture. I'm partial to wicker furniture and I know it, which is why I gave myself a warning: *Not now, big guy.* Even though I could practically feel all that wicker unraveling between my teeth, hard on the outside and much softer within. I have memories like you wouldn't believe!

At the far side of the porch stood a silver-haired dude doing nothing much — talking, sipping, laughing — although from the faces of the people around him you'd have thought he was doing big things, like pulling a rabbit from a hat, for example, something I'd actually seen done when Leda hired a magician at Charlie's birthday party. The absolute truth is I'd seen it about to be done, but while the magician was handing the hat over for the kids to inspect — "Take a good close look, ladies and gents!" — I'd smelled a surprising thing, namely a rabbit hidden in the sleeve of the magician's jacket, and after that had come a lot of action, kind of a blur, although I have a clear memory of what happened when the rabbit — what a funny pink-eyed dude! — with me close behind, reached the back gate of Leda's house, a gate with no space for squeezing under, except the little bugger did, never to be seen again, although I'm sure I could have tracked him down if I'd been given the chance, which I was not.

But that's neither here nor there, as humans often say, totally right in this case, since it took place at Leda's big house in High Chaparral Estates, just about the fanciest neighborhood in the whole Valley, where she lives with Malcolm, her new husband with all kinds of software money and very long toes. The point was I'd seen this same silver-haired man once before, on the little spin I'd taken with Mr. Ferretti, and he'd been doing this exact same thing, namely talking, sipping, laughing, surrounded by a bunch of — what would you call them? Fans? — waiting for him to pull a rabbit out of a hat. Forget that last part: the silver-haired dude, a very smooth-skin dude, except for what I could see of his neck, more on the wrinkly and saggy side — had no hat. What he had was his silver hair, all full and shiny, plus his smooth skin and fine teeth, big for a human and the whitest I'd ever seen. Lizette, towing Suzie behind her, wedged her way through the little crowd.

"General?" Lizette said.

The silver-haired dude paused, one finger in the air, and turned to Lizette. Hey! What was this? A smell started up in both of them? Two smells, human male and female, although kind of the same thing if you get what I mean, probably a long shot since I'm not giving you much help.

"Yes, Lizette?" he said, in the voice a man uses for a woman he sort of knows, but not real well.

"I'd like you to meet a friend of mine," Lizette said. "Suzie Sanchez, *Washington Post* reporter, General Galloway, our guest of honor."

Suzie and General Galloway shook hands. "Pleased to meet you, General," Suzie said.

General Galloway gave her a smile. Those big, white teeth: wow! I found my own mouth opening wide, for reasons unknown to me.

"Call me Trav," the general said.

"Okay," said Suzie, although she didn't call him Trav, or anything, for that matter. Humans meeting for the first time was often a tricky moment. Take Booby "Bonecrusher" Daunt, who ruined so many handshakes that finally we'd had to take him aside, me and Bernie, and in no uncertain —

"And this," Lizette was saying, "is Suzie's friend, Bernie — I'm sorry, Bernie, I've forgotten your last name."

"Little," said Bernie, stepping forward and shaking hands with the general. They were about the same height, although Bernie was bigger, with broader shoulders. He didn't have that smooth skin, but neither was his neck all wrinkly and saggy. In fact, I realized for the first time right then and there that

Bernie had the most beautiful human neck I'd ever seen. But that was Bernie for you: amazements piling up on amazements.

The general had eyes that were on the biggish side, but now they narrowed. "Bernard Little?" he said. "Cadet Bernard Little?"

"Sir," said Bernie.

"Two-hit shutout at Annapolis? The game with those snow squalls at the end?"

"A long time ago, sir."

"But vivid in my memory," said the general. "My good luck to be at a chinwag with Navy colleagues that afternoon. Fully expected to see you in the big leagues after your service obligation."

"Didn't happen," Bernie said.

Was this about baseball? Bernie had pitched for Army until he'd thrown his arm out, although I didn't quite get that part on account of how far Bernie can wing the tennis ball when we're playing fetch, namely a country mile, much longer than a city mile, which I'd finally figured out is because of less traffic.

"Stayed on?" the general was saying.

"Yes, sir."

"See any action?"

"A little."

"Iraq?"

"Yes."

"Where?"

"Different places."

"Fallujah?"

"Yes, sir."

"First or second battle?"

"Some of both."

The general gave Bernie a nod, like Bernie had asked him a question and he was saying yes. Kind of confusing, but whatever was going on, all the people around the general were now looking at Bernie.

"Assume you're no longer on active service?" the general said.

"Retired," said Bernie.

"Rank?"

"Captain."

"And what are you doing now?" the general said. "I'm going to guess there's baseball involved."

"No, sir," Bernie said. "I'm a private investigator."

"Ah," said General Galloway, rocking slightly back on his heels. "Working out of DC?"

"Arizona. We're just visiting."

"We being?"

"Me and Chet, here."

And without warning, all eyes were on me. A bit of warning might have been nice, especially since — and how had this happened? — I seemed at that moment to be gnawing on a nearby wicker leg. I put a stop to that so fast no one could possibly have noticed, but next time, please — a little heads-up.

The general gazed down at me. I gazed up at him. "Nice-looking animal," he said.

Right back atcha — that was my first and only thought. The general was a nice-looking animal, if you left out the neck, and I'm the type who's always willing to cut dudes a break, even some of the perps and gangbangers I'd come across in the line of duty; cutting them a break the first time is what I mean, goes without mentioning. As for nice-looking animals, the very nicest in the room was Bernie, of course, leaving myself out of the competition for the moment, I'm not sure why, because competition and I are like that, meaning tight.

The general turned to Bernie. "In town for long?"

Bernie glanced at Suzie. "Not sure."

A few new arrivals — they brought the smell of outside with them — came up to the general, kind of sweeping him away from us.

"Trav," one said, "you were so fabulous on *Charlie Rose*."

The general looked over their heads at

Bernie. "Hope we can have a nice sit-down sometime," he said. "And thanks for your support."

"Um," said Bernie.

"My support?" Bernie said.

We were out in Lizette's garden now, just me, Bernie, Suzie, and a bartender pouring bourbon for him, wine for Suzie, and water for me in a bowl brought specially from the kitchen.

"A natural assumption," Suzie said. "It is a fundraiser, Bernie."

"Meaning he's definitely running?"

"What kind of country would we have if you had to be definitely running before the money started flowing?"

"A better one," Bernie said.

"It was a rhetorical question," Suzie said. "What I really want to talk about is the battle of Fallujah."

"Why?"

"Why? Because of its historical importance, second, and that you, the man I — that you were there, first. Which I just now found out, despite how long we've been together."

Bernie gazed into his glass, swirled the bourbon around. I had the craziest thought of my life: he'd jump right in that glass if he could.

"There's not much to say," he said.

"How is that possible?" Suzie said.

They looked at each other. Suzie reached out and touched Bernie's arm. Did his eyes go the slightest bit misty? Hard to tell under the flickering light of the lanterns set up in the garden, and that wouldn't have been Bernie, whom I'd seen cry only once, the day Leda took Charlie away to live in the house in High Chaparral Estates. Plus I didn't get a long look because at that moment Lizette came out of the house and hurried over, practically running in her high heels.

"The man of the hour," Lizette said to Bernie.

Suzie took her hand off his arm.

"Uh," Bernie said, "nice party, thanks."

"The pleasure's all mine," Lizette said. "I've never seen the general so charged about meeting someone."

"I didn't realize you knew him so well," Suzie said.

"Not," Lizette said, "personally. But I'm very active politically."

"I thought you were Canadian," Suzie said, "from Montreal."

"French Canadian by origin," Lizette said.

"But I'm a citizen now." She turned to Bernie. "Tell me the story of this famous ball game, the one played in a blizzard."

"More like a few flurries," Bernie said. "Made it much harder for the hitters."

"So — hard for everyone and still you did well?" Lizette said.

Bernie shook his head. "Didn't affect the pitching much." Lizette gazed at Bernie in that big-eyed way some humans have when they're not getting it. "I was a pitcher."

"Forgive my denseness," Lizette said. "I know nothing about baseball."

"Never caught the Expos when you were a kid?"

"The Expos?"

"Montreal's old baseball team — the Nationals now, playing right here."

"Oh, of course, of course," Lizette said. "My family was so completely non-sporty that these things barely registered." She touched Bernie's arm on the exact same spot where Suzie had been touching it. "Tell me all about pitching."

"Well," Bernie said, "it's actually —"

The porch door opened, and a man looked out. "Lizette, the general's car is here."

Lizette hurried off.

"You can tell me all about pitching," Suzie said.

"Stop," said Bernie. He took a nice big sip of bourbon, maybe closer to a gulp. "Montreal's a hockey town, but it's odd she'd never even heard of the Expos."

" 'Completely non-sporty,' " Suzie said in a way that sounded a lot like Lizette, only more so.

"Don't be catty," Bernie said.

Bernie was saying Suzie was like a cat? I gave her my hardest stare, saw nothing cat-like about her. Did she have a look on her face like she was high and I was low? The farthest thing from it. Did that mean Bernie wasn't making sense? I couldn't go there.

"It's just that a powerful man pays attention to you, and all of a sudden you're on her radar," Suzie said. "I didn't realize she was like that."

"Maybe she's genuinely interested in pitching," Bernie said. "It's actually a vast subject."

"Start with the screwball," Suzie said.

They both started laughing. What was this? They'd also both spewed some of their drinks? And then more laughter? What was going on?

The laughter died down. "Some people really are oblivious to sports," Suzie said. "I discussed Montreal with her, and it was obvious she knows it well."

"How so?" said Bernie.

Suzie thought for a moment. "I remember her telling me the best place to stay."

"Which is?"

"The Château Frontenac."

"Stayed there once myself," Bernie said. "On a weekend pass from Fort Drum."

"Nice?"

"Very. The only problem is it's in Quebec City."

"Not Montreal?"

Bernie shook his head.

TWENTY-ONE

The next thing I remember is waking up bright and early the morning after Lizette's party, bright and early being the way I roll when it comes to waking up. The truth is that although we're alike in lots of ways, me and Bernie, how we sleep is probably not one of them. Once he falls asleep — and that can take a while, what with all the turning and twisting, plus a bit of pillow punching to get it in just-right shape — Bernie's out for the night. I'm . . . I'm exactly the opposite, opposite being a tricky thought I'm now getting my head around for the very first time! Just when you think I'm done amazing you, I — whoa! What did I almost get into? Easy, big guy. But the point I'm trying to make, if I can only get out of my own way — wow! Another amazing thought! What a life! Back to the point: I can fall asleep just like that, no problem, but I'm never out for the night. That's not how it works in the nation within, especially if you're the security-minded type, which I am, and big-time. If I'm not paying attention to what's going on around me at night, then I'm not doing my job.

So on the night of Lizette's party, did I actually mess up and sleep right through until dawn, or was I up and down and simply don't remember? Who knows? Not me, amigo, and best not to dwell on it for one more moment, except I kind of recall hearing Bernie and Suzie talking in low voices from her bedroom. Outside her door was where I first settled down, come to think of it, and where I woke up was on the cool tiles of the front hall, meaning that in the night I must have . . . something or other. Hey! Not bad: I'd just come close to figuring out another tricky one, one more reason the Little Detective Agency is so successful, leaving out the finances part.

I opened my eyes and got to my feet in this real slow stretchy way I have for waking up when there's no reason to hurry. Then I gave myself a little shake, walked around in circles for a bit, gave myself another shake, this one more vigorous. I was off to a great start, and not for the first time. Nothing compares to the start of the day, except for the end and everything in between.

I made my way into the kitchen and was heading toward my water bowl in the corner when I heard a faint *whirr-whirr* outside the window. What was this? That strange hovering bird was back, the one with no eyes and wings that didn't flap? Birds are not high on my list of fellow creatures to begin with, which you probably know by now since I've gone on about it ad nauseam, as Bernie says — and that turns out to be all about puking, one of the most fascinating subjects out there, but we just don't have the time right now. What I'm getting to is that I don't like birds in general, and especially didn't like this strange and rather shiny bird particularly. Hey! Could it be? No feathers? No eyes, no feathers, no flapping? I couldn't have been called scared at that moment, fear and Chet being like two something or others passing in the night, but surprised? I admit it. And sometimes when I'm surprised, especially in a real sudden way, the barking in me starts up. Does something like that happen to you?

"Chet! What the hell's going on with you?" I turned and there was Bernie — hadn't seen him in way too long — pulling on a pair of pants and kind of hopping along at the same time, one of the coolest human moves out there. But right now, we had a problem. I turned to the window and amped up the sound level, sending Bernie a message.

"What? What?"

And at last, his gaze went to the window — oh, no: at the very moment, when with no warning the strange bird shot straight up into the air, out of sight! But not out of hearing, that *whirr-whirr* still out there, although distant now, and faint.

"What? What? Something in the yard?"

Bernie stepped up to the window, raised it, peered out. "Don't see anything," he said, sticking his head right out there. "Wait — unless it's that squirrel by the hedge. Gotta ease up on the squirrel obsession, big guy."

Huh? Squirrel obsession? I'd never heard of such a thing. Maybe Bernie was still half-asleep, not quite in the picture, the picture being birds, specifically that very strange one, and not squirrels. I went closer, stuck my own head out the window. And then there we both were, bodies indoors and heads outdoors, me and Bernie side by side. What a nice moment! Why had we never done this before? I was having a lovely thought about staying right here forever — couldn't come up with a single reason why not — when I noticed a black squirrel with an enormous bushy tail standing by the hedge. Just standing there looking like . . . like he owned the place! Which he most certainly did not. I owned the place!

"Chet! Knock it off! I can't hear myself think!"

And crazily enough, I couldn't hear my own self think either. But what was there to think? That enormous bushy tail was the most annoying thing I'd seen in ages, and I'm sure you'd have felt the same. Did I mention how he was gazing right at me with his tiny squirrel eyes? Like . . . like he owned the place! Whoa! Who owned the place? I did! Chet the Jet owned the place!

"CHET! NO!"

A little later — hardly any time at all, really — we were enjoying a nice breakfast in Suzie's kitchen, me, Bernie, Suzie. Bacon and eggs for Bernie, yogurt and berries for Suzie, kibble for me, and no doubt a bit of bacon would be coming my way soon, although Bernie didn't seem in a hurry to make that happen. No way he was mad at me about the squirrel, of course. He had to know I'd done my very best to catch the little bugger, and even though I'd come up short — but I'd actually laid a paw on him, first time in my life! — no one can ask any more of you than your best, as I'd heard

Bernie tell Charlie more than once, down at the T-ball field, for example, which I wouldn't be visiting again anytime soon. But that's another story. Right now, we were getting along beautifully, and Bernie's hands smelled of a very interesting special soap he'd used after finishing up with the resodding.

So: bacon, anybody? Yes, me! I'm anybody and I wanted bacon.

And maybe Bernie was finally having that exact same thought, namely that it was time for the big guy to chow down on some bacon, but at that moment, his phone rang. He glanced at the screen, and his eyebrows — can't miss Bernie's eyebrows, with a language all their own — made a kind of surprised movement, and he said, "Hello."

He listened for a bit. Suzie watched him listen. I watched her. Her thoughts were like Bernie's in that you could sort of feel them in the air, except hers were . . . stronger in some way? What was with that? I didn't want to go down that road, so I didn't.

"Well, sir," Bernie said, "very nice of you to ask, but, ah . . ." He listened some more. "All right, if you put it that way," he said. "I'll just need an address." A bit more listening and then Bernie clicked off.

"General Galloway?" Suzie said.

"How'd you know?"

"Process of elimination," Suzie said. "I've never heard you say 'sir' to anyone else."

"Force of habit," Bernie said. "And it's the rank, not the man."

"What I don't get," Suzie said, "is that in real life you have no respect for authority at all."

"Real life?" said Bernie.

Suzie waved that aside with back of her hand, a cool human move you sometimes saw from Bernie, too. Meaning he and Suzie were alike in some ways? Uh-oh: another road I didn't want to go down. On top of that, none of this back-and-forth was making any sense. All I knew was that no one was paying any attention to me. Am I the type who needs attention twenty-four seven, whatever that may mean? Not at all: I can amuse myself, no problem. I glanced around and saw that the remaining bacon strips were just sitting there in a dish on the table, also getting no attention from anybody. Those bacon strips — not many, although more than two — were in easy reach, pretty much ready for the taking. What would you have done in my place?

". . . but somehow you were a great success in the military," Suzie was saying.

"Where do you get that from?"

"It's obvious from how all the other military types treat you."

"I was average," Bernie said. "Otherwise I'd still be there."

"You would?"

Bernie glanced down — real quick, you'd never have noticed — at his leg, the wounded one. "Doesn't matter," he said. "The point is he asked me, as a personal favor, to come out to his place in Virginia for a little chitchat."

"About what?" Suzie said.

"He didn't want to discuss it on the phone," Bernie said. "You coming?"

"Am I included?"

"Always."

"I meant by Galloway."

"He'll have to lump it."

"Call me 'sir,' " Suzie said.

"I'll try to think of the best time for that," Bernie said.

Sudden change to the feeling in the room? Check. Change in the scents of Bernie and Suzie? Check. Change in the color of Suzie's face, now pinker? Check. I missed none of that, but the meaning, if any, I'll leave to you.

"Let's just finish up breakfast," Bernie said, his gaze moving to the table, possibly narrowing in on the bacon dish, now empty, no getting around that, "and then we'll hit the —" He looked at me. I sat up tall, alert, ready, a total pro, and looked at him right back. He blinked, gave his head a little shake. We were good to go, unless I was missing something.

We got to the car, and right away: a problem. Was this a problem we'd had before? I thought so, namely the problem of the Porsche having a driver's seat for Bernie, a shotgun seat for me, and a little shelf seat thing in the back for Suzie. No problem so far, you're thinking, and you'd be right. The problem was all about this mistake getting made every time, a mistake that led to me on the shelf and Suzie in the shotgun seat. And Bernie was eyeing me in a way that indicated we were headed for mistake territory yet again, when Suzie's phone beeped. She checked the screen, her dark eyes moving quickly back and forth, and said, "Rain check."

Which was exactly what I wanted to hear!

"What?" Bernie said.

"Metro desk," Suzie said. "Someone's out sick and they want me to cover the damn kitchen design show."

"Right up your alley," Bernie said.

Suzie drew back her hand and made a

hard throwing motion at him, but of course, she had nothing to throw so nothing got thrown. But Bernie ducked anyway! What was with that?

"It's not funny," Suzie said. "I'd like to get to know the general."

"Why is that?"

"Because of something Lanny Sands told me."

"Who's Lanny Sands?"

"You haven't heard of the Sandman?"

"Excuse my ignorance."

Suzie touched Bernie's shoulder. "Sorry," she said. "It must be one of those inside-the-beltway things, like we — journos, politicos, lobbyists — are living in a separate country. Lanny Sands is a presidential insider, one of those backroom guys with a reputation for doing what needs doing." She took out her phone. "Here's a picture of him."

Bernie glanced at it. "He wears a suit and a Harvard baseball cap?"

"It's a look."

"Indicating what?"

"Something elitist," Suzie said. "He told me that if the general was the nominee, he might have a story for me."

"What kind of story?"

"He didn't say, just didn't want me to

279

jump the gun."

"What did that mean?"

"I'd like to know," Suzie said.

Was this more like it, just me and Bernie rolling in the Porsche? You bet! But we'd hardly gone more than a block or two when a white cruiser came up beside us, blue lights flashing. We pulled over, the cruiser parking behind us and the cop coming over. Hey! Little raisin eyes? This was our pal Lieutenant Soares, although what kind of pal flashes the blue lights at you, especially when you're real eager to get going?

Soares gazed down at Bernie. "How're you doing?" he said.

"In what respect?" said Bernie.

"The Eben St. John case, what else?"

"I didn't realize I was reporting to you."

"You're not," said Soares. "Just thought we'd have a quick collegial get-together."

"Traffic stops are collegial where you come from?" Bernie said.

"I piss you off, don't I?"

"What's that got to do with anything?"

Soares glanced over at me. "I piss off your dog, too."

"What makes you think that?" Bernie said.

"Something wrong with your hearing? You don't hear that low growl?"

Low growl? News to me.

Bernie glanced my way. "It's not necessarily you," he said. "Could be indigestion."

"Huh?"

I found myself with the lieutenant, out of the picture. Indigestion was what, again?

"From eating too fast," Bernie said.

Eating too fast? How was that even possible?

"I know that one," Soares said. "My girlfriend says I gotta slow down, chew my food."

"You have a girlfriend?" Bernie said.

"What's surprising about that?" said Soares. And then he burped, one of those real gassy burps. He'd eaten sausages, and not long ago, plus there were some Tums in there, Tums being something I knew well from once having snapped up a whole box. I came close to an understanding of what they'd just been talking about and then clouds closed off the part of my mind that was working on the problem and that was that.

". . . let my own hair down first," Soares was saying. It looked to me that he had hardly any at all, but I waited for him to take off his uniform hat, which he did not, so I never got to find out for sure. "We interviewed everyone who'd been on the third floor of 1643 Ellington Parkway either at the time of the attack or the break-in. An accountant across the hall thinks he might have heard the gunshot, but he put it down to some noise on the street. Several people saw the sign painter calling himself Mr. York at work and thought nothing of it. No one remembers the older woman you said was with him, and there's no professional sign painter named York in the district. We're still looking into the rest of metro. Preakness Development is bogus —" Soares took out a notebook, checked a page. "— as you mentioned, and Terrapin Exports was a dead end, as you also mentioned."

"So you're nowhere," Bernie said.

"If you want to put it that way," Soares said. "We're still in the process of interviewing friends and associates of the victim."

"Uh-huh."

"Your turn," Soares said. "What you got?"

"Advice," Bernie said. "Find York and the older woman."

"I'd never have thought of that."

"Start by canvassing the fourth floor."

"The fourth floor?" said Soares. "Why would anyone up there have seen them?"

Bernie looked at Soares, said nothing.

"Who are you protecting?" Soares said. "That asshole Nevins?"

Bernie kept on saying nothing, one of his best techniques.

"Have it your way," Soares said. "What else are you hiding?"

"Nothing."

There was a silence. Soares looked up and down the street. "Where you headed now?"

"Sightseeing."

Soares tapped our hood. Hands off the paintwork: that was my only thought. "Stay in touch."

Bernie nodded.

"One other thing," Soares said. "Let me know if you think you're being watched."

"Being watched?" said Bernie. "By who?"

Soares smiled and turned back toward his cruiser. "Two can play the selective information game, pal."

A game? Who were the two? Bernie and Soares? Soares and me? Me and Bernie? Soares got into the cruiser and sped off, meaning it was me and Bernie. We were golden.

Twenty-Two

"Sweet Virginia," Bernie said. We were in beautiful country, rolling and green, with long white fences, lots of real big trees and broad meadows, plus horses, cows, and even pigs from time to time, to all of whom I gave a piece of my mind as we flew past. As for Virginia, I knew no one of that name, sweet or not, and waited for Bernie to clue me in.

We turned off the pavement and onto a long gravel road that curved over the top of a hill and led down to a nice spread: big white house with red shutters, big red barn, some outbuildings, tennis court, and in the distance a river sparkling in the sunshine.

"Jeffersonian dream come true," Bernie said, as we pulled into a circular drive in front of the house and came to a stop. We hopped out of the car, me actually hopping, and headed for the front door. At that moment, a horse came trotting out of the barn, ridden by a woman in fancy riding getup. She rode away in the other direction, toward a fenced-in riding ring, kind of briskly although not at a pace I'd actually call fast.

"Don't even think about it," Bernie said.

Think about what? I had no idea. I walked right beside Bernie, being the very best Chet I could be. Or even better! I was still trying to get hold of that one when the front door — a huge old wooden one with lots of brass, the smell of brass always welcome, so good for clearing the head, as you may or may not know — opened and General Galloway looked out.

"Appreciate your punctuality, Captain," he said as they shook hands.

"Bernie will do, sir," Bernie said, a moment of possible confusion passing quickly away, the only captain I knew being Captain Stine of the Valley PD, a captain on account of some help he'd gotten from me and Bernie. I made a quick stab at remembering what it was, kind of like one of those bears on Animal Planet when the fish comes though the rapids, and missed, as the bears often do. I've actually had some experience with a real bear, and don't mind at all if ages go by till the next one.

"And in the same spirit, seeing as how we're both retired," the general said, "you can call me Trav."

"Yes, sir," Bernie said. "And after you're elected?"

The general laughed. "Then it's strictly Mr. President. But who said I was running?"

"Just about everyone."

"Just about everyone has been wrong before and will be wrong again," General Galloway said. "Fact of the matter is, I haven't made up my mind. Maybe you can help me on that."

"Don't see how," Bernie said. "I know nothing about politics."

"Best possible recommendation. Come on inside." The general glanced my way. "Think your dog here — Chet, isn't it — would prefer to stay outside?"

"You've got a good memory."

"Know every soldier in your command by name — that's basic."

Bernie smiled.

The general had been smiling, too, and the smile was still there, although now it seemed to be hanging all by its lonesome. Have I mentioned the smoothness of the general's skin? I now picked up a very faint scent of a sort of cream Leda used to slather on lots of, and of which Suzie sometimes dabs on a little.

"Something funny?" General Galloway said.

"Only if you think Chet's under your command," said Bernie.

What was this? Under the general's command? Me? Or somebody else? Had to be somebody else. I'm under nobody's command, amigo. Excepting Bernie's, of course, but even there it depends what we mean by command. My take's always been that it's a kind of suggestion. Bernie makes the best suggestions possible, you can take that to the bank, although not our bank, where we've been having problems with Ms. Oxley, the manager. As for where I wanted to be at the moment? Inside with Bernie — a no-brainer, which is the best of all possible brainers, as you probably know.

"Nice room," Bernie said.

My thought exactly. What had the general called it? His study? Something like that. I really hadn't been listening, occupied as I was by the soft feel of the carpet and the lovely smells that came from the leather furniture and old wooden beams. And I haven't even mentioned the view: the riding ring, where the woman was now taking her horse over jumps, something I'd done myself — meaning take myself over jumps

— on a horse ranch case back in the Valley, and done as well as any horse, as I'd been trying to demonstrate when — But do we have to go there?

"I married rich, the second time around," General Galloway said.

They both looked out the window, just in time to catch a smooth, easy jump, the woman giving the horse's neck a little pat pat on landing. I shifted closer to Bernie, making it easier for a pat pat to come my way.

". . . but that wasn't my motive," the general said. "I'd have married Isobel even if she'd been a pauper. True love, believe it or not."

"Why wouldn't I believe it?" Bernie said.

The general turned to Bernie, his head tilted a bit to the side, the way humans sometimes do, not sure why. "I looked into you," he said.

"Uh-huh," said Bernie.

"Your military record is stellar. Did you know there was some talk about the Medal of Honor for your conduct on the night of November 9, 2004?"

Bernie said nothing.

"Didn't quite think it rose to that level myself," the general said, "although the Silver Star would have been appropriate, in my opinion. Still, the bronze is nothing to sneeze at. Feel you ended up with the short end of the stick?"

"The guys who didn't come home got that," Bernie said.

The general looked away. Then came a silence, broken only by the faint *clop-clopping* of the horse in the ring. The general rose from his chair and went to the window. A man came into view from the direction of the barn. The woman dismounted. The man took the reins and led the horse away. Dog life beat horse life: it was as simple as that.

"As for your present career," the general said, turning from the window, "there seem to be two schools of thought. I'm choosing to believe the second, namely that the positives outweigh the negatives. Bottom line, you're a smart investigator who gets results and knows how to keep his mouth shut. And that's what I need."

"For what?" Bernie said.

"Assistance," said the general, coming away from the window. He stood behind his chair, his hands resting on the chair back. Hands are a big subject, maybe for later, but one thing about them is that small dudes can have big hands and big dudes can have small hands. That was General

Galloway, the second kind.

"In an investigation?" Bernie said.

"Not exactly," said the general. "What I'd like you to do —"

The door opened and the woman came in, still in her riding outfit. She saw me and Bernie and said, "I didn't realize you had company."

Bernie rose.

"Captain Bernie Little, Seventh Cavalry retired," the general said, "my wife Isobel."

Isobel took off her velvet-covered helmet, shook out her hair. Lots of it, all lovely and golden and recently colored, a smell impossible to miss. She looked younger than the general, except for chin area, which looked older, although why I'd all of a sudden be noticing a detail like that is beyond me.

"Nice to meet you," Bernie said.

Isobel nodded. "Is that your dog?"

"Chet's his name."

"A handsome animal," she said, turning out to be a first-class human being, and just when I was starting to think she tilted the other way! "Sorry to interrupt, Trav," she went on. "Just reminding you of that photo shoot — it's in forty-five minutes, down at the boathouse."

"The boathouse?" said the general. "Is that a good idea?"

"Why not?" said Isobel.

"Maybe it's a little too . . . patrician, you might say."

"Since when does that bother the American people?" Isobel said. Totally beyond me, but whatever it was, Bernie liked it: I can always tell.

"I don't want to appear aloof," the general said.

"Wear jeans and a T-shirt."

"You think?"

"Why not?" Isobel said, turning to Bernie. "What's your opinion?"

"On what the general should wear for the photo shoot?" Bernie said.

"Precisely."

"I'm not qualified to have an opinion about that."

"Aren't you a voter?"

"I am."

"Then what would you like to see?" Isobel said.

"Nothing from a photo shoot," said Bernie.

Isobel laughed, a real quick laugh, here and gone, and now looked at Bernie in a new way.

"What is it you do, Captain?"

"Bernie will do," Bernie said. "I'm a private investigator based in Arizona."

"How interesting," Isobel said. "And what brings you here?"

Bernie opened his mouth to speak, but before he could, General Galloway jumped in.

"I brought Bernie in for a quick consult," he said.

"On what?" said Isobel.

"Security."

"Yours or the nation's?"

The general smiled. "My wife has a very sharp wit, in case you haven't noticed. My own security, Isobel. It's too soon to be putting out policy papers."

"I thought Bill Donnegan handled personal security," Isobel said.

"He does," the general said. "I'm looking for an objective critique from someone else in the business. You know Bill Donnegan, Bernie?"

"I know Donnegan's, of course," Bernie said. "But not him personally."

"What do you think of them?" Isobel said.

"Probably what they think of me," Bernie said.

The general laughed. "You're in their doghouse at the moment."

Whoa! Stop right there. Bernie in a doghouse? I'd seen that once before, but that was Bernie on a bet and after a number, more than two, of bourbon shots, the dog-house in question belonging to Spike, a buddy of mine in the nation within who hadn't reacted well on finding Bernie curled up in his personal space. Were we in for another round of that? I sat up tall, ready for anything.

"Why is that?" Isobel said.

"We had some conflict with one of their agents on a recent case," Bernie said.

"An agent now deceased," said the general. "Although I'm not clear on the circumstances."

"He drowned," Bernie said.

Hey! It all came back to me. The long fall off that oil platform and then the two of us, me and what's his name from Donnegan's — a sort of competitor of ours, if I'd gotten things right — plunging down and down into the black water, with only me coming back up, another case cleared by the Little Detective Agency, and the best kind of case-clearing, where we ended up getting paid cash money. What was left of the roll was in Bernie's wallet at this very moment, still smelling slightly of shrimp, a story too long to go into now. Were we about to shake some green out of General Galloway? I got a real good feeling.

"A poor swimmer?" Isobel said.

"You could put it that way," said Bernie.

"And what about you, Bernie?" she said. "Are you good in the water?"

The general gave her a funny look. Bernie gave her no look at all, just said, "Chet's the swimmer on this team."

How nice of him! But that was Bernie, every time. And in fairness, he's no slouch in the water himself. Take our trip to San Diego, for example: we'd surfed, me and Bernie, me on the front of the board, not so different from riding shotgun in the Porsche — my favorite thing in the whole wide world, if that's not clear by now.

Isobel looked my way. "I like how his ears don't match."

My ears don't match? Had I already known that and forgotten, maybe on account of my life being pretty busy? And what did it even mean? Probably something good, if Isobel liked it.

She came closer. "Do you think he'd mind if I gave him a pat?"

"You never know," Bernie said. What a sense of humor!

Isobel stood in front of me. My head was right at her hand level, making us a good fit for patting purposes. She reached out and gave my head a soft pat, right between the ears. It felt nice, although nothing like the pats you get from Tulip and Autumn, two very fine ladies who work at Livia Moon's house of ill repute back home. Then came a surprise, not good. A scent I knew, very faint but there, was coming off her. Old Mrs. Parsons, our neighbor on Mesquite Road but now in the hospital, gave off the same scent, although stronger. Plus Maurice! What was going on?

Still patting me and hardly raising her voice above a murmur, Isobel said, "Must be nice, having a partner like this."

"Wouldn't change it for anything," Bernie said.

Right back atcha! What a pleasant visit this was turning out to be!

"Are the two of you working on anything at the moment?" she said. "Beside whatever Trav's got in mind."

"A security review is what's in mind," the general said, sounding a bit annoyed. "As I mentioned already."

"We're working on a murder case, actually," Bernie said.

"Back in Arizona?" said Isobel.

"Here," Bernie said. "Meaning the metropolitan area. A man was murdered a few days ago, and his father hired us to help with the investigation."

"Sounds interesting," General Galloway

said. "Who was the victim?"

"A consultant named Eben St. John," Bernie said.

All at once, I could hear Isobel's heart pounding away, loud and clear, and feel the pulse in her hand.

"Is that someone we know?" the general said.

"No," said Isobel, her eyes on me but not in a seeing way, her hand no longer in patting mode, more like gripping, like she was holding on.

"I hope that case won't preclude you from doing other things," the general said.

"It depends on the other things," said Bernie.

Isobel let go of me, squared her shoulders — a human move I always like to see. "I'll let you two discuss it," she said, crossing the room without looking at either of the men and going out.

"See you at the boathouse," the general called after her. He waited for an answer, and when none came, rubbed his hands like he was warming them up and turned to Bernie.

"We don't have much time," he said, leaning forward and closing the distance between them. "What I'm looking for is someone to help me preserve my tiny island of privacy. I'm aware that if I'm elected, privacy is not an option, but until that happens, I want to enjoy a taste of normal life."

"So you're running?" Bernie said.

A few pink spots appeared on the general's smooth cheeks. "I didn't say that. Everything is fluid at this point — thought I'd made that clear." He sat back a little in his leather chair, smallish hands kind of tight on the armrests. "Suppleness of mind is what I need from you."

"You can't get that from Donnegan's?" Bernie said.

"You can't get that from any big organization, right on up to the government of our wonderful homeland," the general said. "I assumed that was common knowledge."

Bernie gave him a long look. "I'll need specifics."

General Galloway sat back somewhat farther. "Fair enough," he said. "Should I start with the money?"

"The money comes last," Bernie said.

Oh, Bernie: that was my thought. The general seemed to be thinking, too. He opened his mouth and was about to speak when a man in a white uniform of some kind appeared in the doorway.

"Sorry, sir," he said. "Mrs. Galloway says it's time. She sent a change of clothes." He came in, handed the general jeans and a T-shirt, and left.

The general rose, started unbuttoning his shirt. "To be continued?" he said.

"You've got my number," said Bernie.

TWENTY-THREE

The dude in the white uniform showed us out through a side door. For some reason, Bernie didn't seem to want to circle around the house to the driveway. Instead, he kind of wandered the other way, past the tennis court and through a small apple orchard, red apples hanging from the trees, reminding me of Christmas, although I couldn't think why. Oh, but the smells, so lovely! I could have stayed there all day, except Bernie kept wandering, so I wandered with him, snapping up a fallen apple and making quick work of it. Apples aren't bad at all, especially the crunchy kind, which this one was, maybe the crunchiest I'd ever scarfed down. Were we on a roll? I had no doubt.

From the far end of the orchard, we could see down to the stream. A narrow gravel road that came from the direction of the house wound down to another white building on the near bank, which had to be the boathouse, on account of having a dock in front of it. A nice-looking wooden boat with a big cabin was tied to the dock, and some guys were down there, unloading light stands from a van and setting them up near the boat. A golf cart rolled into view on the gravel road, General Galloway at the wheel, now wearing jeans and a T-shirt. He parked by the boathouse, jumped out of the golf cart in an energetic sort of way, and strode onto the dock.

Footsteps sounded in the orchard behind us. I turned and there was Isobel, emerging through the trees, still in her riding outfit. Her boots smelled pretty wonderful. Suppose I was left alone with them for a reasonable amount of time? Couldn't hurt to dream.

She came up to us, and for a moment or two we all watched the activity at the boathouse.

"What do you think?" Isobel said.

"About what?" said Bernie.

"His outfit."

"Looks good to me."

"But you're not qualified, quote end quote."

Bernie turned to her. Her face looked older out here in the light. It was a face I liked, hard to say why, although you couldn't call it gentle. But what does that say? You couldn't call Bernie's face gentle, either, and they don't come any gentler than him. "You got that right," he said.

"The fact is, he never wears jeans and a T-shirt in real life," Isobel said.

"Real life?" Bernie said.

"When he's not running for president."

"Some people might say it doesn't get any realer."

"Would you?" Isobel said.

"Nope," said Bernie.

"Me neither." She reached up, plucked an apple from the nearest branch. Down on the dock, the general now had his face turned up to the sky. A woman was patting it with a powder puff. "It twists you out of shape," Isobel said.

"Just the protagonist?" Bernie said. "Or those around him, too?"

"I won't let it happen to me," Isobel said.

"You don't want to be First Lady?"

Isobel laughed. "I'm already miserable enough, thank you."

"Why is that, if I'm not out of line?"

"You are." Isobel took a big bite of her apple. A jet of spray came flying out, landed on Bernie's face. "Oh, I'm so sorry," she said, taking out a tissue.

But Bernie had already wiped it off on his

sleeve. "Not a problem," he said. They exchanged a quick look, way beyond me to understand, but there was nothing comfortable about it.

Down at the boathouse the general stepped onto the cabin cruiser. "Can't make out the name on the stern," Bernie said.

"*Horsin' Around*," Isobel said. "It's actually mine, a birthday present from my father."

"Sounds like a generous person."

"He was that."

A man spoke to the general. The general put his hands on the wheel — just like Charlie does when he's pretending to drive the Porsche — and faced the camera.

"So," said Isobel, "will you be joining us, meaning the team?"

"Not sure yet."

She took another bite of the apple, turning away this time. "Because of this other case you're working on?"

"Partly."

Isobel tossed away what was left of the apple. I had it on landing and was back in a flash. "Wow," she said. "He's an athlete, if some dogs can be called athletes. I know horses can."

"Dogs, too," Bernie said.

I lowered myself to the ground, the half-eaten apple between my front paws, in a convenient position for leisurely snacking.

"Tell me about the other case," Isobel said.

"What do you want to know?"

"Nothing specific. It sounds interesting, that's all. A consultant, you said?"

Bernie nodded. "In global economics, as far as I can make out. He ran an outfit called World Wide Solutions. Ever heard of it?"

Isobel put her hand to her chest. "Me? No. But the town is positively infested with consultants, all scheming away."

"Eben's scheming days are over. Someone put a bullet in his head."

"What was his last name again?"

"St. John. He was a Brit."

"I wonder if the ambassador knew him," Isobel said. "We're going there for drinks tonight."

"Ask him," Bernie said. "And while you're at it, ask him if he knows a man called Aubrey Ross."

"Who's he?"

"Just someone who turned up in the case."

Isobel nodded. "All right," she said. "I will. This is kind of exciting. How do I reach you?"

Bernie handed her our card.

"I like the flower," Isobel said. "Do all

private eyes have flowers on their business cards?"

"It's the law," Bernie said.

Down at the photo shoot General Galloway was still at the wheel, now gazing into the distance while the crew made their adjustments, moving the light stands around and placing a big foil reflector. It caught the sun and flashed a glare all the way up to us.

"Doesn't it look unbearable?" Isobel said.

"Ambitious people make sacrifices."

"He would've been smart to make a few more."

"Like what?" Bernie said.

"Nothing," Isobel said. "Have you got any suspects?"

"No."

"What about motive? Any clues?"

"If so, I haven't connected dots."

"What's your gut?" Isobel said, her voice getting brighter in a strange way, like we were getting ready to play some sort of game. "Robbery gone bad? Crime of passion?"

Bernie was quiet for a moment or two. "I think he was killed because of something he knew."

Isobel gazed down at the ground, which was right where I happened to be. I gazed up at her, but she wasn't seeing me, might not have been seeing anything: her eyes had that look humans get when they think they might have heard something far away. "Like what?" she said, her voice quiet, even soft, her game-playing mood now gone.

"That's what we're going to find out," said Bernie.

Meanwhile, I was listening for faraway sounds. So many to choose from: a quacking duck, a splash in the stream, chimes in the breeze, someone slamming on the brakes, a siren, the general saying, "Is this a better angle?" Had Isobel heard all of that? Any of it? Some? I had no idea.

"You know what I keep thinking about?" Bernie said as we drove away from General Galloway's place.

Lunch? That was my best guess, and really, what could be better?

" 'Intelligence for the masses,' " he said, losing me completely. "That was Eben's goal, according to Aubrey Ross. What do the masses want to know the most?"

When lunch was happening? I couldn't take it farther than that. This was very hard to follow. Besides, wasn't it time for him to shift gears? The engine sound was getting awful whiny.

"I'll tell you what the masses want," Bernie said, speeding up a bit, which drove the whininess to almost unbearable levels.

Shift the gear! And all at once, Bernie did just that as though . . . as though he'd read my mind? I was struck by a new idea, maybe the best idea of my life: maybe I could make it happen again, make Bernie obey my thoughts! Right away, I started thinking about lunch and only lunch, with all the power in my mind.

"They want to know," Bernie said, "that everything's going to be all right. And the person who most makes them feel that is the one who, for example, gets elected president." We rounded a long, down-sloping curve and sped through a golden patch of sunlight. There's all kinds of beauty in life. What we had now was the golden patch, Bernie's hand on the gear shift, the scent of honey in the air, and that was just for starters. I stopped thinking with all the power in my mind, which had turned out to be surprisingly tiring.

Bernie glanced over at me and a smile began to form on his face. "How about we stop for a quick —"

And then the phone buzzed. A quick what? Snack, by any chance? Had it actually worked? Could I get Bernie to do things just by thinking them? Newness can happen in life, baby!

A voice came through the speakers.

"Bernie Little?"

"Yup," Bernie said.

"Maurice St. John here. I haven't heard from you."

"No."

"I would have supposed, being the client, that there'd be more communication."

"We're working the case," Bernie said.

"Have you anything to report?"

"I prefer to do that at the end."

There was a silence. Then Maurice said, "Very well." More silence.

"Okay, then," Bernie said.

"One other thing, if you have a moment," said Maurice.

"I'm listening."

"Although unrelated to the case, there's something I'd like you to do. You can bill me for the extra time."

"We'll see," Bernie said. "What is it?"

"Eben's tack," said Maurice.

"Didn't get that."

"His tack," Maurice said. "His riding equipment — boots, saddle, helmet. I'd like to have them."

"Eben rode horses?"

"Splendidly. The stable sent me an email asking what to do about Queenie."

"The queen?" Bernie said. He smacked the nearest speaker a couple of times. "The Queen of England? I'm not hearing you too well."

Maurice raised his voice. "Queenie was Eben's horse. She's to be sold, but I'd like the tack, as I mentioned, which perhaps you could forward to me."

"Where's the stable?" Bernie said.

"In Virginia," Maurice said. I heard a tiny rustle of paper, and then: "Great Falls."

Bernie fished under the seat, found a balled-up map, did some swerving back and forth, but not too far across the center line. He sort of spread the map on the steering wheel and said, "Tell them we'll be there in twenty minutes."

"This here's Queenie," said the stable kid, a tall kid, almost Bernie's height but real skinny, with a backward baseball cap and lots of pimples. I liked him from the get-go.

"Nice-looking horse," Bernie said.

"She's a sweetheart," said the kid.

We stood on one side of a fence in a green meadow, watching Queenie. Queenie stood on the other side, watching us and flicking at a fat, slow-flying fly with her tail. Whenever her gaze wandered my way, her nostrils got real wide. I tried to find something nice or sweet or merely acceptable about her and failed. Horses — and I've had a lot of experience — are prima donnas, each and every one. True, it makes them easy to spook, and Queenie would be at the easy end of easy, but I got the feeling we were on the job, meaning I was in total pro mode, no worries in that regard and no possible need for Bernie to say, "Chet! Knock it off."

But he was! Why the —

"The growling, big guy. Zip it."

Growling? What growl—

The growling — if that low and rather pleasant sort of burr could be called growling — wound down in a way that I found almost musical.

"Chet, huh?" the kid said. "I bet everyone calls him Chet the Jet."

"Just my son does, actually," Bernie said.

What about me? I call myself Chet the Jet. Don't I count?

"How old's your son?" said the kid.

"Almost seven. And you?"

"Fifteen."

"In high school?"

"Yeah."

"Surviving?"

"Kinda."

"It gets better," Bernie said.

"Yeah?"

"No guarantees, of course."

The kid smiled. "That's what my mom says."

"She own this place?"

"Runs it. The owners live in Europe most of the time."

Bernie nodded toward Queenie. "What's the price?"

"For Queenie? She already got sold."

"Yeah?" Bernie said. "When was this?"

"Couple days ago or so," said the kid. "Lady who trains here sometimes bought her."

"How much?"

The kid's face went sort of blank. "My mom didn't say."

"None of my business," Bernie said. "It's just that I'm acting for the family of the previous owner."

"Eben?"

"That's right. You knew him?"

"Yeah. Is it true he got murdered?"

"Yes."

"Do they know who did it?"

"No."

The kid reached in his pocket and took out . . . a big fat sugar cube? I'm not really a fan of sugar cubes, but I wanted this one quite badly. In fact, I couldn't think of anything else. The kid reached through the fence and held the sugar cube out for Queenie. At that moment, I felt Bernie's hand on the back of my neck, not heavy, just there, most likely Bernie just being friendly. Queenie lowered her head, got the sugar cube between her lips, worked it back into her mouth and out of sight.

"He was a nice guy," the kid said. Then he fell silent, watched Queenie making chewing motions. Bernie has this patient way of standing, like nobody will ever be in a hurry again. He was standing that way now. After a while, the kid went on, "Some of the riding folks are kind of snotty. And Eben had that British accent."

"Snotty times two," Bernie said.

The kid laughed. "Yeah, but he wasn't snotty once you got to know him. Not like he was a barrel of laughs or anything. Just nice."

"You and he talk much?"

"Not really. He talked a lot to Queenie."

"Yeah?"

"Saddling up, washing her down. You'd hear him saying 'Who's a beautiful girl?' 'What's your pleasure today?' — like that."

And then we were all back to looking at Queenie again, a somewhat annoying development, in my opinion. "Will Queenie be staying here?" Bernie said.

"Not sure," the kid said. "The lady who bought her has a big spread not too far away."

Bernie hadn't moved at all or changed his stance in the slightest, but the whole patience thing was over. I could feel it, simple as that.

"What's her name?" Bernie said.

"Mrs. Galloway," said the kid. "Her and Eben rode together sometimes." He glanced at Bernie. "She's more the snotty kind."

"Nobody's perfect," Bernie said.

Except for him, or course, but he was too perfect to say so. With my mind on that, I didn't realize until we were back in the car that I'd forgotten to spook Queenie, maybe chase her around the meadow a bit. Would we be coming back here? I sure hoped so.

Twenty-Four

"This," said Bernie, the two of us back in the car now, and possibly driving in the direction we'd come from — I'd only know for sure if that golden patch appeared again — "is a time for playing your cards close to the vest. But since we haven't got any, let's go full frontal."

Full frontal? I hoped with all my heart — which is my MO when it comes to hoping — that full frontal wasn't in the plans. It had only come up once in our career — the case having to do with a stolen sombrero and a nudist colony, nudist colonies being totally new to me back then, a happier time in that way and that way alone. The less said about nudist colonies the better, but clothes are a fine invention when it comes to humans, let's leave it at that. For the rest of the ride, I kept a close eye on Bernie, waiting for him to start unbuttoning his shirt, but that didn't happen, meaning maybe he'd reconsidered. Sometimes you catch a break in this business.

We pulled back into the driveway at General Galloway's place, went to the front door. The white-uniformed dude opened up before Bernie even knocked.

"They're gone for the day," he said. "Did you forget something?"

"The general mentioned they were going out," Bernie said. "I didn't realize it was so soon. Remind me where they went again?"

Nothing changed on the white-uniformed dude's face or in his voice. He just wasn't as friendly anymore, impossible to explain how I knew. "Sorry," I said, "I don't do the schedules."

"Who does?" Bernie said.

"One of the assistants."

"Is he around?"

"She," said the white-uniformed dude, the sound of less friendliness now in the air. "And no, she's not. Is there any message you'd like me to pass on to the general?"

"No," Bernie said. "But you can tell Mrs. Galloway we came back."

"Yes, sir. You came back. Anything else?"

"That's it," Bernie said. "We came back."

"Messed that one up, but good," Bernie said as we drove away, although I didn't see how, all humans in the scene remaining clothed, for one thing. " 'We came back.' It was supposed to sound like the voice of doom, but I bet he started laughing the moment the door closed."

What was this about? I had no idea. My mind was pleasantly blank for a spell, and then, with no warning, I thought: lunch!

"Hey, big guy, what's up?"

Up? Nothing was up. I did seem to have a paw pressing down on Bernie's knee, but in the nicest way.

"Need a pit stop, huh?" Bernie said.

Which wasn't the case at all, until . . . until all of a sudden I did need a pit stop, and in the worst way!

"All right, big guy, hang on — hang on, for God's sake."

Bernie pulled into a little roadside clearing. I hopped out, sniffed around a bit. The place smelled unmistakably of pit stop, clearly one of the busiest in my experience, popular with humans of both sexes, and same for the nation within, a cat or two, plus foxes, deer, squirrels, raccoons, and what was this? A bear? Plus another creature or two I didn't even know! I laid my mark here and there, finally settling on a tree stump with white mushrooms growing on the top. There I was, watering mushrooms and therefore doing good, all the while gazing at the sky in that relaxed frame of mind you often get toward the end of a successful pit stop, when out from behind the crown of a nearby tree came the strange bird, the shiny hovering bird with no eyes, no feathers, and wings that didn't flap. It glided down in a long slow arc, passed right over Bernie's head — he was standing outside the car now, leaning in through the open door and digging around under the seat, meaning he was searching for a cigarette, of which there were none, as I knew from the total lack of tobacco smell in the car — and then rose straight up in the air and hung motionless, at about treetop level or so.

I finished up what I was doing, gave myself a quick shake, what Bernie calls my head-clearer — "like slapping your face with aftershave," which sounds unpleasant, in my opinion — but time enough to forget all about the strange bird, trot over to Bernie, watch him rooting around under the seat, and then — whoa! — remember again about the strange bird. Was it still up there hovering? Oh, yes.

Bernie straightened, turned to me. "What are you barking about?"

The strange bird, of course. What could be more obvious? I amped it up.

"What? What? You needed a pit stop, we took a pit stop. Thirsty maybe?" He reached back into the car, dug out my portable bowl and a bottle of water, filled the bowl, laid it on the grass beside me. I have a thing I sometimes do, hard to say why or even describe, that involves backing up with my legs real stiff and barking in a quick rat-a-tat-tat machine gun way that's hard to ignore.

"Drink, for the love of God! You're not thirsty? What do you want?" Bernie raised his hands, looked up, spoke to the sky, a human thing you see from time to time, the sky never answering, in my experience. "What does he want? What the hell does —"

Bernie froze, his gaze at last on the strange bird. I went silent. It got very quiet in our little pit stop area, nothing to hear but the faint *whirr-whirr* of the strange bird. Bernie watched the bird. I watched Bernie. At first, his face looked surprised. Then his mouth opened very slightly, a sign he was understanding something. Next, his eyes got hard.

He glanced at me. "Good boy, Chet. Way ahead of me again, huh?"

Of course not! How could anyone ever be ahead of Bernie?

Bernie opened the trunk of the Porsche

and took out the tire iron. That was unexpected. We were going to do some work on the car? Were we even having any problems with it lately? Not that I'd noticed. And the truth is that car repairs are not our best thing. You wouldn't believe how long it takes to get a coat like mine clean if it happens to get splashed with all the oil that's in the tank and then some. But if Bernie said car repairs, then car repairs it would be. Except now he was stepping away from the car, his head tilted up, eyes back on the strange bird. He patted the end of the tire iron once, twice on his open hand and then — and then came maybe the most exciting moment of my career, so far. Bernie drew back his throwing arm — he's got a cannon, as I must have made clear by now if I'm doing my job — and flung that tire iron high in the sky. It spun up there, glittering in the sunshine and whirling so fast I could hear the rush of air, closing and closing on the strange bird, which just went on hovering, maybe too stupid to know that big trouble was on the way — on the way with bells on, amigo! whatever that might mean, my apologies for even throwing it in there — and then: *WHACK!* What a lovely sound, solid, metallic, satisfying. The strange bird came down in a jerking spiral and landed right beside us with a jangly thud.

"Easy, big guy, easy."

Uh-oh. Was I jumping up and down? I made my best effort to get that under control, at least eliminating the up part of the jump, if that makes any sense. Meanwhile, Bernie was crouched over the strange bird, which was now in pieces, more than two, and not a bird at all, or even a creature of any kind, but a machine, with insides that reminded me a bit of the insides of Bernie's desktop computer, the day that Charlie figured out how to get the back off. The fun we'd had! And I'd ended up pooping out that one missing piece — a little green plastic square if I remember right — the very next day, so no harm, no foul. But no time for any of that now. Eye on the ball, big guy, which is what Bernie always says, although when it comes to playing fetch all our tennis balls and lacrosse balls are covered in my scent, so nose on the ball gets it done for me.

Where were we? Oh, yeah: the strange bird that turned out to be a machine. Bernie poked through its remains, and I squeezed in my closest to give him every bit of support I could. He picked out a tiny round glassy thing, turned it between his finger and thumb.

"Camera lens, Chet," he said. He glanced up at the sky, now empty except for a few gold-tipped puffy clouds, and then looked all around. A pickup went by, towing a horse trailer, the horse's tail sticking out the back. No getting away from horses in these parts. The tail flicked in an irritating way, and then we were alone again, me and Bernie.

He rose. "What we're going to do, big guy, is wait right here." He checked his watch, not his grandfather's watch — our most valuable possession and always either in the safe back home or at Mr. Singh's, our favorite pawnbroker, and don't forget his lamb curry — but his cheapo watch, that had actually cost nothing, Bernie having found it in a trash barrel while we were working some case about which I remember nothing else. "How about we time this?" he said. "Test the efficiency of our spooks, if you see what I mean."

I most certainly did not, nor, if spooks were involved, did I want to. Hadn't Suzie said something about spooks a while back? If so, you already know my stance on Halloween.

"First, let's take out an insurance policy," Bernie said.

A fine idea. Once we'd had a fire in the circuit breaker box in the garage, not long after Bernie had figured out a cool way to do something or other with the wiring, and pretty soon we'd learned all sorts of lessons about insurance. But so worth it, those dudes from the fire department turning out to be a fun bunch.

Meanwhile, Bernie was snapping pictures of the remains of the strange bird with his phone. I love how he closes one eye when he does that!

"We'll just send these to Suzie," he said, pressing a button. Then he found a paper shopping bag in the trunk of the Porsche, paper always his response when asked that plastic or paper question, and tossed all the pieces of the strange bird inside. After that, we just sat in the car and listened to some of our happiest tunes: "Sea of Heartbreak," "Born to Lose," "The Sky Is Crying," "It Hurts Me Too." Bernie sang along, and I chipped in from time to time as the spirit moved me — and it did a whole bunch of times, which is one of the things about me — with this *woo-woo-woo* thing I can do, nose pointed to the sky. We know how to sing a song, me and Bernie, and were singing our very best when two black cars, a sedan and an SUV, came up the slope, turned into our little spot, and parked on either side of us. We got out of the car, both of us moving as one, no communication. A situation like this starts up, you don't just stay there on your butt like . . . like a sitting duck. I've had some exp—

But no time for that now. We stood side by side. The doors of the SUV opened, and a man and a woman got out, both of them in dark business suits. A lot of suit wearing went down in this part of the country. I was still wondering whether that thought was going to lead me anywhere when a man got out of the sedan. He too wore a dark suit, but there was one difference, namely that I knew him. It was Mr. Ferretti, pushing his energy wave on ahead. Did I have anything against Mr. Ferretti? Not that I could think of. Besides being on the good-looking side for a human, with that big bony nose, even bigger and bonier than I remembered, hadn't we had a fun car ride together, not so long ago, a car ride that included some steak he was nice enough to share with me, and share in the nicest way, meaning I got most of it? So why would anyone be surprised that my first move was to trot over to him, tail wagging and all set for a hiya-pal-how-ya-been kind of pat? But surprise was what I saw on the faces of the two people from the SUV, and also from Bernie. Mr. Ferretti looked more bothered than surprised, frowning the way humans do when a problem suddenly crops up. I tried to identify a problem and pretty soon actually came up with one, which doesn't happen every time. The problem? I wasn't getting any pats from Mr. Ferretti. I headed right back to Bernie.

The man from the SUV walked off on his own, stopping around the spot where the strange bird had landed and toeing the grass. He turned to Mr. Ferretti, shook his head. Mr. Ferretti gave the woman a tiny nod. She came closer. Her hair, nice and thick, was tied up in one of those buns, one stray bit hanging loose at the back. That stray bit perked me up for some reason, and just at the right time, on account of those non-pats being a bit of a letdown, even for a dude as naturally perky as myself.

"Are you in possession of an object that doesn't belong to you?" she said.

"I paid for it with my taxes," Bernie said.

Oh, no. Tax time already? I really hoped not. Tax time was the worst, balled-up papers wall-to-wall, ink on Bernie's nose, calculators bouncing off the ceiling.

"Maybe you don't realize the gravity of the situation," she said.

"Normally, you'd be right," Bernie said. "But we just had a demonstration of gravity on this very spot, so it's fresh in my mind." No idea what that was about, but it seemed to make Bernie very cheerful, so I felt cheerful, too.

The woman eased back one side of her suit jacket, revealing a holster on her hip, gun butt showing out the top. When I'm cheerful, I sometimes do things I don't realize I've done until they're over, like . . . like snatching that gun right out of its holster! A voice in my head — Bernie's, of course — said, *Not now, big guy.* I got a grip. Not now means maybe later, with quite possibly no maybe about it, at least from my understanding of how things shake down.

"Hand it over," the woman said.

Bernie smiled. "You guys from a model plane club?"

She didn't like hearing that, and neither did her buddy from the SUV, but Mr. Ferretti laughed. He came forward. "I'll handle this," he said. He turned to Bernie. "What do you want?"

"Not to be spied on," Bernie said.

"Can we have a grown-up conversation?" said Mr. Ferretti.

"Sure," said Bernie. "Start by telling me who murdered Eben St. John. Even money it was you."

"You'd lose that bet," said Mr. Ferretti. "Plus it's a damned ungrateful thing to say."

"Ungrateful?" Bernie said.

Mr. Ferretti stepped forward, put his arm over Bernie's shoulder, and led him away, although not away from me, since I was right beside Bernie from the get-go. "I was hoping you'd go back to Arizona," he said.

"When was this?" said Bernie.

"After I sprung you."

Bernie stopped, turned to Mr. Ferretti, studied his face. I could feel Bernie thinking real fast. "So you do know who killed him."

"Negative," said Mr. Ferretti. "I just know it wasn't you."

"How?"

"Can't you figure it out?"

What a question! Of course, Bernie could figure out whatever it was. Wasn't he always the smartest human in the room? I waited. And waited some more. A little smile appeared on Mr. Ferretti's face. Was there a problem? All at once, it hit me: We weren't in a room! We were actually at this pit stop, in a kind of invisible soup of piss smells, the invisible part pretty meaningless to me, although probably not to you. The terrible point — I shrank from even letting my mind think it, but good luck with that, my mind so often being its own boss — was that perhaps, at this particular pit stop, Mr. Ferretti was the smar—

No! No! It couldn't be. The sun rises every day. Bernie's Bernie. That's all there is to say.

Twenty-Five

"You don't know who killed Eben, but you know it wasn't me," Bernie said.

"Correct," said Mr. Ferretti. "So therefore . . ."

Whoa! Mr. Ferretti was going to take a swing at a so therefore? Didn't he know so therefores were Bernie's department?

Bernie didn't let that happen. Before Mr. Ferretti could say one more thing, Bernie said, "So therefore, your name's Ferretti, two R's, two T's."

Good for Bernie! Although kind of confusing: didn't we already know that? I certainly did. Sometimes humans were . . . a little slow? No, no, not possible. What a crazy thought! I made it go away and hoped my hardest it would never come back. If humans were a little slow, then we were all in big trouble, and who wanted that?

Mr. Ferretti laughed. "You've got a smart girlfriend," he said. He glanced at me. "And a smart pooch. Even a cool car, at least in my eyes. All adds up nicely. Go home, Mr. Little. Enjoy your life."

"I'm enjoying it right here," Bernie said.

"Then you don't know what's in your own best interest," Mr. Ferretti said.

"That's still up to me," Bernie said, "unless there are new laws I'm unaware of."

"New laws you're unaware of? That's a given. To say nothing of the old ones. For example, the law gives me the power to arrest you on the spot for practicing your craft in this jurisdiction without a license."

Bernie reached into his pocket, took out a folded-up sheet of paper, handed it to Mr. Ferretti. "Can I sue you for defamation?" Bernie said.

Mr. Ferretti snapped the sheet of paper out straight with a flick of his wrist and gave it a quick glance. "Soares gave you this?"

"Uh-huh."

Mr. Ferretti sighed. Sighs are interesting. Bernie's mom, for example, a real piece of work who sometimes comes for a visit — please not again anytime soon, the fact being I do not shed, whatever she happens to believe, and if I do, it's no biggie — is a champion sigher, and we've got plenty of sighers in the nation within, but I haven't figured out what sighs are all about. Did

Mr. Ferretti and Bernie's mom have something in common? She'd had a sort of big bony nose at one time — nothing on the scale of Mr. Ferretti's, of course — but then some work got done, and more work after that. The truth was, she looked like a whole new person every time I saw her. No problem for me and my kind: her smell remained exactly the same, somewhat reminiscent of Bernie's, which was the best thing about her.

"Too many cooks," Mr. Ferretti said, giving the sheet of paper back to Bernie.

Mr. Ferretti was right about that. Cooks were better all by their lonesomes, as Bernie and I had learned when we'd attended the Great Western Chili Burger Cook-Off as guests of Cleon Maxwell, our buddy who runs Max's Memphis Ribs, best ribs in the Valley, bar none. Some cook had peed in some other cook's special top-secret barbecue sauce, or maybe it was the other way around, and the next thing we knew, the air was full of flying cleavers and we were on the run, both of us packing a burger, me in my mouth and Bernie . . . in his mouth, too! At least in my memory.

". . . any reason your recipe's better than his, following up on your cliché?" Bernie was saying, losing me completely and all at once, meaning he was now at his most brilliant. The case was as good as solved or even better. I tried to remember who was paying.

"Is that a serious question?" Mr. Ferretti said. "Soares is just a local cop."

"And you?" said Bernie.

Mr. Ferretti tilted up his chin a bit. I felt that energy wave of his, the chin movement sort of nudging it along. "You know what I am," he said.

Bernie didn't move at all but seemed to close the distance between the two of them, maybe just by getting bigger, hard to say how, exactly. "It doesn't scare me," he said.

"No?" said Mr. Ferretti.

"Not personally," Bernie said. "But for the future of the republic, yeah."

"A subject above both our pay grades," Mr. Ferretti said.

Bernie was about to reply when the woman called to him. "Boss?"

We all turned to her. Hey! She and the other dude were way too close to the Porsche — our ride! — and the other dude was reaching — reaching inside! — and . . . what was this? Taking out the shopping bag with the remains of the strange bird? Our shopping bag? One thing and one thing only was clear: I had no time to think. The good news is that's when I'm at my best. No bad

330

news comes to mind. Bernie says I'm a bowl-half-full type of guy, whatever that might mean, although at that moment he was saying something else, like, "Chet!" Or possibly, "CHET!"

Here's a funny thing. There have been times in my life when from the face of someone, Bernie, say, you can tell that shouting is going on, but what I'm actually hearing is more of a whisper or nothing at all. Does that ever happen to you? No matter, the important point being this was one of those times. I was vaguely aware of Bernie whispering my name as I charged my very hardest and fastest — way too long since my last hard and fast charge — right at the dude with the shopping bag. He saw me coming — there's a look humans get in their eyes when they see me coming in full-charge mode, a look I love! — and then started flailing around in a clumsy way, hands coming up, body half-twisting, shopping bag pinwheeling away, all those bird pieces taking separate flight, in short, the exact kind of reaction you want from a chargee, if chargee makes any sense, probably not. And so: I launched! The wind in my ears, the pounding of my heart, the taste of blood any moment now: hard to beat a moment like that, even if you live forever, which has always been my plan.

But right at the highest point of my leap, well above the heads of all humans concerned — which is a nice angle to have on humans, as I'd learned before and was learning again — I caught sight from the corner of my eye of an unwelcome development, namely the woman opening her jacket and going for her pea shooter, a pea shooter I now knew for sure I should have taken off the table when I had the chance. Lucky for me, I'm capable of kind of writhing around in midair and changing my flight plan, which is what I did, snatching that gun — which from the surprising weight must have been more of a stone-cold stopper than a pea shooter — right out of her hand —

"OW!"

— and trotting it over to Bernie. He took it just as Mr. Ferretti was reaching into his own jacket. Bernie turned to him, gun held loose, pointed at the ground, and Mr. Ferretti stopped with the reaching thing, holding his hands nice and steady, out where we could see them. Over by the car, the dude was staring down at the front of his shirt, which had somehow popped all its buttons, and the woman was dabbing at her wrist with a tissue, a tissue that looked just about pure white to me, give or take.

A comfortable silence descended on the pit stop area. I'm sure we were all thinking pretty much the same thing: what a beautiful day, the sky so blue, the leaves on the trees all sorts of colors, a soft breeze. Bernie tucked the gun in his pocket. At last! Going so long without a peacemaker had made me nervous, even though I hadn't realized it at the time. And now? I was back to feeling tip-top, and I knew it, which made everything just that much tip-topper.

"The thing is," Bernie said, "Chet feels kind of possessive about our car."

Mr. Ferretti nodded. At the same time, his two helpers were stepping away from the Porsche, kind of rapidly, as though they expected it to blow up any moment. Not a crazy thought on their part! We'd had a Porsche — the one before this, or the one before that, hard to keep it all straight in the mind when your life is on the adventurous side — blow up on us, in some ways a beautiful sight. And in the end, we'd made somebody pay and pay good, although who, exactly, wasn't coming to me at the moment.

Bernie moved over to Mr. Ferretti, put his arm over his shoulder, just the way Mr. Ferretti had done to him at the start of their little walk and talk. "How about your assistants take a moment or two in the SUV?"

Mr. Ferretti nodded. "Coffee?" he said to Bernie.

"Black," said Bernie, taking out his wallet.

"That won't be necessary," Mr. Ferretti said. "Guys?" he said to the others. "If you will? Coffee run. Black for Mr. Little."

"Uh," said the man with the open shirt, "we're kind of in the middle of nowhere."

"Even the middle of nowhere has coffee these days," Mr. Ferretti said. "Warms the heart about this land of ours."

The man and woman got in the car.

"If you get a chance," Bernie called after them, "Chet's fond of Slim Jims."

Fond? I was flat-out crazy about them! Ever tasted one? Then you know.

The SUV drove off. Bernie walked over to the Porsche, started picking up the bird remains all over again. "Mind bringing that shopping bag?" he said to Mr. Ferretti.

Mr. Ferretti went and got the shopping bag from the far side of the clearing where the breeze had taken it. Nothing shabby about his retrieving skills, although not in my class, hardly bears mentioning. He held the shopping bag open while Bernie dumped the pieces inside, Mr. Ferretti gazing at them kind of sadly. For a few moments they worked together real nice, like good pals. Hey! It turned out that Mr. Ferretti had beautiful hands, although not as beautiful or as big or as anything as Bernie's; also not bearing a mention. But here's something about me: I kind of like mentioning things that don't bear mentioning! What's with that? I'm even tempted to mention whatever it was one more time.

Meanwhile, the last piece of the strange bird was dropping into the shopping bag with a soft clank, and a good thing — I never wanted to see that bird or any part of it again. Mr. Ferretti extended his hand, like he was expecting Bernie to give him the bag, but Bernie did not, taking a step back instead, which reminded me of a sort of a game that one of Charlie's little buddies played with him once, a game that was all about holding out an ice cream cone and then snatching it away every time Charlie reached out for it, and that had led to a miniature brawl between them, stopped but pronto by Chet the Jet, who also ended up with the ice cream cone.

Forget all that. The point is Bernie held on to the bag. "How about we make a deal?" he said.

"To get my own property back?" said Mr. Ferretti. "That doesn't strike me as friendly."

"We're not friends," Bernie said. "More like the opposite."

"Oh?" said Mr. Ferretti. "Even after I got you out of jail? Seems a tad ungrateful."

"I'll explain," Bernie said. "Stop me when I go wrong. You knew I didn't kill Eben, but you say you don't know who did, meaning you're sure my alibi was solid. No other possibility that I can see. But my alibi is the kind that almost never holds up. I was asleep at Suzie Sanchez's place, no witnesses. Makes it a real good bet that you had a drone outside her window. No way you'd have been keeping an eye on me — I'd just come to town. You've been spying on Suzie. Suzie's my girlfriend. So therefore, we're enemies, you and me."

What a great moment in my life! Mr. Ferretti had tried to take the so therefores away from Bernie, and Bernie had snatched them back, just like . . . an ice cream cone. An ice cream cone? An odd thought. I pushed it aside, tried to pay attention.

"You made just one mistake," Mr. Ferretti said. "We weren't spying on Suzie."

"The drone just happened to be outside the bedroom window?"

"Pretty much. We had a drone in the vicinity — not this one, by the way, if taking revenge on an inanimate object is motivating you — but its mission had nothing to do with Suzie Sanchez or you."

Then came a long silence. I could feel Bernie's thoughts zinging around, short and choppy, not like his usual thoughts. Mr. Ferretti watched him think for a while and smiled. I myself puzzled over "drone," a new one on me.

"So therefore," he said, "we aren't enemies, you and I."

What was this? Mr. Ferretti had snatched the so therefores right back? Bernie! Do something!

Which Bernie did, although it was the last thing I expected: he handed over the shopping bag.

"Much obliged," said Mr. Ferretti. "I'll take my colleague's firearm, while we're at it."

"Whose side are you on?" Bernie said, the gun remaining in his pocket.

"Side?"

"One of the political parties, maybe? The president? Some candidate?"

"Oh, no, nothing like that," Mr. Ferretti said. "I'm here to protect the country in the long term."

"Now you've got me scared," Bernie said. "I'll be keeping the weapon."

TWENTY-SIX

"Nice job on the gun, big guy," Bernie said as we zoomed off down the road, just the two of us back on our own, the way we like it. "Interesting that you and Ferretti seemed to know each other already." He glanced over at me. "How and when did that happen?"

Not an easy question. I searched my memory. Nothing there at the moment! Meaning there was no choice but to look to the future, not a bad outcome, all in all.

"Must have been while they had me locked up downtown," Bernie said, "but how —"

The phone buzzed.

"Bernie?" It was Suzie, but sounding not quite herself, her voice higher and thinner.

"Hey, Suzie. You all right?"

"No. I mean yes. Mostly yes. But something's come up and I think you should —"

"Suzie? Suzie? Are you still there?" We

listened hard, me and Bernie, his hand tightening on the wheel, the knuckles getting yellow. I heard a click, and then nothing.

Bernie pressed a button. The *beep-beeping* of a phone call trying to get started came through the speakers.

"Suzie, pick up."

But she did not.

Bernie turned to me. " 'Mostly yes.' What does that mean?"

I had no clue. Bernie stepped on the pedal.

"What was she covering? A flower show?" We roared up a hill, almost took off at the top. Way in the distance, I could see the city, a big white dome sprouting like a mushroom in the center. "Design show, that was it," Bernie said as we blazed down the far side of the hill, even faster. "What's the name of that editor of hers? Sheila? Sherry? Charlotte?"

I didn't know. Plus all these questions were making me nervous, and so was Bernie's voice, which was nervous, too, no doubt about it. That hardly ever happened, but when it did, it spread to me every time. I started panting. Sometimes you can pant the nervousness right out of yourself. That didn't seem to be happening this time. So: stop with the panting, right? Except I couldn't.

". . . Sheila, maybe," Bernie was saying in that louder voice he uses for being on the phone even though everyone tells him to tone it down. "Or Charlotte. Don't know her last name. She's Suzie Sanchez's editor, and Suzie was trying to reach me and —"

"One moment, please."

We topped another hill, the city closer now, the blue river running through it shining like a huge snake. Oh, what a terrible thought! Why now?

"Metro desk."

"This is Bernie Little. I'm . . . I'm a friend — a good friend — of Suzie Sanchez."

"Yes?"

"Can you tell me the location of the design show?"

"Design show?"

"The design show you asked her to cover."

"I didn't ask her to cover the design show."

"Maybe I've got the wrong person. Can I speak to her editor?"

"I'm her editor, and she's not covering the design show."

"But someone's out sick," Bernie said. "Didn't you text Suzie about taking over the assignment?"

The woman's voice got snappy. "No one's out sick, and we're not even doing the design show this year."

"But I was right there! How the hell —"

Bernie took a deep breath. I'd seen him take this kind of deep breath before, always when he was trying to control himself. These control struggles were always the best time for feeling Bernie's strength, even better than when he was throwing down with some huge drooling tough guy. Explain that! Nothing wrong with drooling, of course, wish I'd left it out.

"Sorry for the misunderstanding," Bernie said, quieter now. "Where is the design show?"

"Franklin Court," said the woman, still snappy. "But she won't be there."

We drove into the city, went downtown, and soon I was catching glimpses of that strange stone tower again. It popped up a lot, taller than just about everything else around; I turned my head this way and that to keep the tower in view.

Bernie glanced my way. "What's with you and the Washington Monument, Chet?"

I didn't know, wasn't even sure I understood the question.

"Kinda makes sense," Bernie said. "He was a fan of the nation within. Had to be — those Virginia gentlemen were into foxhunt-ing in a big way."

Fox hunting? I knew foxes, of course, had run one or two off the property back home, sneaky little buggers and surprisingly shifty. We were going to hunt some of them down? That sounded wonderful! Only one problem, namely that foxes have a scent you — meaning me, no offense — can pick up a mile away, and way more if it turns out a mile isn't very far, and I was smelling absolutely none of it, like there wasn't a single fox in the whole town.

"Smell something?"

Bernie was watching me again. I had my nose pointed up, and yes, I was smelling something, in fact, many somethings.

"Food, I'll bet."

Sure, but that wasn't the point. The point was the absence of fox scent when I'd just been promised a foxhunt. What was up with that?

"Easy, big guy — we'll get you fed."

Fed? But I wasn't the slightest bit —

We parked in an underground garage. What is it about those places that I don't like? Easier to name the things I do, which is only one, specifically the smell of human piss, almost always male. Kind of a mystery, since I'd never caught a human in action in an underground parking garage, but action went on, no doubt about that, and this garage was no exception. It put me in a very good mood, hard to explain why, or maybe I was in a very good mood already. We went up to the street and entered the lobby of a tall and fancy building, all human piss smell gone, except for the tiny trace you find when old people are on the premises. Did a lobby count as premises? I had no idea, but there were a few old people around, all of the well-dressed, slim, and sort-of-young-looking type — "if you don't look at their necks," as Leda used to say.

This lobby was maybe the nicest I'd ever been in, full of sunshine, with polished stone all over the place. Along all the walls were — what would you call them? Sort of rooms, except they weren't real, since the real room was the lobby? Whoa! Way too complicated!

Lots of people were clustered around the unreal rooms — kitchen, living room, office, closet, TV room, others I didn't know the names of, all filled with shiny things, lots of them breakable if you happened to have a tail. I followed Bernie across the lobby, my tail up and as motionless as I could make it. He walked up to a woman with a clipboard.

"Can I help you?" she said, glancing at me with a nice smile. "Pet design's on the fourth floor, room four one six."

"Pet design?" Bernie said.

"Doghouses, bedding, doggie door entrances, the latest in bowls, leashes, calming vests, collars, booties, you name it."

Wow! I couldn't wait! Booties? What an idea!

"Actually," Bernie said, "we're looking for Suzie Sanchez. She's a reporter for the *Post* who —"

A line or two appeared on the woman's forehead. "I'm not sure what's going on with that. They need to get their act together."

"What do you mean?"

The woman's nice smile was gone. "First," she said, "we were told they wouldn't be covering us this year. Then she shows up at the last moment, no warning. Fine, we can work with that. Next, five minutes later, out the door she goes, not a word of explanation. Although not before I'd blogged that the *Post* would be doing a story after all, damn it."

Bernie took a real quick glance around the lobby. "Did you see her leave?"

"Are you saying I'm making this up?"

"Not at all," Bernie said. "Was she alone?"

"She was with some guy."

"Did she come in with him?"

The woman shrugged. "Maybe. I don't know."

"What did he look like?"

"Some guy." Her phone beeped. She checked it, tapped at the screen with the tips of her silvery fingernails. "I wasn't paying a lot of attention." She looked up, the are-we-done-here? look on her face.

"One more thing," Bernie said. "Who's handling security?"

"The building — it's included in our deal."

"I'd like to talk to whoever's on duty at the moment."

"Why? What's going on? I don't understand."

Bernie's voice did that hardening thing where it actually gets quieter. "If this wasn't important, I wouldn't be bothering you."

The woman gave him a new kind of look, like . . . like she was seeing Bernie now, and not just any dude, although how anyone could ever get Bernie confused with just any dude made no sense to me. She tapped at her screen, put the phone to her ear, and said, "Security?"

We rode — uh-oh — an escalator upstairs.

Bernie didn't exactly hold me by the collar the whole way, more like he rested his hand on it in a pally sort of way. There are many great human inventions — the car, the tennis ball, the barbecue pit, just to name two or more — but the escalator is not one of them. Suppose you slipped at the top and got swept underneath, gone to who knows where. You must have thought of that or maybe had bad dreams about it and then had trouble getting back to sleep and ended up tired the next day. If you haven't, I hope that kind of thing doesn't start up now on account of me bringing it up. I'd feel bad about that.

We were lucky this time, getting off with no problem — "Did good, big guy, I know it's not easy" — and walking down a hallway. Bernie knocked at the first door we came to; a man called, "Come in"; and we went in, me forgetting all about escalators, if I hadn't done so already.

Big buildings, sports stadiums, airports: they all have security offices somewhere inside, a fact you learn early in our business. No matter what the rest of the place is like, the security office tends to be on the shabby, stripped-down side, but not this one, which had nice furniture, a floor of polished stone just as in the lobby, a wall of flat-screen monitors, and a little white desk with spindly legs. The dude sitting behind it was kind of the opposite of the desk, if that makes any sense, huge and dark.

His eyes went to Bernie, then to me, and didn't look too happy about something or other. Then he took a closer look at Bernie and everything changed.

"Bernie?" He rose, even huger than I'd thought, with a body like an oil drum, only way bigger. His voice was kind of like an oil drum, too, deep and booming.

"William?" Bernie said.

They moved toward each other, met in the middle of the room, shook hands, Bernie's big strong hand practically disappearing inside this William dude's. William's other hand was the machine type, metal and plastic, which didn't bother me at all. Lots of guys I knew at the VA hospital back home — where we sometimes went for visits, me and Bernie — had hands like that, and some of them could do fun tricks with those machine hands, like shuffling a deck of cards — Bernie had bet fifty bucks against that one — or peeling a grape, which had cost us a C-note.

"You haven't changed," William said.

"Neither have you," said Bernie.

William held up his machine hand and

laughed.

"So we're both bullshitters," Bernie said. "They couldn't save it?"

"Came close," William said.

"Why didn't you let me know?"

"I was stateside by then." For a moment, William's eyes got a faraway look. "Got into some other things. Besides, you were still back there, and, you know . . ."

"Yeah," said Bernie.

They let go of each other's hands.

"Going good now?" Bernie said.

"No complaints," said William. "I run security for this place and some others up toward Logan Circle." He turned to me. "And who's this good-lookin' hombre?"

Just one of the many good things about Bernie: he had topnotch buddies all over the place, William clearly being at the very top of the notch.

"This is Chet," Bernie said.

"He partial to treats of any kind?"

"Partial's putting it mildly."

William went to his desk, opened a drawer. "Thought I had a . . . guess not." He rummaged around. "Think a Slim Jim would do? I snack on them myself, truth be told."

Wow! The kind of buddy who just got better and better. As for Slim Jims, they would always do. And somehow, without being aware of the actual journey, I was now sitting right beside William, possibly on one of his feet. A moment later — but what a long moment! — I was in a small Slim Jim world of my own.

". . . private investigation," Bernie was saying. Then came something about Suzie and the *Washington Post* and —

"She's your girlfriend?" William said.

"Why the surprise?"

"Nothing. I read her article on those Neanderthal reenactors. Funny stuff."

"So? I can't appreciate funny stuff?"

"Sure you can," William said. "And why so touchy?"

"Sorry," Bernie said, and he got started on a long explanation of what we were doing here, which I tried to follow in the hope of learning a thing or two but got undermined by my concentration, which was elsewhere.

By the time I'd polished off my little snack, Bernie and William were over by the wall, studying one of the monitors. On the screen was a picture of the lobby. And hey! There was Suzie! Couldn't wait to see her! We were going to zip on down there ASAP, right, even if it meant the escalator? Only we didn't. Instead, we just stood still, watching Suzie. She started walking past the little pretend rooms, taking a look around, and then a man stepped up to her. A slicked-back-hair sort of man with a face made of slabs, a man we knew: Mr. York. They talked for a moment or two and then turned and headed out the front door of the lobby, side by side.

TWENTY-SEVEN

"That help, at all?" William said, turning from the monitor.

"Yes and no," Bernie said.

Yes and no? I hate when that comes up, can never get my head around it. Is it okay, for example, to gnaw on a chair leg? Isn't that yes *or* no? Either it's cool to gnaw on the chair leg — "lookit ol' Chet workin' on that damn chair leg," — or it's uncool — "CHET!" But yes *and* no? How can you gnaw and not gnaw at the same time?

Maybe William was having the same problem, because he'd started rubbing his forehead the way humans do when they need more help from up inside there — rubbing with his machine hand, by the way, a very interesting sight that made me forget all about what I was doing, which seemed to be . . . gnawing on one of the spindly legs of William's little white desk? When had I even gone over there? I put a stop to that gnawing, but pronto.

"That was Suzie?" William said.

"Yup," said Bernie.

"And the guy?"

"Goes by the name of York." Bernie took out his phone, tapped it with his finger, listened. "She's not picking up."

"I've got an exterior camera," William said, "covers the main entrance and a small segment of the street." He switched on another monitor, picked up a remote. I saw the entrance where we'd come in. People were going in and out much faster than normal. Then things slowed down and out came Suzie and Mr. York. They crossed the sidewalk and got into a small white car parked by the curb, Mr. York behind the wheel, Suzie in the shotgun seat. The car drove out of the picture. William fiddled with the remote and the car drove back into view and froze in the middle of the screen. He fiddled some more and closed in on the license plate. "Make that out?" he said.

Bernie nodded. He was writing on the back of one of our business cards — I saw that bothersome flower on the front. Why not a gun, or cuffs, or an orange jumpsuit? Nothing against flowers. Their smell can practically knock you out sometimes, but not in a scary way, and we can be scary, me and Bernie, just another one of our techniques at the Little Detective Agency.

"Want me to run that plate?" William said.

"If you can," said Bernie.

"Would I be any good at my job if I couldn't?"

William got on the speakerphone with a woman named Belle or possibly Maybelle who told a story about a dude on his driving test and how he'd ended up crashing right through the wall of her office at the DMV, leading to a couple of nice days off, but now she was back and happy to help. Not long after that, she was saying something about a white Honda registered to a Jean-Luc Carbonneau of Fenwick Street. William asked about her boyfriend, and she said she'd thrown him out on his worthless ass, which got them both laughing, her and William, and then they said good-bye.

"Much appreciated," Bernie said.

"No need for that between you and me," said William. They shook hands again. "That Fenwick address is in Ivy City," William said. "Not the best area."

Not the best area? So what? We worked in bad areas all the time. Did William think we were soft? It had to be that flower, a real bad influence in our lives. What could I do about it? Chew up all our business cards?

Hey! A plan! Back to tip-topdom, except for a paint chip or two caught under my tongue. I had them all coughed out by the time we were back in the Porsche.

"You getting sick?"

Me? I leaned across the front seat, rested some of my weight on Bernie, just so he'd know how good I felt.

"Can't breathe like this, big guy."

And we were off.

Bernie drove in silence. He's one of those drivers who sit back in the seat, nice and comfortable, even when we're chasing some perp who still doesn't realize it's game over. And so many of them don't, even when they're cuffed! Some try to make a deal, like the dude who offered us a weekend at his time share in New Jersey, wherever that may be. But what I was getting at is that if Bernie's very worried about something, he sits more forward in the driver's seat, not so nice and comfortable, which was how he was sitting now. What was he worried about? Couldn't have been because we were heading into a bad part of town — we work out in Vista City, where they sometimes throw grenades off the rooftops — so it had to be the flower.

He turned to me. "Sighing, Chet?" he

said. "I'm worried about her, too."

Not the flower, then, but some female person? I went over the female persons I'd been in contact with recently — Isobel Galloway, Lizette, Suzie — and decided it had to be Suzie. I'd never want anything bad to happen to her, wanted nothing but good for her with all my heart. I sat far forward, my front paws on the dash, which usually makes the car go faster. But we were pretty much bumper to bumper and ended up going slower, if anything. My heart speeded up, maybe just so something would be going fast.

Bernie gave me a pat. "Easy, now," he said. "No jumping to conclusions — there's lot of possibilities. Starting with Carbonneau, for example, not exactly a common name in these parts. Lizette Carbonneau and Jean-Luc Carbonneau, alias Mr. York. Gotta be related. Brother and sister? Husband and wife? So therefore?"

I waited for the payoff on the so therefore, Bernie's department. When I got tired of waiting, I went back to my last memory before that, the no-jumping thing. No real need for Bernie to give me a heads-up on that subject: I knew the downside of jumping from moving cars, having done it twice before, once chasing a perp and once getting away from one, and hadn't the slightest desire to do it on this particular outing; okay, maybe now that Bernie had mentioned the idea, a slight desire.

"Sticking your head a bit too far out there. Cool it."

Somebody had their head stuck too far outside? What were they thinking? And who could be that stu— And then in no time at all, I boiled that somebody down to me and took care of business. Meanwhile, we were rolling in a bad part of town, bumping over rusted train tracks, boarded-up houses on one side and grimy warehouses on the other. Bernie turned a corner, and we pulled up in front of a low brick building with dirty barred-over windows and a cracked and broken sidewalk out front.

"It's a bar?" Bernie said.

No doubt about that: bar smells were in the air, big time. We got out of the car, and right away, a red-eyed dude appeared from down an alley and came toward us, although not in a direct line, the scent of his booze cloud reaching us first.

"Hey," he said.

"Hey," said Bernie.

"That your dog?"

"In a manner of speaking."

The dude thought about that, also did a

bit of weaving back and forth, as though the ground had gone wobbly under his feet. "I getcha," he said. "Does he bite?"

"Only for a reason."

"Uh-huh. I'm the same way myself. How about I watch your car while you're inside?"

"It's a free country," Bernie said. "I can't stop you."

The dude thought that was funny, started to laugh, and then hawked a glob that didn't bear too much looking at into the gutter. "Talkin' here," he said, wiping his mouth on the back of his arm — uh-oh, the kind with needle marks — " 'bout the kind of watchin' that's more the protectin' kind."

"Think that's necessary?" Bernie said.

"I don't think." The dude tapped his forehead. "I know."

Bernie reached into his pocket. Was he about to draw down on this dude with our new piece, the one I'd — how would you put it? Borrowed maybe? — yes, borrowed from Mr. Ferretti's lady pal? Nope. Instead, out came Bernie's wallet. The dude leaned toward it, like something was pulling him that way.

"How much?" Bernie said.

"Call it twenty," said the dude.

Bernie held out a bill. "Let's call it five for now and five on delivery of service."

"An' here I thought you were a nice guy," the dude said.

"Think again," said Bernie, which had to be one of his jokes, Bernie being the nicest guy you'll ever meet. He started to put the bill back in his wallet, but the dude grabbed it first.

"We got a deal," he said.

"Done," said Bernie. He glanced at the bar. "Know this place well?"

"Coulda owned it by now, for all the money I spent inside."

"Ever run into a guy named Jean-Luc Carbonneau?"

"Nope."

"About your size, thirty-five or forty, slicked-back hair."

"I don't have no slicked-back hair. Look never appealed to me at all."

"With you on that," Bernie said. "He might also go by the name of York."

"York? That's different."

"You know him?"

"By sight. Who's the Frenchie?"

"That's not important," Bernie said. "Tell me about York."

Sometimes humans use their chins for pointing. It took me a long time to get that one. This boozy dude — an employee of the Little Detective Agency at the moment? I hoped not for long — was doing it now, pointing at the top story of the bar with his chin. "Rents a room on the second floor," he said. "Not around much."

"What does he do?" Bernie said.

"Do?"

"Everybody does something."

"Like I drink, for example?"

"Yeah."

"I don't know. Maybe he does drugs. Drugs or drink — a choice, not an echo, you know what I mean. I tried both — drink's better."

Bernie gave him a look. At first, I thought it was one of his hard looks; then I wasn't so sure.

We went inside. No one there except for a short round woman standing on a stepladder in front of the bar. She had a lightbulb in her hand but couldn't reach the socket in the ceiling, although she was trying her hardest, which you could tell from her grunts, pretty much the loudest I'd heard from a woman.

"Help you with that?" Bernie said.

The woman turned toward us, and — oops — she and the ladder both got a bit unsteady, the ladder tipping one way and she another, and don't forget the lightbulb, also airborne. Bernie can move real fast when he has to — but of course he hardly ever has to, not with me around — and this was one of those times. He crossed that floor — a sticky kind of floor, which you find in a certain kind of bar — in two steps, and snatched that lightbulb right out of midair! He also caught the woman, almost, uh-oh — but no, he didn't drop her, just lowered her safely down, and if not gently, then pretty close.

A round woman, about chest-high on Bernie. She looked up at him. "That was kind of amazing," she said.

"Um," said Bernie.

"Not often I run into a man who can carry me bodily," she said.

"Me, uh, either," Bernie said.

The woman laughed. She had a jolly sort of laugh. Also jolly was the fact, fact beyond doubt, that she had a biscuit treat or two in the pocket of her jeans.

"How about I . . ." Bernie said, standing the ladder back up, climbing the first step or two and screwing in the bulb. The woman watched his every move. I got myself a little closer to her. When were we going to start up with "This your dog?" and stuff like that?

Bernie climbed down the ladder.

"Your dog's sniffing at my pocket," the

woman said.

"Chet!"

"That's all right," the woman said. "I have biscuits in there."

And after hardly any more chitchat at all, they were mine.

"Got a dog yourself?" Bernie said.

"Until recently. Their lifetimes don't match up very well with ours."

Bernie nodded, like that made sense to him. As for me, I had no clue, but the biscuits were delish, just about the best I'd ever tasted.

When I tuned in again, Bernie was saying, ". . . actually looking for a man named York. I believe he rents a room upstairs."

The woman didn't look quite so jolly. "Rents it from me," she said. "You a cop, by any chance?"

"No," Bernie said. "Why do you ask?"

"No reason," the woman said. She glanced my way. "Your dog looks like the K-9 type."

Again? Why did I have to hear that again? Yes, I am the K-9 type, and I was especially the K-9 type until I flunked out of K-9 school on the very last day with only the leaping test left, and leaping was then and is now my best thing. A cat was involved: that's all I can tell you.

"Any reason you might be expecting the

cops?" Bernie said.

"This is the kind of neighborhood where we're always expecting cops," the woman said. "Except when they're needed."

"Has Mr. York done something that would interest them?" Bernie said.

The woman looked away. "Not that I know of."

Bernie took out his phone, flicked his thumb on the screen, held it up for her to see. "Recognize this woman?"

"No."

Bernie handed her our card.

"You're a detective?"

"Working in cooperation with DC police. The woman on the screen has disappeared, last seen with Mr. York. Time is crucial in situations like this. Why have you been expecting the cops?"

She looked at Bernie, then at me. "Not expecting, really," she said. "I wouldn't have been surprised, that's all."

"Why?" said Bernie.

"On account of this guy who was killed last week. I used to see him around here and then I look in the paper and somebody shot him."

"You're talking about Eben St. John?"

"Didn't know the name," the woman said.

"But I recognized the face. He used to come visit Mr. York."

TWENTY-EIGHT

The woman, name of Jeannine — if I got that right, conversation zipping back and forth at a rate that's not the best for me — locked the front door of the bar and led us upstairs and down a dark and dim old corridor that made me want to be outside. But indoor work is part of what we do at the Little Detective Agency, and I'm a total pro, so I forgot all about the great outdoors, or almost. But no one ever says "the great indoors." I'll leave it at that.

We came to a door at the end of the corridor, a peeling-paint kind of door with one kicked-in panel repair that had no paint at all, a sight you see from time to time in this business.

"He hasn't been around in a few days," said Jeannine, "maybe not since I saw that story in the paper, come to think of it." She knocked on the door.

"Then why are you knocking?" Bernie said.

"Where I'm from, it's polite to knock."

"Where is that?"

"Here," said Jeannine. She shot him a glance. "All the poor people in DC are natives. All the rich hail from someplace else." Jeannine took out a ring of keys, stuck one in the lock, opened the door.

"Looks like someone beat us to it," Bernie said.

"I don't understand," said Jeannine.

But I did. What we were looking at was a room turned upside down. We'd turned rooms upside down plenty in our time, me and Bernie — a time that was just getting started! — on account of it being a great way to nail the kind of perp who leaves evidence behind. I started sniffing around while Bernie explained things the way I've just done, more or less, quite possibly less.

"But how did they get in?" Jeannine said. "There's only two keys, mine and his."

The room had one window, the kind with a barred metal grille on the outside. Bernie and I went over and looked out. Down below ran a narrow alley — amazingly rich in the department of piss smell — with a boarded-up building on the other side.

"A child couldn't squeeze through those

bars," Jeannine said.

Bernie nodded. Then he put his hands on the grille and with no effort at all lifted it out of the frame, tipped it sideways, and drew it back into the room.

Jeannine came closer. "Somebody climbed a ladder and unscrewed the grille?"

"But not a perfectionist, because they didn't screw it back in on the way out," Bernie said.

He leaned the grille against the wall, turned to the room, and started going through all the scattered things — clothes, papers, books, pillows, plus the insides of stuff: mattress, couch, TV. What was this? We were turning upside down a room that had already been turned upside down? Wouldn't that mean in the end we'd have put everything back to . . . my mind teetered on the verge of some big thought, and then withdrew. I gave myself a quick shake and headed in the direction of the only interesting smell in the room, other than piss scent rising up like fog from outside. Meanwhile, Bernie was kneeling by a hole in the floor where the boards had been torn out.

"What are you looking for?" Jeannine said.

"Does the name Jean-Luc Carbonneau mean anything to you?"

"No. Why?"

"How about Lizette Carbonneau?"

"No. What are —"

"Did York ever have any female visitors?"

"Not that I saw," Jeannine said. "But who —"

"Did York sign a lease?"

"No. He came here a couple of months ago, had a look around, and paid a year's rent."

"Sounds about right."

"In what way?"

"In terms of the picture of him we're building."

"Who's we?"

"You and me," Bernie said. "You've been a huge help so far."

Whoa! And what about me? I stopped what I was doing, namely following one of the real important scents in our business, a trail that had led me into a corner of the room where a floor lamp, now on its side, the shade torn to pieces, was plugged into a wall outlet. Keeping your distance from wall outlets was the way to go — if you get too close a strange temptation to stick your tongue in them overcomes you, as you may or may not know — but at this moment I had to overcome the overcoming, if that makes any sense. Meanwhile, I'd put the brakes on the whole thing, on account of:

what about me?

". . . don't want any trouble," Jeannine was saying.

"All the trouble here has already happened," Bernie said.

"How do you know?"

"No one comes back after something like this. They either found what they came for or figured it wasn't here in the first place."

Jeannine nodded in that way humans have when they're not really buying it, and then her gaze fell on me.

"Why's he standing with his front paw up in the air like that?" she said. "And looking back our way?"

"Not sure," Bernie said. "He does that sometimes."

Humans — and I mean this in the nicest way — can be a little . . . slow sometimes. But at least I was now being included, which is how I like to roll. Just imagine if things were happening and you were stuck on the shelf. What a nightmare that would be!

I barked once or twice — no particular reason — and got back to work, which in this case meant going right up close to that wall socket and pointing it out to Bernie, meaning I went stiff, nose at the socket, tail way up.

"Chet? Found something, big guy?"

He came over, knelt beside me, peered at the socket, unplugged the lamp. "Got a screwdriver, Jeannine?"

Jeannine reached in her pocket, produced — hey! — a Swiss Army knife. We had one just like it at home, taken off a perp who'd tried to stab Bernie but had fumbled out the corkscrew attachment instead. We'd made him pay anyway — tempers rise in situations like that. Bernie unscrewed the socket cover and removed it. Now we had a nice little space, with a socket on one side — I kept my tongue off it, took hardly any effort at all — and a jar on the other, the sort of jar that might contain peanut butter — not a favorite of mine, way too sticky at the top of my mouth — although this jar was for something else, which was the whole reason I'd sniffed it out.

"Nice work, champ," Bernie said.

A powerful breeze arose, even though we were indoors. In no time at all I realized my tail had started up, kind of . . . bringing the outdoors inside? Wow! Was my mind on fire, or what? Plus my tail had a mind of its own, and it was on fire, too, so . . . so that was as far as I could go on this one.

"What is it?" Jeannine said.

Bernie lifted the jar out of the little space

in the wall and got to his feet. "Empty jar of hair gel," he said. "Country Gentleman brand, sixteen-ounce size." Bernie unscrewed the lid. Inside was a small envelope. Bernie slit it open with his fingernail, making a soft ripping sound I liked and don't hear often enough. He removed a little black silver-tipped gizmo of a kind I'd seen before on office desks.

"Flash drive?" Jeannine said.

"Have you got a computer?"

"Downstairs," said Jeannine. "But how did your dog know it was there?"

Now they were both looking at me, and just at the moment when I was seeing how far out I could flop my tongue. I tried to get things back to normal and pronto, but unflopping a tongue like mine takes time.

"I'm not really sure," Bernie said.

"Maybe flash drives give off a smell we're not aware of," said Jeannine.

Where to even begin? With smells humans aren't aware of? We'd never come to the end, no offense. How about flash drive smells? Of course, flash drives have a smell, pretty much the same plastic smell that comes off so many human things, a smell you can hardly ever get away from. But just because the hair gel jar was out of hair gel didn't mean it was out of hair gel scent, which was what I'd picked up. And wasn't hair gel part of the case? Chet the Jet, just doing his job. It wasn't that complicated.

"What's he doing with his tongue?" Jeannine said.

"Not sure about that either," said Bernie.

Jeannine opened her laptop on a table in the bar, stuck in the flash drive. Two pictures popped up on the screen. Hey! The people in the pictures looked kind of familiar. What a day I was having!

One of the pictures was an outdoors scene, a man and woman all dressed up and hugging each other on a snowy day, a strange building topped by two green party-hat sort of towers in the background.

Jeannine pointed to the man. "York?" she said.

"Ten or fifteen years ago, I'd estimate," Bernie said.

"I could swear I've seen that place before."

"Red Square," said Bernie. "In Moscow."

Jeannine pointed to the woman. "Is that a wedding dress under her coat?"

"Yup," Bernie said. "Their wedding day."

"York never mentioned a wife," said Jeannine.

"Here she is more recently," said Bernie, eyes shifting to the second picture.

Lizette? Yes, for sure, even though the picture was a bit blurry. But it was hard to miss her red hair, blown by a breeze. She was standing on a boat and not wearing much in the way of clothes. A silver-haired man stood at the wheel, his back to the camera.

"Looks like Chesapeake Bay," Jeannine said. "I can't quite make out the name on the stern."

"*Horsin' Around*," Bernie said.

"You've got great eyesight."

"More hindsight, in this case." He pocketed the flash drive.

"What do you mean?"

"Just that I'm slow," Bernie said, meaning he was giving Jeannine a little demonstration of his sense of humor. He counted out some money, laid it on the table. "Enough to fix up his room?"

"More than enough," Jeannine said. "But you don't have to do this."

"I'm the new tenant," Bernie said. "If anyone else wants to see the room, tell them to call me."

"Do you think that will happen?" Jeannine said.

"No."

We went outside. Our red-eyed pal was buffing the hood of the Porsche with a dirty rag.

"Got your shades?" he said. "You'll need 'em, shine I put on this."

"Uh," said Bernie, gazing in an unhappy way at that rag.

"Lots of riffraff been around, but I had your back."

"Thanks," Bernie said. "Here's the five bucks."

"How about ten?"

"We had a deal."

"Maybe, but it turned out harder than I thought."

"What are you talking about?"

"Din't I mention the riffraff?"

"I don't see any riffraff."

"Only because I put the fear of the lord in 'em." Our boozy buddy reached down his pants, pulled out a surprisingly long knife.

"Put that away."

The dude slid the thing back in his pants, maybe saying "ouch" as he did. All of a sudden he got angry, the way boozy buddies do. "Goddamn you, anyway. Child of privilege."

Then came a shock, namely Bernie getting angry, too. He grabbed the dude by his shirtfront, lifted him right off the ground. "You don't know what the hell you're talking about."

The dude's red eyes got very big, not a pleasant sight. "Okay, okay, put me down. Din't mean it, more like I was exaggeratin' for effect."

Bernie put him down.

The dude brushed himself off, gave Bernie a careful sideways scan. "Wasn't just riffraff neither."

"Huh?" said Bernie.

The dude looked down the block. "Major operator in a Mercedes come by, gave your ride the once-over, big-time. Mafia, trust me. I know all the made guys."

"Please," Bernie said.

"Think I'm talkin' through my hat?" said the dude, proving he didn't know Bernie at all. As if Bernie wouldn't notice the dude wasn't even wearing a hat? Bernie doesn't miss a thing like that, amigo. Meanwhile, the dude was pointing down the block again. "Speak of the devil."

The devil comes up from time to time in our work, but I hadn't actually met him yet, so the big silver car rolling slowly our way had all my attention. Then, as it came close, the driver hit the pedal and zoomed right past us, a little action sequence I'd seen before, always when some perp recognizes who's out there — namely us — too late.

Zoom, but not so zoomy that I didn't catch a glimpse of the man in the car, kind of a disappointment since it wasn't the devil after all. Instead, it was Suzie's suit-and-baseball-cap pal, the man rocking the interesting narrow-shoulder, big-head combo. The Sandman? Lanny Sands? Something like that.

We hopped in the car. What was this? Bernie actually hopping over the closed door? But that was Bernie. Just when you think he's done amazing you, he amazes you again.

"Where you goin'?" said the boozy dude. "What about my money?"

"Here's ten — you earned it," Bernie said, thrusting a bill at him and stomping on the gas.

"What the hell?" the dude shouted after us.

I looked back. The dude was waving some reddish bit of paper. Bernie checked the mirror. "Christ," he said. "Did I give him a fifty-pound note?"

A fifty-pound note? I wondered what that might be. Something not good: that was clear from the way the dude was ripping it to shreds and flinging those red shreds to the wind, a pretty sight. There's all kinds of beauty in life.

Twenty-Nine

"Château Frontenac's in Quebec City, not Montreal, Chet," Bernie said, as we sped after the silver car, a Mercedes, if I was getting this right. "And would it be possible to live there and not know of the Expos, no matter how — what did she say? Unsporty? — no matter how unsporty your family was? See where we're going with this?"

Did I see where we were going? Absolutely! We were going after that silver Mercedes, meaning this was a car chase, one of our specialties, and it had been way too long since the last one, which had ended, I now remembered and wished I hadn't, with the Porsche we'd had then flying off a cliff, with both of us in it, at least for a moment or two.

Nothing like that was in our near future. No cliffs around, for one thing, and Lanny Sands was not much of a wheelman — easy to tell by the way he took the turn at the end of the block, fishtailing across to the wrong side of the street. A good wheelman — and Bernie's the best there is, goes without mentioning — doesn't let the car take over — Bernie says that every time he gives Charlie a driving lesson, always so much fun, me in the shotgun seat, Charlie in Bernie's lap, his little hands on the wheel, Bernie's own hands in his pockets — even makes you feel you're going slower than you really are. Then you happen to glance to the side, and everything's a blur! That'll get the fur standing up on the back of your neck, no matter who you are.

We came to the end of the block, took the turn with a kind of snapping motion that shot us down this new street even faster than we'd come in, all this with Bernie sitting back, just a couple of fingers on the wheel. Meanwhile up ahead, Lanny Sands checked his mirror, swerved one way, then another, straightened out, and flew down a long slope crossed by railroad tracks at the bottom, faster and faster. Faster and faster, but we homed in anyway, nice and gentle, practically right on his bumper. Bump him, Bernie! Lanny Sands checked his mirror again, didn't look happy to see us so up close and personal. Bernie didn't bump him, even though we've had a lot of success with bumping dudes in the past, instead made the pat-pat slow-down motion with his hand.

"Don't want him to get hurt," he said. He glanced at the road ahead. "Hope no damn tra—"

I never got to hear Bernie's hope; too bad, because his hopes turn into my hopes, and I like having a hope or two in mind. I was just picking between bacon bits and steak tips when a *ding-ding-ding* started up at the railroad crossing, the red light flashed — but don't take my word for it on the red part, Bernie's belief being that I'm not at my sharpest when it comes to red — and the black-and-white barrier swung slowly down. And Lanny Sands? He was glued to the rearview mirror again! Or still!

"For Christ sake!" Bernie said, as a train rumbled into view, a towering sort of train, or maybe it just looked towering because we were so close. He started honking the horn, waving his arms around, pointing at the train, now pounding into the crossing. At last, when it was almost too late, Lanny Sands faced front, saw what was happening, and hit the brakes with everything he had — easy to tell when a guy hits the brakes with everything he has by how he rises right up out his seat, head ramming the roof — and the next thing I saw was the Mercedes doing doughnuts as it spun right into the crossing. But no, not quite right in: at the last moment, just when something really bad was about to happen between car and train, the Mercedes struck the post that held up the barrier, knocking the whole contraption to the ground, and came spinning back toward where we'd come to a complete stop, near but not too near the track, rocking very slightly. But spinning right at us — that was the point — and almost on us! Bernie reached over and grabbed me and — was it possible? — threw me right out of the car, to the side and out of danger. I was still in midair when the Mercedes hit the curb in front of us, changed direction, slammed into a phone pole, and came to a dead stop, the hood popping up and steam boiling high. The train roared on through and things got quiet.

We ran over to the Mercedes, me and Bernie, side by side. The driver's-side door opened with a horrible shrieking sound — the kind that rips through my ears and all the way down my spine, buzzing inside me — and fell right off. Lanny Sands came squeezing out from between the airbags, and stood up in a wobbly sort of way.

"Easy, there, Lanny," Bernie said. "Are you all right?"

A bit wobbly, baseball cap knocked sideways, like he was some kind of gangbanger, and a tiny trickle of blood at the corner of his mouth, but Sands looked all right to me. Nice neat suit, tie knotted and straight, clean shirt that was basically blue except of the white collar and white cuffs, shoes shined and gleaming.

He glared at Bernie. "You're the worst kind of asshole," he said.

"The kind who thinks he's smarter than he is?" said Bernie.

"That, too," said Sands. He dabbed at the corner of his mouth, gazed at his hand, wiped it off on a curve of the airbag that was sticking out of the car. "I meant your whole cowboy approach, so yesteryear."

Bernie a cowboy? What a crazy idea! His opinion of horses had to be the same as mine — prima donnas, every one — and he'd only been on a horse once in his life, the reason those lovely eyebrows of his didn't match, one with a scar through the middle, quite tiny and hardly noticeable.

"Then help me out," Bernie said. "Show me the modern way."

"What are you talking about?"

"Start with Suzie Sanchez."

"What about her?"

"Where is she?"

"No idea," said Sands. "Is she missing?"

"You didn't know?"

"Why would I? All I know is that I told her to be patient. Evidently she ignored my advice."

"Patient about what?"

"Not going to get into that," Sands said. "I promised her the story when it was time. Can't do any more than that."

"A story about General Galloway?" Bernie said. "Or sleepers? Or both?"

Sands said nothing.

Bernie reached out and straightened his cap, Sands leaning away but too slow.

"Did you actually play baseball for Harvard?" Bernie said.

"I covered sports for the *Crimson,*" Sands said. "Not that it makes any difference."

"No?" said Bernie, moving slightly closer to Sands. I did the same, got the sweet moving-in feeling that often came before grabbing the perp by the pant leg, which was how our cases usually ended. Sands backed up, but not far, what with his car, still steaming, right behind him. "How come you were sitting on that place, York's or Carbonneau's or whatever his real name is?"

"Sitting on?" said Sands.

Whoa! He didn't know "sitting on," one of our best techniques at the Little Detective Agency? Bernie explained what it was. I didn't really listen, more interested in that trickle of blood at the corner of Sands's mouth, which seemed to have started up again. His blood had a strangely powerful smell, way too strong for that tiny amount, if that made any sense, and it didn't, not at the time.

"I happened to be passing by," Sands said.

"I'll throw you a bone," said Bernie. Now we were getting somewhere! I crouched, ready to spring in any direction. But no bone appeared. Instead, Bernie went on, "If you've been keeping an eye on him, you can stop. He's gone and he's never coming back."

Sands shook his head. "The moron. He fell for the dream."

"What dream?" Bernie said.

"The American dream, what else?" Sands said. "There's never been a plan that couldn't be screwed up by human emotions."

"Such as?

"Jealousy, in this case."

"York got jealous?"

Sands opened his mouth to answer but at that moment got distracted by something on the front of his shirt. What was this? A tiny piece of metal, like the end of a narrow pipe? He gave it a gentle tug, and out it came. Not so tiny. And then: blood. It gushed out like from a hose on full blast.

Sands sank to his knees and toppled over onto the reddening street. Bernie knelt beside him, pressed his hands on Sands's chest. Blood poured right through his fingers, a terrible sight, on and on. Sands gave Bernie a look like he was going to ask for something. Then his eyes stopped seeing, the blood stopped flowing, and he lost the smell of the living.

Bernie found a coat in the trunk of the Mercedes, covered the Sandman from the top of his head to about his knees. I sniffed at the blood on Bernie's hands. It bothered me. He wiped them off on the coat, then took out his phone and called Lieutenant Soares. We didn't stick around.

"Suzie? Suzie?"

No answer.

We were back at Suzie's place, going from room to room, opening every closet, finding zip. I could smell Bernie's sweat, not the nice, fresh kind that goes with hiking, but the sharper kind that goes with being nervous. Some humans are nervous all of time, all humans are nervous some of the time, and no human, not even Bernie, although he's close, are nervous none of the time. I pressed against him every chance I got, just letting him know . . . something or other; I couldn't think what.

He looked down at me.

"We're lost, big guy."

That had to be a mistake. I'd been lost once or twice before in my life, but always when I was alone. How could I be lost now? I was with Bernie. And he was with me.

Bernie went to the sink in Suzie's kitchen, splashed water on his face. I went to my water bowl in the corner and lapped some up. Water helps you feel better, as I hope everyone knows.

Bernie looked at me, his face wet and glistening. He can look frightening at times, if you don't know him. "Come on, Chet," he said. "Let's get aggressive."

I loved the sound of that! It was a kind of love I felt most strongly in my teeth, impossible to explain why. We marched over to Lizette's house and pounded on the door, Bernie doing the actual pounding, me pounding in my mind.

THIRTY

In pounding-on-the-door situations, you have to be ready for just about anything. Shotgun blast right through it, for example? It happens. But not this time. No shotgun blast, no huge shaved-head dudes bursting out with cleavers raised high, no drunk shouting, "Nobody home" at the top of his lungs. Instead, we had silence. Bernie leaned forward and — what was this? Put his ear to the door? Like — like he was listening real hard for some sounds inside. I wondered what he was picking up. All I heard was a running toilet, no surprise, toilet running being a big human problem, found in just about every house I've ever been in. Once Bernie had gotten so fed up, he'd tried to install a new toilet on his own. What a day that had been! I've always been interested in toilets, by the way. Sometimes you can find the very freshest water in them — and sometimes not.

"Quiet as a tomb," Bernie said, possibly missing that running toilet. He took out a credit card. Hadn't I come close to seeing Bernie's credit card move recently? I sort of remembered it in his hand, and then some door had opened and out had come a UPS dude, making it easy for us. I hoped that wasn't about to happen now, although I'm fond of UPS dudes in general, especially the ones who drive around with treats in their pockets. No need to stop or even slow down, UPS buddy — just toss it out the open door! And all at once, I really was hoping a UPS dude would step out of Lizette's house.

Bernie stuck the credit card in the crack at the side of the door and popped it right — but no. The door didn't pop right open. Whoa! This was a first, and not of the good kind. Bernie worked the card up and down, wriggled it around, took a breath, started over. Taking a breath and starting over was one of our best techniques at the Little Detective Agency, much more Bernie's thing than mine. How do you stop once you've started? A complete mystery to me. Meanwhile, Lizette's front door wasn't opening.

Bernie stepped back. "This is no ordinary door, big guy," he said. He stepped back a little more and lowered his shoulder. That meant Bernie was about to smash the door to smithereens! You see smithereens in my job from time to time, one of my favorite sights. Was I up on my back legs, kind of jumping up and down with excitement? Uh-oh. Not professional: I got a grip, and pronto. Bernie lunged forward and then came a deep thud that seemed to shake the whole house, and Bernie — Bernie bounced straight back? "Ow," he said. The door looked exactly the same as before, not a smithereen in evidence.

"Nothing ordinary about it," Bernie said, rubbing his shoulder. "And why would anyone even the least bit ordinary have a fortified door like this?"

I had no answer, in fact, couldn't recall the question. All I knew was that the running toilet now sounded a bit louder.

"What are you barking about?"

Me? If I was barking, no sure thing, although I amped it right down just in case, it had to be on account of that running toilet and how thirsty it was making me.

"Someone's inside after all?"

Not exactly, but maybe close enough. We're a team, me and Bernie, and always will be.

We walked around the house to the

screened-in porch. Bernie peered inside. "See that door that leads into the house? You can bet the ranch it'll be a clone of the front one."

At the moment, we didn't have a ranch, although Bernie often said he'd like one someday. But how would we ever have a ranch if we lost it in a bet before it was even ours? This was confusing.

". . . sake of argument, let's suppose," Bernie was saying, "we just went ahead and did something that was bound to trigger the alarm system. Think the cops'll come barreling up?" With no warning at all, he threw a beautiful right cross at a section of the screen. We've watched a lot of boxing in our time — don't even get me started on the Thrilla in Manila — plus Bernie knew what he was doing with his fists, so it was no surprise that the screen ripped wide open. We went right through that opening, me — after a brief moment of confusion — first.

Bernie glanced around while I had a quick hard listen, picked up the running toilet as well as a new beeping, very quiet, somewhere in the walls. "And if tearing out the screen didn't trigger the alarm," Bernie said, striding across the room to the door that led into the house, "how about this?" He took out the gun. The gun? Which one was this? So many to keep track of. First, before we'd even gotten started, there'd been our .38 Special, now at the bottom of the sea; after that, the pink-handled popgun, found in the flower pot by Mr. Ferretti; and the gun now in Bernie's hand, taken from Mr. Ferretti's woman pal by me, Chet the Jet. Wow! Had I remembered the whole thing? The case was as good as closed. How about right now we grab Suzie, hop in the car, and zoom on back to the Valley, music blasting all the way, starting with "The Road Goes On Forever and the Party Never Ends"? A great idea, one of my very best, but . . . but where was Suzie? That was when I realized we had a problem. My tail realized it, too, and went all droopy. I got it back up, nice and stiff. We were pros and on the job, after all, my tail and me.

Meanwhile, Bernie had the gun pointed at the inner door, right near the knob. "Cover your ears," he said, which had to be one of his jokes. How would I do that, exactly? I was still wondering when he pulled the trigger. *BLAM!* Cover my ears even if I could? No way! Not with gunplay sounds in the air. Plus we had the bonus sights of splintering wood, the whole knob and lots of metal parts flying here and there, and the door sagging open. There's all kinds of beauty in life, sorry if I'm mentioning that so soon after the last mention. But controlling when beauty shows up? Who can do that?

Back inside Lizette's house, and everything seemed different from the night of the party. Was it just because then was night and now was day? That's always a big deal to humans, not so much in the nation within. How about the fact that there'd been lots of noise and now we had silence, except for the running toilet, the faint beeping behind the walls no longer sounding. Maybe, but there was more to it than that. Call it a feeling. We sometimes get feelings in the nation within, feelings that come out of nowhere, but no time for that now.

"Where do people like to hide things, big guy?" Bernie said. What a question! I'd seen just about everything, including a perp who hid a diamond ring up his nose. We were just about to let him go when he turned out to be allergic to me and my kind — something I really don't like in a human — and had a sneezing fit, the diamond ring caught by Bernie in midair . . . "basements and bedrooms," he was saying. "Let's start in the basement."

Not a lot in the way of basements where I come from, so this was new to me, and I'm always up for new, except for doors not smashing to smithereens when Bernie bashes them. Were all basements like Lizette's, with washer and drier and water heater and some other machinery I didn't know over on one side and lots of boxes, furniture, suitcases on the other? I had no clue, just knew it was nice and cool down here, plus the running toilet sound was much louder, coming from behind a door behind a rack of dresses.

That was where Bernie started, with the dresses. He looked through them, checking the labels. "Kind of pricey, is my guess," Bernie said. "What does she do, ostensibly? Something in IT?" He moved on to another rack, this one hung with men's suits. "These would be Jean-Luc's," he said. "Also pricey. Left over from their married life? Or waiting here in case their married life resumes? Meanwhile, he's been living in that crap hole above the bar." He turned to me. "See where I'm going with this?" I did not. "Actually," he went on, "I'm not sure I do myself." Had to love that Bernie! Not just because of how alike we were, but also on account of all the interesting things he said, like "crap hole," for example.

He turned to the boxes and suitcases, started going through them. All sorts of stuff came out and was soon scattered around the basement — more clothes, books, sheets, blankets, CDs — but Bernie didn't seem interested in any of it. "Is this a we'll-know-it-when-we-see-it?" he said. "I hate those."

Whatever they were, I hated them, too. I made my way toward the running toilet sound. By now that water had to be as fresh as it comes, and my mouth was drier than a dust storm, of which I'd seen plenty.

"Chet? What are you doing over there?" Bernie came closer. "Smell something?"

Well, of course I smelled the water, one of the best smells there is — although easy to forget, on account of it being in the air most of the time — but really it was the sound that had drawn me.

Bernie cocked his head, like he was trying to hear better. "Is that a toilet running?" He drew the gun, walked up to the door and threw it open, gun raised for trouble waiting on the other side.

But there was no trouble, just a small empty bathroom with a toilet and a sink and a bare towel rack. The toilet cover was down. Bernie raised it, gazed into the bowl, jiggled the handle, first step in toilet repair. The toilet kept running.

"Imagine how much water gets wasted

this way," he said. "A big system, yes, but finite. What's so hard to understand about that?"

All of it, in my opinion, and even more, if that makes any sense. I nosed around Bernie, dipped my head in the bowl and lapped up cool, clear water, just about the best I'd ever tasted. This burg — Foggy Bottom, if I was getting things right — had lots going for it. Lovely water, for starters, and after that . . . I'm sure something will come to me eventually.

Bernie reached over me, took the lid off the tank, something in the tank often being the problem, and I certainly hoped so this time, because the next step — removing the whole toilet — was where the trouble began.

Bernie peered into the tank. I got my head right next to his and did the same, and there we were, peering together, side by side, our heads touching, our minds practically . . . one! What a thought!

The only water in the tank was at the bottom, a tiny trickle running in from one side and draining out under a raised flap in the middle. "Float stuck, as per usual," Bernie said. "What are we dealing with here, eighteenth-century technology? How many ball cocks are jammed just like this in the country right now? Hundreds of thousands?

We're doomed." He reached into the tank, grabbed the round metal thing — had to be the float — and raised it.

"That's funny," he said, pausing, hand still on the float. "Did I feel something shift in there? What's in a float except air?"

I had no idea. Bernie unscrewed the float, held it up, peered into the little hole. "Hmmm," he said. Then he put the float on the floor and stamped on it, not hard. The metal flattened out, came apart. Bernie bent down, went through the pieces, picked up a baggie. Inside were two sort of books, thin and small, with reddish covers. Bernie took them out, leafed through them.

"Russian passports, big guy," he said. "What would I do without you?"

I didn't understand the question.

Bernie turned the pages of the passports. "Mostly in Cyrillic, but there's some English here and there, maybe a *glasnost* development."

Wow! Whatever was going down, this was Bernie at his smartest. The air in the little bathroom felt just the way it does before lightning flashes across the sky. I crouched down on the floor, no fan of lightning, myself.

"His real name is Alexei Urmanov, and she's Yekaterina Urmanova, meaning the marriage is genuine. Genuine Russian sleepers, Chet, plus . . ." He tapped the passports on his palm, glanced at me. "What are you doing down —"

I barked, real loud, real sharp. Bernie jumped back. "Whoa! You scared me."

Oh, no! How was that even possible? But no time to think about it now because I'd heard knocking on the front door. I raced out of the bathroom, through the basement and up the stairs, Bernie following, to judge from the huffing and puffing at my heels.

THIRTY-ONE

I got to the front door before Bernie, stood straight and stiff, all my muscles taut — a nice feeling when you're the physical type. Outside a woman called, "Lizette? You there?" I went back and forth on the question of whether to bark, and was still doing it, faster and faster, when Bernie caught up. He stuck the gun in his pocket, keeping his hand in there, and opened the door.

Yes, a woman, a very interesting woman who brought with her scents of the nation within, plus cats, gerbils, parakeets, horses, and also guinea pigs, which was no surprise, since she was carrying one of the little critters in a cage, a chubby dude with a white face and eyes that looked alert and stupid at the same time, if that makes any sense. There's one kind of human who smells like this woman and one only, namely the vet kind. Parked in the driveway was a typical vet sort of van, decorated with a panel picture showing one of my kind who appeared to be cuddling with a cat, which is a typical sort of vet van picture, hard to explain.

"Uh, hi," the vet said, looking up at Bernie. "Is Lizette home?"

"Not at the moment," Bernie said.

"That's funny," the vet said. "I told her I'd be dropping by with Barnum." She raised the cage.

"I can take him," Bernie said, removing his hand, now gunless, from his pocket.

The vet hesitated, her mouth open and ready for speech but none coming out. Her gaze fell on me. And it was a sight she liked! I could see it in her eyes.

"Say hi to Chet," Bernie said.

The vet smiled. "He's quite the looker."

And so was she, despite those extra chins!

"Lizette did mention something, come to think of it," Bernie said. "I'm an old friend."

"Oh?"

"Of both of them, actually — Lizette and Jean-Luc."

The vet stopped smiling. Her face darkened and her eyes narrowed, plus her neck went red.

"Is there a problem?" Bernie said.

"Tell him to keep his goddamn hands off her," the vet said.

"I'm sorry?" Bernie said.

"Maybe I shouldn't be saying it, but somebody has to," the vet said. "The bastard gave her a black eye last month."

"She told you that?"

"I saw it," the vet said, "the first time she brought Barnum in with his problem. She wouldn't admit it, of course — that's how these things work. I volunteer at a shelter for abused women."

"All right," Bernie said. "I'll tell him."

"You will?"

He nodded.

"Thanks," said the vet. "Men have to get involved."

"Uh-huh."

There was a pause, and then she handed over the cage. "Barnum's been fed for today," she said. "Just make sure he's got water."

"Okay," said Bernie. Barnum looked up at Bernie, made some squeaky sounds. "What was his problem?"

"Running lice," said the vet.

Bernie put the cage on the floor — quickly, but nothing you could call simply letting go.

"A stubborn case, which was why I kept him three days," the vet said, "but I won't charge for the last one." She headed for her van, got in. We watched her drive away.

"Not what I expected, big guy," Bernie said.

I was with him on that. No way I'd expected Barnum. He made some more squeaky sounds, squeakier than before, his alert, stupid gaze glued to me, as though . . . as though I might be fixing to pounce on the cage, possibly upending it and pawing the door open and after that the way would be clear for anything I wanted to —

"What I'd expected was whoever's on the end of Lizette's security system," he went on, losing me immediately. "Instead —"

A car — and not just any car, but a Porsche, and although maybe not as old as ours, it was still nice enough: you can't have everything, as humans often say, actually a bit of a puzzler to me — came down the street, slowed, and started turning into Lizette's driveway. At that moment, the driver saw us, meaning me, Bernie, and Barnum — in the doorway. What was this? She was having a bad reaction, mouth opening wide, like we weren't a pleasant sight? My first guess: it was somehow on account of Barnum. Then I noticed those strange glasses she was wearing — cat's-eye, not a look that appeals to me, but not the point. The point was I'd seen this woman — an older woman of a certain type — hey! Bernie's mom was that same certain type — with swept-back wings of white-and-black hair, a very nice color combo, in my opinion, and not just on account of it being mine, too, although mostly. But forget all that, forget the whole thing going back to the cat's-eye woman and the fact that I'd seen her before. I was trying to remember when and where, or at least one of them, when she swerved out of the driveway entrance and shot off, maybe even heavier on the pedal than Lanny Sands, but there was not even a hint of fishtailing in her case.

"C'mon, big guy," Bernie said. "This is starting to make sense."

What great news! We hopped into the car — me behind the wheel, kind of crazy, how had that even happened? — got everything sorted out, wheeled around and —

And a patrol car came roaring up the street. It braked to a shrieking stop, blocking the driveway. Lieutenant Soares jumped out of the passenger side door. Bernie turned the wheel hard, cut across the grass, passed Soares and his ride, and we were almost on the street when another cruiser blew in, blocking us again. Bernie pulled over. Cops swarmed toward us, guns drawn. Bernie didn't even look at them: his gaze was distant, up the street in the direction the cat's-eye woman had gone. He leaned forward, squinting at her car. "HNX four nine one?" he said. The cat's-eye woman rounded a corner and vanished from sight. "Or was that a seven?"

The cops surrounded us. Bernie touched the back of my neck.

"Easy, big guy."

Soares stepped forward, his raisin eyes like two dark specks of rage. Whoa! What a horrible thought! I wanted to look away but couldn't.

"What the hell are you trying to pull?" Soares said.

"Who writes your dialogue?" Bernie said, losing me completely, but maybe not Soares. His arm came up like he was going to give Bernie a backhander across the face. I'd once seen a dude actually do that to Bernie; he'd regretted it the very next thing, and maybe Soares knew that, because he lowered his hand. He also lowered his voice, but the anger still came out, if that makes any sense, in the form of flying spit spray, always an interesting sight.

"Any idea who you abandoned on the road up in Ivy City?"

"I abandoned a dead body," Bernie said. "And I called it in."

"Like that's good enough?" Soares said. "Hand over that goddamn license."

Bernie gave him a folded-up sheet of paper. Soares ripped it to shreds. Everyone was ripping things to shreds on us these days. Was there any way that could be a good sign?

"You don't need me to tell you he was speeding and didn't see the train until it was too late," Bernie said.

"True," Soares said. "I need you to tell me why he was speeding."

"You haven't figured that out?" Bernie said.

"You were chasing him."

Bernie nodded.

"Why?" Soares said.

"Because I suspected he had information regarding the murder of Eben St. John. The fact that he ran confirms it."

Soares leaned in a little closer, lowered his voice some more. "Why would someone like him know anything about this case?"

"That's the question," Bernie said.

Soares leaned in even more. From that distance, they could have almost . . . kissed each other, a thought that made no sense at all. Then Soares said, "You know your problem? You're too cute." And for a crazy moment, the kissing idea did sort of make sense. But then no kiss happened, and also the truth was that although Bernie was pretty much the best-looking human on the planet, you really couldn't call him cute. "Get out of town," Soares said. "Don't come back."

He and the rest of the cops got into their cruisers and drove off. The kissing thing hadn't made sense after all, although I wasn't sure why. Given enough time, I might have figured it out, but there's never enough time, so I didn't even try.

Were we getting out of town? I wasn't sure about that either. For a while, we just sat there at the end of Lizette's driveway, me and Bernie alone with his thoughts, all of them dark and anxious. After a while, he got on the phone.

"William," he said. "Bernie here. I'm going to push our friendship a bit."

William's deep and booming oil-drum voice came through the speakers. "Don't see how that could be possible," he said. "But try me."

"I want to run another plate."

"Nothing easier. Putting you on hold."

We waited. Bernie stopped thinking, leaving just the two of us, me and him. What a peaceful moment! Would I have minded if it had gone on forever? Actually, yes. Wouldn't we get hungry eventually? There was no food in the car. I went back to enjoying the peaceful moment, but it was gone.

William came back on. "That's a diplomatic plate, Bernie. Registered to one Ludmilla Lysenko, employed at the Russian-American Investment Advisory Council. That's on A Street. Here's the number."

"Thanks," Bernie said, writing it on the palm of his hand. "And I'm happy to pay your contact at the DMV whatever you think is right."

"Not necessary," said William. "But I'll pass on your thanks when I see her."

"You see her?"

"Possibly tonight."

"Ah."

"Russian-American Investment Advisory Council," Bernie said, parking in front of a nice-looking brick row house on a shady block of nice-looking brick row houses. "Could it sound more innocuous?"

I had no idea. I did hear plenty of sounds, but they were the normal street sounds you pick up in a big city, none of them coming specifically from the Russian-American Investment Advisory Council row house. We got out of the car, went up to the front door. Bernie pressed the buzzer. I heard it buzz inside the house, but no one came. Bernie tried the knob. The door was unlocked, kind of a surprise. We went inside.

It turned out to be kind of homey. First came a softly lit hall with a thick rug, lovely-smelling flowers in a vase, pictures on the walls, most of them showing dressed-up people shaking hands. Then on one side, the space opened up into an office where a young gum-chewing woman sat at a desk, eyes on a screen, hands on a keyboard, ear buds in her ears, music leaking out in a tiny sort of way.

"Hello?" Bernie said, as we approached her desk. She tapped away at the keyboard, eyes still on the screen, and popped her gum, a sound I happen to like very much. Pop it again, young lady! But she did not. Bernie rapped his knuckles on the desk.

The young woman looked up gasping and putting a hand over her chest, the way humans do when you startle them. I'd once seen a dude swallow his gum in exactly this kind of situation, but the young woman, maybe a better gum chewer, had it under control. She whipped out the ear buds.

"Oh, my God," she said, taking us in, Bernie first, then me. "You scared me."

"We buzzed," Bernie said.

"Sorry," the young woman said. She took a tissue from a box on the desk, brought it to her mouth, sort of tongued the gum into it, and tossed the balled-up tissue into a wastebasket. It took all my self-control not to go nosing over there. "Can I help you?" she said.

"Your English is very good," Bernie said.

"Thanks," she said. "I went to college here in America."

"Which one?"

"Go Buckeyes."

Bernie laughed. "What's your name? I'm Bernie and this is Chet."

"What a beautiful dog! My name's Sonia."

Sonia? A very nice name, and she was clearly a very sharp young lady. Our friendship was off to a great start.

"Ludmilla Lysenko's English is good, too, but not like yours," Bernie said. "Where did she go to school?"

Or maybe we weren't off to quite the start I'd thought. Sonia sat back in her chair, not so friendly anymore, also looking somewhat older. "I'm not sure I understand your question."

"Not a problem," Bernie said. "I'll ask her myself. Is she in?"

"I — I'd have to check."

"Please do. Here's our card."

Bernie handed it to her. Sonia spent what seemed like a long time reading it, then said, "If she's in, can I tell her what this is in reference to?"

"Sure," said Bernie. He took out the two red passports we'd found in the float of Lizette's basement toilet and opened them so Sonia could see. "It's in reference to the Urmanovs."

Sonia opened her mouth, closed it, tried again. "Maybe I should take those with me, just in case she's in her office?"

Bernie shook his head.

Sonia rose, left the room, went in the hall. I heard her climbing stairs, and then came the sound of low voices from the floor above. Bernie went around the desk, started going through the drawers. I took a step or two over to the wastebasket, took out the balled-up tissue with the gum inside, nudged it around for a bit, felt better about everything.

Sonia returned, saw what Bernie was doing. "Excuse me?" she said.

Bernie closed the drawer, in no hurry at all. He gave her his empty gaze, the scariest of all Bernie's gazes. Sonia tried to meet it and failed, like so many others, no shame there. Bernie moved toward her. She backed away.

"Ms. Lysenko is not in. Is it money you want?"

"No," Bernie said. How true that was! For the very first time I really understood why our finances were such a mess. And always would be! Whoa! "But I'll trade the passports for Suzie Sanchez."

Sonia picked up the desk phone, spoke words I didn't understand at all, except for "Suzie Sanchez." She hung up, turned to Bernie. "We know no one of that name."

"Who's we?" Bernie said.

"The Russian-American Investment Advisory Council," said Sonia.

Bernie laughed. I wasn't sure what he was laughing at — and Sonia looked pretty clueless on that score, too — but it was always nice to see him in a good mood.

"Do svidaniya," he said, a totally new one on me.

We went outside, got in the car, drove down the block, did a U-ee, and parked in a shady spot with a not-too-distant view of the Russian-American Investment Advisory Council town house.

Day started to fade. Bernie and I sat side by side, just enjoying darkness taking over. After a while, a big black car double-parked by the town house, had barely stopped before the town house door opened and two men hurried out, both carrying roller bags. They jumped in the black car and it took off.

"Next stop, Moscow," Bernie said. We stayed where we were. I went over the Moscow thing in my mind, and was still going over it when the town house door opened again and Sonia came out, wearing a backpack. She crossed the street and walked our way real fast, eyes straight ahead, everything about her intense. Bernie got out of the car and stepped onto the sidewalk. Sonia almost bumped into him. He grabbed her wrist, held it in a way I could tell was not particularly forceful for Bernie, but her struggles got her nowhere.

"Let me go," she said.

"Scream for help," said Bernie.

But Sonia did not.

"You should have gone with the others," Bernie told her.

"The goddamn flight was full," Sonia said. "I'm on the next one."

"Nope," said Bernie. "And your life as you knew it is over."

THIRTY-TWO

This is how we like to roll, and almost always do: Bernie behind the wheel and me, Chet the Jet, in the shotgun seat. Sometimes — not very often, you might say, but way too often, in my opinion — we need room for one more. That means somebody — Bernie, this extra and somewhat troublesome person, or me — has to ride on the little shelf in the back, which is where I now was, Sonia having taken my place in the shotgun seat. Bear in mind that I'm a hundred-plus pounder, and Sonia was one of those slender young ladies who'd topple right over if just bumped lightly. The problem of how to administer that light bump from where I was occupied all my thoughts.

Meanwhile, we hadn't actually moved, were still parked on this nice shady street, like we had nowhere to go and nothing to do. I knew that wasn't right. First of all, where was Suzie? Second of all, there were lots of other problems, too many to sort out.

"Ever killed anyone?" Bernie said, eyes straight ahead.

Sonia, who'd been staring straight ahead as well, turned quickly in his direction. Was that a tear track on her face? I hadn't heard her crying; maybe she was one of those silent criers, a mysterious kind of subgroup. All I knew for sure was that tears taste salty. "Of course not," she said. "What do you take me for?"

Bernie turned to her, but slowly. "That's what we're determining," he said. "Ever cause anyone to be killed?"

"No."

"Ever fail to prevent someone getting killed?"

Sonia's gaze, still aimed in Bernie's direction, took on a faraway look. Bernie's gaze did the reverse, if that makes any sense, closing in.

"No," Sonia said, at last and very softly.

"Close call, huh?" Bernie said. Sonia's neck turned red, something you see in women but never men. What was it about? You tell me. "Don't worry about it," Bernie said. "If people could just get the easy calls right, we'd be fine."

Sonia nodded, very slightly. "What are you going to do with me?"

"That's what we're determining." Hadn't Bernie just said that? Once I had a dream where a bowl of steak tips appeared and I scarfed them all up and then — presto! The bowl was somehow full again. This was like that, except not so tasty.

"I don't understand," Sonia said. "I don't even know who you are."

"I'm the loose cannon," Bernie said.

How great did that sound! But why just him? I wanted to be a loose cannon, too. I thumped my tail on the horrible shelf where I was marooned, just once, but heavy enough to send a message.

Bernie's eyes flickered my way, and he went on. "What's going to happen to your two buddies from the office when they get back to Moscow?"

Sonia shrugged.

"I'm guessing their careers are over," Bernie said.

She nodded, just a little nod, hardly noticeable.

"Do you have family back there?"

"Not close."

"You like it here?"

Another very slight nod.

"Here's the deal," Bernie said. "Help us find Suzie Sanchez, and I'll do what I can for you."

"What does that mean?"

"Not much. But what's your alternative?"

"You could let me go."

"Not happening."

She glanced sideways, toward her door.

"And that would be pointless," Bernie said. "No one outruns Chet."

You won't hear anything truer than that, amigo! I was considering unwedging myself from my perch and giving the back of Bernie's neck a quick lick, when Sonia looked my way.

"I always wanted a dog."

"Breeders contact me about Chet from time to time."

Breeders? About me? I wondered what that was about. It sounded extremely interesting, definitely something to sort out, nail down, get my mind around. While I got going on that, a back-and-forth started up between Bernie and Sonia.

". . . and I could have one of the puppies?" she was saying when I tuned back in.

"Pick of the litter," Bernie said.

Then came a long silence. A strange feeling came over me, a feeling of being very small and cuddled up in a sort of ball with others of my closest kind, also very small. Not sure what that was about, but I could just about smell it; in fact, I could.

Sonia took a deep breath. Was this an interview? Was Sonia a perp? I watch for deep perp breaths when Bernie's doing one of his interviews: it means we're winning. We like winning, me and Bernie.

"I never knew anything about Lizette and Jean-Luc, other than rumors of their existence," she said. "None of us did, except for Ludmilla."

"That's what you called them? Not the Urmanovs?"

Sonia nodded. "By the time they surfaced, they'd been in so deep and so long they weren't really the Urmanovs anymore."

Bernie turned the key. "Where to?" he said.

"It's only a guess," Sonia said.

"I bet you're a good guesser."

"That makes you one of a kind," said Sonia. "But there's a place they use, Ludmilla and Lizette."

Bernie put us in gear and we were on the move, the seating arrangement still messed up. But at least Sonia was sharp enough to realize that Bernie's one of a kind. Me, too. We're one of the same kind, if I haven't mentioned that already.

Chesapeake Bay? Was that it? I tried to keep track of what Sonia was saying, not easy with so much to look at now that we were out in dark country, water over on Bernie's side, darker than the land except when the clouds moved away to let the moon shine down, and then countless tiny watery moons appeared. All that, and I haven't even gotten to the smells, many of them salty, and probably won't have time. But here's something interesting: when the moon went back behind the clouds, the smells got stronger. What's that all about? The moon sniffs up lots of smells so there's less for everybody else? That was as far as I could take it.

". . . sleepers," Sonia was saying. "It was an operation that dates back several administrations in our bureau. They lived completely normal American lives, had no contact at all with any kind of control. And then Lizette finally found something useful to do."

"Who knew about it?" Bernie said.

"What Lizette was up to? Only Ludmilla at first, then the rest of us."

"Meaning at your cute little setup on A Street."

Sonia nodded.

"What about on our side?" Bernie said.

"Our side?"

"The American side. Did anyone on this end know about Lizette and Jean-Luc?"

Sonia was silent.

"Eben St. John, for example," Bernie said.

Sonia turned to him. "I knew nothing. Not until after the fact."

"You're protesting your innocence too much," Bernie said. "It arouses doubts."

"I'm telling you the truth," she said, her eyes tearing up. The moon came out and shone on a tendril of hair that wound around her ear, a very nice sight.

"It's your only hope," Bernie said.

She pulled back, as though trying to increase the space between her and Bernie. Who would want to do that?

"How did Eben find out?"

"I don't know," Sonia said. "Please believe me."

We entered a small town — gas station, motel, a few stores and houses, nothing lit up except the motel.

"Slow down," Sonia said. "It's the next left."

"And then?"

"First gravel driveway after you reach the bay. The house is on a bluff."

Bernie stopped the car. "Any chance Ludmilla's gone back to Russia?"

"Only if she's found Jean-Luc. She's been looking for him twenty-four seven."

Bernie backed up, into the motel lot,

empty except for us. "Rent a room. Don't leave. We'll come back for you."

"And if you don't?"

"Then you're screwed," Bernie said.

Sonia got out of the car and turned to Bernie. "I'll — I'll do anything you want," she said.

"You're losing me," he said, stepping on the gas. I wriggled through the small space and onto the shotgun seat before anybody could change their mind about anything.

We took the next turn. The road led down a gentle slope to the water — what had Sonia called it? The bay? — and then followed along beside it, and right away I saw a fish jump out of the water, all silvery in the moonlight — so close Bernie almost could have reached out and caught it — and plopped back in, leaving silvery ripples behind. When it comes to eating fish, they sometimes have very annoying bones inside, which I learned the hard way once, and after that the hard way again.

"Is there a Sonia in *Crime and Punishment*?" Bernie said. "Had to write an essay on it at West Point. C minus, as I recall, but it might have been worse."

Missed all that, except for crime and punishment. No missing crime and punishment: it was our bread and butter. As for bread and butter, I prefer just the butter, right out of the package, or even in the package if pressed for time.

"Here we go," Bernie said, turning into a gravel driveway that appeared on my side. It took a long curve, headed back toward the sea, and there on a bluff overlooking the bay stood a small house, no lights showing. Bernie stopped the car and we walked the rest of the way, Bernie with the gun in his hand, me the way I am when the gun is in the picture, namely at my most alert. We reached the house, stopped, listened. I heard the lapping of little waves, an owl hooting far away, almost out of range, and nothing from inside the house. We started walking around it, passing a kayak leaning against the wall and a trash can smelling of sour milk, and came to the back.

There was a lot to take in at the back of this house, and take in quickly. First, the view, a wide-open view of the bay, with a boat not far off, a boat with a big cabin and light glowing inside. I thought I remembered that boat: something about horses, wasn't it? Also in the view was a little rowboat, on its way out to the cabin cruiser. Moonlight gleamed on the slicked-back hair of the rower, and the planes of his face were clear: Mr. York, a.k.a. Jean-Luc and maybe a.k.a. something else, a.k.a. being an annoyance that comes up in our business from time to time. A woman sat in the bow, facing toward the cabin cruiser and therefore away from us, but I knew it was Suzie, just from how she was sitting.

Nothing more to take in on the water, but out on the deck behind the house we had something else going on, what Bernie would call a complication, namely the cat's-eye woman, Ludmilla, standing by the railing that overlooked the bay, one of those cameras with a big long nose on a table beside her, the cat's-eye glasses perched up on her head, and a rifle in her hands. At least we knew all of the people in the scene, but no other positives came to me.

Steps led to the deck from the side. We went up them at our very quietest, losing sight of Ludmilla for a moment. When we got to the top, Ludmilla had the rifle in firing position, drawing a bead on the rowboat. *Pop,* before we could take another step: the soft pop of gunfire when a silencer's in play. A silencer takes away the sound, but not the power, a fact that surprised me in my rookie days. The power's still there, take my word for it. Out on the water, Mr. York went still and then slid down out of sight, the oars slipping from his hands.

Now we were on the move, big time. Ludmilla stuck another round — it looked like gold in the moonlight — into the chamber, and resighted very slightly, the muzzle now pointing right at Suzie. She was rising to her feet in the bow of the rowboat, eyes wide open, huge and dark. Ludmilla's trigger finger started to tense just as we hit her and hit her hard. Another *pop,* but the rifle was pointing straight up by then, knocked loose from her hands. Before it even hit the ground, we had Ludmilla pinned nice and motionless under us, although it took her a while to accept the motionless part. She even spat at Bernie, something I hate to see in a perp.

Bernie rose and jerked Ludmilla to her feet in his roughest way. We looked out toward the bay, but the moon was covered up again, and there was nothing to see except the glow of the cabin cruiser lights. Bernie put his free hand to his mouth like he was going to shout something, but then lowered it, staying silent.

"Your fucking dog's biting my ankle," Ludmilla said.

"Shut up," said Bernie. He looked at me. "Good job, Chet. That's enough for now. C'mon, boy."

Meaning what?

Not long after that, I figured it out. Bernie was suggesting I let go of Ludmilla's pant leg. Nothing I'd done to her could possibly qualify as biting, which was where the confusion came from. I let go, got rid of a few bits, or possibly swaths, of khaki material that had somehow gotten caught in my mouth, and then we took Ludmilla inside the house.

Most houses have duct tape somewhere around the place. Ludmilla's was under the kitchen sink. We duct-taped her to a chair, feet, hands, and chest, Bernie doing the actual work and doing it fast.

"Why did he go rogue on you?" Bernie said, also talking fast. "Jealousy? He forgot the point of the exercise?"

"Beyond reminding you of my diplomatic immunity, I've got nothing to say," Ludmilla said.

Bernie taped one last piece over her mouth. We'd duct-taped a perp name of Roly Polinski just like this some time back, and as we'd left Bernie had told him to sit tight, but he didn't do that with Ludmilla.

Out on the deck: no moon and nothing to see on the bay but the cabin cruiser's glow. We went around to the side of the house, picked up the kayak, and carried it down to the water. I knew kayaks from our trip to San Diego — we'd surfed, me and Bernie! — although I'd never actually been in one. But boats in general were coming up a lot lately in my career, and one thing was clear: riding in the bow — which is boat lingo Bernie taught me — is a lot like riding shotgun in the Porsche. In short: heaven, even if I'm not sure what heaven is, except I seem to be in it a lot.

There were two seats — like bucket seats only deeper — in the kayak, bow and stern, stern being more boat lingo in case you're new to this. Bernie tapped the side of the bow seat. "In you go, Chet. And not a sound."

I hopped in, making no sound, and stood tall, facing the bay. Bernie got in the stern — far from silently, sorry to have to point that out — and pushed off. He got going with the paddle. It, too, made some sound, but lovely, all burbles and swishes.

The cabin cruiser — *Horsin' Around,* if I was getting this right — took shape despite the darkness, got bigger, and then we were right beside it. Bernie glided us around to the stern. A platform hung down, and the rowboat was tied to it. Bernie made a little clicking sound in his mouth meaning jump onto the platform, so I did. He jumped out, too — more like he wriggled out — and pulled himself onto the platform, then dragged the kayak up with him. We glanced down into the rowboat. Mr. York lay on the bottom, totally still, a small dark pool spreading beneath him. We climbed onto the deck of *Horsin' Around* and approached the cabin door, the kind of door with slats. Light leaked out and so did sound. I heard General Galloway saying, "I'm completely baffled." Bernie drew the gun, and we burst in, hard and heavy, the door flying off the hinges.

"Hold it right there," Lizette said, her voice rising, but not much — reminding me of how Bernie would be in her place. A weird thought, but there it was.

The cabin was like a living room with a couch and two chairs. General Galloway sat on the couch, wearing tightie whiteys and nothing else. Suzie sat on one of the chairs, wearing jeans and a T-shirt. Lizette stood at one side of the room, wearing a long man's shirt and bare-legged. Not sure why I'm including all this clothing information: it seemed important at the time, no telling why, at least by me. Way more important was the gun in Lizette's hand, pointed at Suzie, although Lizette's eyes were on us.

"Drop it or I kill her," Lizette said. "It's very simple."

"The Château Frontenac's in Quebec City," Bernie said. "Not Montreal." He lowered the gun.

"Don't, Bernie," Suzie said. "She's going to kill us anyway."

"Not me, surely?" said the general, rising to his feet.

Lizette laughed. "That's the funniest thing you've ever said."

"What do you mean?" he said. "I don't understand what's going on. What's happened to you?"

"Try this," said Lizette. "The orgasms, quote end quote? Faked, each and every one." The general staggered, and his skin went white; he slumped back on the couch. Lizette gestured at Bernie with the gun. "I'll count to one half."

Bernie dropped his gun. Nobody did anything, but wasn't it a time for doing something? I was gathering my strength beneath me, when a terrifying kind of human figure appeared in the doorway, stepping between me and Bernie. Something real bad had happened to his nose, and his hair, not gelled now, was still slicked back, although with blood. A moment passed before I realized it was Mr. York, a shoeless

Mr. York, leaving red footprints on the deck. He picked up Bernie's gun, gazed at it like he didn't know what it was.

"Look at you," Lizette said.

Mr. York turned that same unknowing gaze on her.

"You've fucked up everything," she said. "And for what? You couldn't be more Russian. Didn't you just hear what I told him? He's a toad. The orgasms were faked, each and every —"

Mr. York shot her right in the middle of her forehead, the sound so loud I thought the boat would break up around us. Lizette fell to the floor and lay still. I considered taking the gun from Mr. York, the right move for sure, but instead found myself moving away from him. Bernie was doing the same thing.

"Russian?" said the general. He covered his mouth with both hands, the first time I'd seen a man do that.

Mr. York shifted his gun toward him in a slow and wobbly way. "Is there any point . . ." He paused there, tried to breathe, had trouble.

"In shooting me?" said the general. "No, none at all. Didn't you hear her? There's no cause for jealousy. I didn't even know she was married until —"

Mr. York's voice rose. "Speak of her with respect!"

"Of course! I was. Please don't misconstrue —"

Mr. York waved the gun at the general, like a man shooing flies. Somehow, the action took him with it. He lost his balance, toppled over, landed hard, and lay motionless on the floor, blood and more blood everywhere. I could smell nothing else.

Silence. Bernie knelt and put his finger on Mr. York's neck. Then he went over to Suzie and held her close. Engine sounds rose up on the bay.

"What's that?" said the general, moving toward a window.

"Trouble for you," Bernie said. He stroked Suzie's hair.

"I thought you were on my side."

"That would be a lonely place," said Bernie. "You're not even there yourself."

Not long after that, we were in Ludmilla's house, although some of Mr. Ferretti's guys had already taken her away. Others were out working on the boat. A car came and drove the general home. That left us — meaning me, Bernie, Suzie, and Ferretti — alone in Ludmilla's kitchen.

"He didn't actually abduct you?" Ferretti said.

"I went willingly," said Suzie. "He promised the story of my life."

"But he made you hand over your cell phone?" Ferretti said. "That sounds coercive."

"Only in the sense that I wanted that story."

"Suppose I asked you not to print it."

"That's for you to take up with the paper," Suzie said. "But I'm writing it tonight."

"Starting with the affair?" Bernie said.

Suzie nodded. "Isobel Galloway got Eben going on that, when they met at the stable. That led to Eben contacting Jean-Luc, far gone with jealousy."

"And the carriage house?" Bernie said. "Why did Eben want you there?"

"He must have been using me to keep an eye on Lizette," Suzie said. "But Lizette already had a close eye on him, complete with access to his office. Jean-Luc sent me the keys, of course." She shook her head. "I made so many mistakes, Bernie."

"Not that I can see," Bernie said.

"Telling Lizette about you, for example. You, and Chet, and the Porsche, and your adventures — all that."

"So?"

"Including the glove box."

Bernie shrugged. "You didn't know what she was." He turned to Ferretti. "I get that Lanny Sands was waiting to see if Galloway won the nomination, with the idea of blowing him out of the water deep in the campaign, but how did he find out in the first place?"

"No idea," said Ferretti.

"From you?"

"We stay out of politics — I told you that."

"Maybe not everyone on your team. Maybe Sands had a buddy in one of your cubicles, tapping away at a keyboard."

Ferretti's eyes shifted.

"Maybe there are all sorts of unimagined ramifications to what you do," Bernie said.

"Easy to say from a seat in the audience," Ferretti said. "But suppose Galloway had gotten himself into the White House."

"You'd have turned Lizette and fed the Russians anything you wanted," Suzie said.

"That's off the record," Ferretti said.

"Is it also off the record that you and your people would have been in position to run the White House?" Bernie said.

Ferretti smiled. First time I'd seen him smile: he had small teeth, nice and even. "Isn't that on the melodramatic side?" he said. "But information is power. That's not my fault."

"Here's the piece of information I'm interested in," Suzie said. "Was the president aware of all this?"

"I have no facts on that," Ferretti said.

"But what do you think?" said Suzie. "Sands was close to him."

Ferretti nodded. "The president's totally broken up about his death, from what I hear, bawling his eyes out. He's got his top speechwriters working on the eulogy."

"You didn't answer the question," Bernie said.

"Here's your answer," Ferretti said. "It depends on the definition of the word *know*."

Bernie gave him a look and said, "So long."

"Do I thank you or do you thank me?" Ferretti said.

"Neither feels right," Bernie said. "But you could do me a favor." He told him about Sonia. "Get her a new identity, put her somewhere safe."

"Can do," said Ferretti. "Especially if there's some cooperation on Suzie's end."

"I can keep your name out of the initial story," she said. "You'll be a high-ranking officer."

"Let's go with midlevel, if you don't

mind," said Ferretti.

Bernie and Suzie started toward the door, hand in hand. Was that a wrap? It didn't feel like a wrap to me.

"Chet?" Bernie said. "What are you doing?"

"He seems to have grabbed my pant leg," Ferretti said. "I thought he liked me."

"Chet!" Bernie said, but he wasn't angry at all, far from it. Had knowing come up in their conversation? I know pretty much all there is to know about Bernie's voice.

We made tracks. I reached the car way before Bernie and Suzie, but it made no difference. I was back on the shelf. For a while, I did some pawing of the seat backs. Bernie and Suzie leaned against each other, shoulder to shoulder, and ignored me. How could that be? Wasn't seat-back pawing an annoyance, big time?

I tried to think of something even more annoying. That made my eyelids heavy.

ACKNOWLEDGMENTS

My grateful thanks to Judith Curr, Peter Borland, Ariele Fredman, Daniel Loedel, and all the people at Atria who have been such strong supporters of Chet and Bernie.

The employees of Thorndike Press hope you have enjoyed this Large Print book. All our Thorndike, Wheeler, and Kennebec Large Print titles are designed for easy reading, and all our books are made to last. Other Thorndike Press Large Print books are available at your library, through selected bookstores, or directly from us.

For information about titles, please call:
   (800) 223-1244

or visit our Web site at:
   http://gale.cengage.com/thorndike

To share your comments, please write:
   Publisher
   Thorndike Press
   10 Water St., Suite 310
   Waterville, ME 04901